THE BITTER CORE

Denise Robins

CHIVERS LARGE PRINT
BATH

British Library Cataloguing in Publication Data available

This Large Print edition published by Chivers Press, Bath, 1997.

Published by arrangement with Severn House Publishers Ltd.

U.K. Hardcover ISBN 0–7451–8966–0
U.K. Softcover   ISBN 0–7451–8967–9

Photoset, printed and bound in Great Britain by
Redwood Books, Trowbridge, Wiltshire

PART ONE

PART ONE

CHAPTER ONE

Venetia Sellingham woke up on her forty-fifth birthday and lay still for a moment without moving. She felt ill.

There was nothing radically wrong with her. She was particularly healthy for a woman of her age, and as those who liked her continually said, Venetia is a marvel—she looks about thirty. Nobody would dream that she is a widow and the mother of a great girl of fifteen.

But this morning Venetia faced the fact that she was, after all, forty-five; that she was Maybelle's mother; that Maybelle was just about to enter for School Certificate. Added to which, Venetia did *not* feel as young as she looked.

She had had too many of Mike's strong cocktails. Darling Mike *would* mix them with a kick that hit one suddenly. All very subtle to start with and one went on sipping and letting him pour one out another. What a party it had been!

'To celebrate your thirty-fifth birthday, my sweet,' he had said, significantly stressing the '*thirty*'.

Venetia pressed her fingertips against hot eyelids. Mike's party had taken place in the flat he shared with his friend and business partner, Tony Winters. Venetia's best friend, Barbara

Keen, had arrived, as usual, later than anybody else, looking thin, beautiful and incredibly well dressed; with that slightly hungry look characteristic of Barbara.

As Mike had once said to Venetia:

'Barbara always looks as though she is about to devour people. She sticks her face right into yours when she talks to you and plucks at your arm with those long coloured talons. You feel that she is after *something*—if not you. She is the most predatory female I have ever known; not like you, Venetia darling—you're so subtle and reserved, so calm and aloof. Drop a pebble into your personality and you'll watch the shining ripple widen. Drop one into Barbara's and it will sink to the murky depths like a plummet and you'll never see it again.'

That was true in a way. Barbara was restless and exhausting; and far too exacting. She had already had two husbands and several lovers. She was only a year older than Venetia. But she had her good points and there was a side to her nature before which Venetia bowed; the courageous industrious side. One had to admire Barbara. She had had real tragedy in her life and was bitterly frustrated, but she presented to the world the spectacle of a gay, self-satisfied creature who could boast that she had built up one of the best businesses in the cosmetic trade. Using the last syllable of her name, 'Bara', she had launched a really

4

attractive campaign to attract the attention of women who needed 'slimming' and reasonably priced cosmetics. BARA products were now known in America as well as in Great Britain. The Bara Salon in Bond Street had been succeeded by branches all over the provinces.

Barbara had said to Venetia last night:

'Look, Venetia, you're supposed to be an intelligent woman. Have you gone out of your mind?'

Venetia answered:

'No. Must one be deranged before one decides to marry for the second time?'

Barbara's curt reply, 'I'll come along and talk to you when I've got a moment,' was enough to damp Venetia's enthusiasm a little but no more. She was far too happy. It had been hard making up her mind. Now, having made it up, she was relieved and delighted. Last night she and Michael had announced their engagement. Everybody in the crowded flat had surged around to toast them in champagne amid cries of *'Congratulations— how marvellous, Venetia, darling. How splendid, Mike. Oh, what a thrill!'* and so on.

Venetia had felt quite light-headed in her pride and satisfaction as she felt Mike's hand gripping hers, and compared him with the rest of the men in the party. He was perfectly wonderful to look at; not very tall but slim-hipped and broad-shouldered—racily built and he glowed with health. He looked what he

5

was—a man who lived a great deal out of doors. Mad about horses, he rode superbly. The flat was full of his trophies. What hadn't Mike won at point-to-points, in jumping contests, at horse shows? He was a member of the Southdown, great friends with all the hunting chaps. He spent his week-ends at his old home—a fine old Queen Anne manor house near Lewes. The estate consisted of twenty-five acres and a farm, but unfortunately Mike had no money with which to keep the place up. It was in bad repair. The stables were letting in water. Mike had only one horse. He needed two. Lack of money had been the trouble ever since before the war when his mother had died. His father was now hopelessly crippled with arthritis. Venetia was not unaware that people might imagine that Mike was marrying her for the money that poor Geoffrey had left her. Money that was not even entailed because there had been no need for Geoffrey to provide for his little daughter. Maybelle would come into her grandfather's fortune. Lady Sellingham (she had been a Miss Occulton) had her own money which had come to her from old Thomas Occulton. He had founded an iron and steel works that paid nearly fifty per cent to its shareholders today. And old Lady Sellingham held two-thirds of the firm's shares. All that would one day belong to Maybelle; a portion after her twenty-first birthday and the rest

THE BITTER CORE

when her grandmother died.

Supposing, Venetia reflected, Mike *did* need her money. Why not? Why not be sensible and accept the fact that in his impecunious state he needed money? On his own admission, he had had many love affairs. But he 'couldn't afford to marry'. She, Venetia, could help provide the things that he wanted. She would enjoy doing it and, besides, Maybelle would like having a stepfather who rode so well. She, too, adored horses.

Venetia and Mike had fallen in love with each other at the Hunt Ball, last Christmas. She had gone down to it with Geoffrey's cousin, Dick. Venetia had never been to a Hunt Ball before. She used to avoid such entertainment. She did not really like the hunting crowd. She had never cared for strenuous exercise. She came from a family of musicians who lived quietly, were immersed in their art. She had married the man of her heart soon after her twenty-third birthday. Geoffrey had been at that time the junior partner in a firm of publishers—the kind that published educational works and technical manuals. He was a sweet, rather dreamy type of man who had come through the Second World War with the loss of his left arm—blown off in the woods of Caen. Fortunately for him he had money of his own and no need to struggle. Venetia had loved him as devotedly and deeply as he loved her. Theirs had been a perfect marriage and some years later a daughter had been born after Venetia had wondered if the joys of parenthood were to be denied her. She had been blessed not only with the ideal husband but a delightful mother-in-law. A most intelligent and charming woman. The birth of little Maybelle, so called after Geoffrey's mother, completed their happiness.

But it had been too perfect a union, Venetia had mused in the bitterness of her sorrow— nothing so splendid could last, and it had ended suddenly when Maybelle was nine. One of those ghastly tragedies which seemed to be without reason or meaning.

It had been during Maybelle's first term at boarding-school, and the first time that Venetia and Geoffrey had felt that they could take a long holiday alone without their precious child. They visited Italy. Geoffrey particularly wanted to see Rome.

Within a week of their arrival, he had been struck down with a fatal germ; to this day nobody quite knew what it was. And to this day Venetia tried not to remember too vividly the awfulness of the week that had followed. That evening when Geoffrey had been seized with stomach cramp and taken to his bed. A hastily summoned doctor failed to diagnose and, after a frantic telephone call through to Geoffrey's mother, Venetia had had her husband flown back to London on a stretcher, and taken straight to a clinic. He had died there at the end of the week. It had been a horrifying experience for Venetia. She had, until then, led a protected and blessed life with her husband.

She was forced to watch Geoffrey change with terrible rapidity from a good-looking, well-covered man into a gaunt spectre with cadaverous eyes and suffering mouth. In appalling pain he never complained; only clung to her hand and begged her to stay near him.

His heart had given out before the doctors really had time to complete all the pathological investigations: the laboratory analysis; the tests and injections. He had an unsuspected coronary weakness. So he had died and left her and Maybelle alone. And Venetia had wondered how there could be a God so brutal—so greedy of human life that He must take a man of thirty-seven who had everything that he seemed to want on earth. It had struck a double blow at his mother, too. Lady Sellingham had only recently lost her husband. But the older woman had shown great courage, that patience which only seems to come with age and experience. She, although mourning an idolized son, had helped Venetia to live through those first bitter months of loss and loneliness.

'You have your little daughter—she is so like Geoff. She must be your comfort,' Lady Sellingham would say when Venetia continued to weep—inconsolable.

9

Maybelle was an enchanting child with Geoffrey's grey dreamy eyes and her mother's ash-blonde hair. For a while mother and daughter stayed in the lovely cottage facing Richmond Park to which Geoffrey's mother had retired after his father died and their old home had been sold up. It was a sunny, peaceful little house, full of the antiques and books that Geoffrey had loved. Not for a year did Venetia re-open her own home which she and Geoffrey used to share. It was a small but elegant house in a *cul-de-sac* close to Kensington Gardens. Geoffrey was particularly fond of Kensington Gardens and some of the happiest moments Venetia could remember were when Maybelle was small, and they used to take her to the Round Pond to sail her boats, or feed the ducks on the Serpentine. One day, when he retired, Geoffrey used to tell Venetia, they would buy a house in the depths of the country and segregate themselves from the world. But during the early years of their marriage they both loved the little white house with the yellow doors and windows, and the glimpse of the Albert Hall. Geoffrey had decided on all the decorations and helped Venetia choose the furniture. After he died she could not bear to break up that home. Once having got over the initial shock, it comforted her to stay amongst his things; and to imagine that she could see him sometimes, strolling across the room—the dear familiar figure with the one empty sleeve pinned across the breast and the one good hand ever outstretched to *her* or to their child.

The memory of that love had sustained Venetia for the first two or three years after his death. She had finally grown accustomed to being without him and able to do what she thought the right thing—which was to continue sending Maybelle to boarding-school. Not for selfish reasons, so that she, the mother, would be free to have a good time, but because she was convinced that it was bad for an only child always to be at home with her mother. Maybelle inherited so much of Geoffrey's erudition. She liked school and her studies and the holidays were fun when mother and daughter returned, refreshed, to each other.

Many men had wanted to marry Geoffrey Sellingham's widow. A beautiful woman of forty with money behind her is a desirable prize. Apart from the money Venetia was truly lovely, her fair hair only touched with grey, her tall body still firm and slim. The pure oval of her face, the fine dark brown eyes set at a slightly slanting angle fascinated people. She dressed well; she was a good hostess; a polished conversationalist. Without having any great technique she played the piano and sang charmingly. Her friends said that Venetia was always an asset at any party. And she gave good parties of her own.

Venetia continued to lie in bed, thinking, remembering, on this her birthday morning. And for the first time in her life it was reluctantly that she considered the fact that this marked the end of her forty-fourth year.

Before meeting Mike she had never minded about the passing of time. Like any woman who has been beautiful, she was anxious to retain the illusion of youth and beauty as long as she could, but the idea of ageing did not worry her, even when the crow's feet made a little net-work around her eyes; when tummy muscles sagged and the waist-line thickened a little and, searching the mirror, it became obvious that she could no longer be called *young*. Now she might cry with the French: *'Forty is the old age of youth, but fifty is the youth of old age.'*

Fifty! That made even Venetia squirm a little this morning as she considered that in another five years she would have reached her half century. *And* Mike would still be under forty. At forty a man was in his prime.

She thought of Mike as she had first seen him in his hunting 'pink', waltzing superbly with the girl with whom he had at the time been involved.

'You know how it is,' he had explained at a later date to Venetia. 'One has to pay some woman compliments and kiss her and run around with the orchids. I, in particular, keep a love-affair going in self-defence; it checks the pursuit of the females with whom one *doesn't* want to get involved!'

Typical of Mike and his colossal egotism. He had looked devastating in that pink coat; the brown of his neck very brown against the white stock, and the blue of his eyes very blue in his tanned face; rather narrow laughing eyes. Mike did a lot of laughing. His most engaging quality was his 'sense of fun'. He could be sweet and friendly, too, and that boyish side to Mike went to Venetia's heart. He was a man with no family ties, except a bed-ridden father who, like Mike, had, at one time, been on the Stock Exchange. Mike had not, so far as Venetia could see, made a great success as a stockbroker. This applied also to his partner, Tony Winter, whose flat he shared. Both the young men seemed to find it hard to make a decent living. All the same, Mike managed to hunt and get down to the South of France in the summer.

From the moment that he had first taken Venetia in his arms, she had surrendered to his long kiss with a frank passion that seemed to enchant him.

'You are so very stimulating, Venetia,' he had told her. 'You don't pretend. Not a trace of the coquette about you, my sweet. You want me as much as I want you—don't you?'

Her answer had been 'Yes'.

This morning she recalled vividly all that had happened that evening.

13

CHAPTER TWO

Mike had come round to her house for drinks before taking her out to a show. They had then known each other less than a month, during which she had seen quite a lot of him. She knew that he admired her. So far he had not made love to her. But she had been subtly conscious of his rising passion.

At first she had been afraid; the difference in their ages frightened her.

Venetia had had to do a lot of thinking about it all. But all the thoughts had scurried like autumn leaves before a strong wind, scattering in all directions once she discovered that she was in love with him.

That fateful evening she had put on a new grey ballet-length skirt and pale grey velvet blouse—off-the-shoulders—just showing the cleft between small breasts of which she was justifiably proud. They were still as firm as a girl's. The only colour in her appearance was in the pink orchids which Mike had sent her and which she wore pinned to her belt.

Michael had given her one swift glance and then without his usual smile or jest, said in a hushed voice:

'By God, you are a beautiful woman, Venetia—you knock the girls absolutely for six!'

14

She had bowed her head in dignified acceptance of his compliment and with that lack of archness that he so admired.

'But the girls still have that something which I haven't got,' she said, with a smile.

'Name it.'

'Youth,' she said. Without envy, she had said it as an indisputable fact.

But she was glad that he found her beautiful. In BARA's Bond Street salon that morning they had induced her to put more blue than usual in the rinse they used for her hair. It certainly made it look attractive; the colour of woodsmoke with a pale gilt sheen. It was long straight hair. She had never worn it any other way but this—parted in the centre and drawn into a coil at the nape of her neck.

'What time have we got to be at the show?' she had begun to ask Mike, dropping her blue mink stole over a chair and picking up a cigarette.

It was then that Mike took two steps across the room, caught her wrists and looking more serious than she had ever seen him said:

'I'm crazy about you, Venetia—*I can't go on* . . .'

For an instant she stood still. She looked up at him amazed.

'Mike—what is it?'

'You must know that I am terribly in love with you,' he said.

The way her heart had jerked then and her

15

knees begun to tremble had warned that she was not at all indifferent to his passion—on the contrary. But for a moment she had tried to keep her head.

'Hadn't you better have a drink, my dear?' she asked.

After that she was not given any further opportunity to think or analyse her emotions. She was in his arms and he was kissing her with a hungry passion to which she responded, both arms around his neck. They had continued to kiss, deeply, insatiably. Mike, as a lover, was not to be dealt with lightly. His were the sort of kisses Venetia had never before experienced. Geoffrey had not been that kind of lover; he had been more gentle; ever careful of her. Even during his most passionate moments he had never seemed entirely to lose his head. He remained sensible of her feelings—over-careful perhaps not to jar her susceptibilities. She had thought him wonderful and been satisfied by his embrace. His chivalry and idealism had seemed to her correct and admirable. Only *now* in Michael's embrace she knew what a woman could be made to feel.

Her life had been empty of all passion for five long years and she was quite appalled to discover how much she needed *this sort of thing*. She found herself more primitive than she had realized, and if there was a fierce and demanding quality in Michael Pethick's love-making, *she enjoyed it*; and returned it. It was

16

as though all her pent-up feelings were released in his arms. There was a lifting of a burden from her spirit, too. The burden of widowhood and of the solitary confinement in which she had placed her physical self. Besides, it was enormously flattering to have a lover like this when one was nearing forty-five, this young man—twelve years younger—vowed that he must possess her or die. Venetia had had to insist that he should let her go—regained her own lost dignity, put some ice in the cocktail-shaker and mixed a drink, then made him sit down beside her on the sofa and smoke a cigarette.

Of course they never got to the show, and Mike tore up the tickets. They didn't even get out to dinner till ten o'clock. They sat talking and talking, with Michael making periodical attempts to make love to her, each one of which she resisted.

'I'm going to be stubborn, darling,' she said. 'We *must* keep our heads.'

His very blue eyes had laughed at her.

'Why?'

'Don't be silly, Mike. We can't just plunge into a kind of cataclysm and not mind where it is landing us.'

He drained his glass and said:

'I only wanted to lead you to a registrar's or to church—anywhere—so long as you marry me.'

Venetia, embarking on her second cocktail,

felt the tumultuous beating of her heart, but spoke quietly:

'Mike, you're not seriously proposing to me?'

'What do you think? I'm in love with you. Of course I want to marry you.'

'Mike—are your sure you haven't just gone crazy?'

'Oh, I have—about you. But I'm asking you to marry me as soon as it can be arranged, my darling.'

That had been the beginning of two hours' controversy. She had brought up every possible argument against such a marriage. Of course, she hadn't enjoyed doing so. It had been like dragging out all her most sensitive feelings and dissecting them there before Mike; laying herself bare for his scrutiny, trying to strip him of illusions. But she had done it because she had thought it her duty. It was her age she kept harping on until Mike sprang to his feet quite white with anger and snapped:

'For God's sake don't keep reminding me that you are nearly forty-five and that I am only thirty-three. I *know* it. You've never made any bones about your age—that's been one of the things I like. I hate women who dye their grey hairs and pretend they are chickens. In any case you haven't really reached the age when you need to start pretending to be younger than you are. You've no need to. You don't look a day older than I do; in fact, in spite

18

of all my hard riding, I'm the sort that will soon run to fat and I bet I'll look fifty when I'm your age.'

'And then I'll be over sixty,' she reminded him with a pitiless honesty.

He had argued that down, too. They had twenty years to go, he said. She wasn't the kind to age rapidly, with those slim greyhound lines of hers. She had, too, that sort of calm disposition that helps a woman to retain her youth. It was the worrying grieving sort that gets so haggard, he said. The hard-drinking, racing, card-playing types. Venetia lived a normal healthy life and drank and smoked normally—far less than most women in his set! Why should she ever grow old?

'But I *shall*,' she argued, 'and whatever you say, darling, there is still twelve years' difference between us—on the wrong side.'

'I don't care,' he had almost shouted the words. 'I love you. Wash out all my arguments and admit that you are likely at any moment to totter into old age—I shall still love you.'

That had warmed her heart. She had felt tears sting her eyelids as she looked at him. He was certainly not just about to totter into old age! He had a thin hard body and a boy's face with its slightly impudent turned-up nose. 'Jack Buchanan', Barbara had called him— well, not unlike.

The debate continued.

She brought up other reasons why it was

19

ridiculous for her even to contemplate marrying him. Not only because of this difference in their ages, but in their tastes. She was a book-worm, she said, and liked her piano. When on holiday she liked to go abroad and see lovely places—stay in mountain retreats—listen to music—visit museums. He was a sportsman. All his tastes were for out-of-doors pleasures. Apart from hunting he liked tennis—he was almost Wimbledon class. An exuberant schoolboy who needed to rush around and play games in order to get rid of his superfluous energy. And when she came to think of it, she said she had never really seen him sit still for longer than a few moments. He had to get up and turn on a radio or look out of a window or glance at his wrist-watch, as though he feared that time was flying by and he needs must fill every moment of it.

Venetia reminded him that she could not play tennis and did not hunt. Geoffrey had been the perfect companion for her. But how would it work out for two such opposite types to live together?

'Don't let's bury our heads in the sand,' she told Mike. 'Let's be adult and intelligent. I'll confess that I'd adore to marry you. When you're not with me, I miss you terribly and look forward so much to our next meeting—but is that enough? We know that physical passion does not last, and—'

Here he had interrupted her.

20

'That isn't always true. When you were telling me about your husband, you said that you were still in love with each other right up to the time he died.'

She had to confess that it was so and to agree that certain other couples they both knew, and who had been married for a long time, seemed to remain in love. But in her opinion, she said, it was necessary that there should be more than physical love if a marriage was to be a success.

Then Mike appeared hurt. There *was* more between *them*, he protested. And he was quite fond of reading and listening to music. As for glamour girls, he could have chosen a dozen if it was just a question of wanting youth and beauty.

Venetia knew—everybody knew about Jix Lawson, who had hunted with him for the last couple of years. It was an accepted fact in their set that he and Jix had been more than friends. But he had put an end to their affair soon after meeting Venetia.

'You are everything that a woman should be. I admire you mentality,' he said. 'I'll fit in with all that you want to do and you won't mind my hunting.'

For an instant Venetia thought about Jix Lawson. She could well remember seeing her dancing with Mike at that Hunt Ball. Someone had pointed out Mike as 'Our glamour boy of the Hunt' and Jix as his 'girl friend'. Venetia did not particularly care for Miss Lawson's

21

type, but she was attractive. Small, with short dark brown hair waving like a boy's back from her forehead, and rather narrow light blue eyes, and the fresh complexion of a woman who lived out of doors, she was narrowly built. They said she looked superb on a horse and rode like a jockey. She was amusing and a first-class mimic. Certainly, she amused Mike. But now, to Venetia, Michael said:

'Jix was the sort of girl one enjoyed going to bed with, but nothing in the old brain-box. And I was certainly not *first* with her. She'll never get married. She tries too hard.'

That made Venetia feel uncomfortable. It wasn't pleasant to hear a man talk about any girl that way. Also it had to be remembered that the Lawsons had no money and that Jix had to groom her own horse and curtail all other expenditure in order to go on with her riding. Venetia was a little sorry for the girl; and especially when Dick Sellingham had told her the other day that Jix really seemed hard hit when Mike had walked out on her. But Mike had said to Venetia:

'There was no question of marriage between us—she knew that when our affair started. Jix would drive me crackers. We'd always be hopelessly in debt and, if anything, she sinks more gin than I do. I need your restraining influence, Venetia.'

Was that a good reason for marrying a young man—in order to become his guiding star?

22

Then came the question of Maybelle.

That was a much more serious impediment to the marriage. And even Michael flinched when Venetia brought up the subject of her daughter. Maybelle was fifteen: half his age. A bit odd, perhaps, to take on a step-daughter half one's age. He grumbled:

'I can never sort of connect you with a huge schoolgirl. I suppose it's because I have never seen you together. You just *don't* look as though you could have such a grown-up daughter.'

That had made her smile. Relentlessly she pressed half a dozen photographs of Maybelle in his hands and forced him to look at her. He had studied them indifferently. Maybelle was not a 'huge schoolgirl'. She was at the awkward age—but she promised to be a beauty. She had grave eyes like her father's and two fair pigtails. Venetia's cheekbones were high and marked. Maybelle's face was round and childish. But in another few years, as Venetia said, she would be a lovely girl and she was already almost as tall as her mother.

Michael had shrugged his shoulders and muttered something to the effect that he was quite sure young Maybelle could never be as beautiful as her mother. Anyhow, he did not mind about Maybelle. He wasn't going to lose the woman he loved and wanted just because she had a growing daughter.

23

'Mind you, darling,' he said, 'I don't think I'm much good with kids. I'm not at all paternal. I couldn't stick having babies around the place.'

'Well, you certainly won't have a baby around the place with me,' she said, 'which is one of the reasons why I shouldn't marry you. Surely you want a son and heir?'

'Heir to what? A crumbling manor house and a neglected estate?'

'Darling, there's your name to carry on and all those good looks which ought to be reproduced.'

'Are you telling me you are too old to have a child?'

'Almost too old,' she had said quietly, 'but I had an operation soon after Maybelle was born; I didn't produce her very easily you know, and I had to wait eight years for her. The specialist told me at the time that I would never have another.'

At that Michael had given his schoolboy grin.

'Better and better. No need to worry. I tell you I don't want children. A ready-made step-daughter will suit me fine.'

'I think you'll get on well with Maybelle. She adores horses.'

'Good. I'll teach her to ride.'

'She can ride already. Her grandmother hired her a pony on her tenth birthday and she's ridden ever since.'

24

Then he put his hands on Venetia's shoulders and looking deeply at her, said:

'Okay, but it's a good thing she'll be at boarding-school for another couple of years. I couldn't stand even your beautiful Maybelle always around the place. I want you and I want you to myself.'

At the time the first phrase of that remark had troubled her in spite of the ensuing flattery. She had felt it would be disloyal to Geoffrey's memory and unfair to their little daughter if she married anybody who did not want Maybelle. Openly she said so, and immediately Michael covered himself by saying that he would do his utmost to be step-father, brother, friend, anything she wanted him to be to Maybelle. That never, *never*, would he let the child feel unwanted.

'It's just that I'm mad about you and can't think about anybody but you,' he had finished.

He had insisted then on drawing her back into his arms. That put an end to intelligent survey of the situation and it also set the seal on Venetia's desire to fall in with Mike's wishes. They were so much her own. She was utterly charmed and enslaved and found herself trembling like a foolish girl under his hot passionate kisses and exploring hands.

Before the evening ended, she had promised to marry him. But she forbade him to make the news public before she had written to Maybelle.

'I insist on getting her letter back and making sure that it won't distress her to know that I'm putting somebody in her father's place.'

That had drawn a frown of perplexity from Michael.

'You certainly have got a strong mother complex, darling.'

'You mustn't mind,' she had smiled, 'because I love my daughter very much and she adores me. If you don't feel you can take us both into your life, it would be much better for *me* to stay out of it.'

He answered that he would do anything on earth that she wanted except let her go. As for their difference in age—she was never to mention it again. It was to be forgotten.

'Others won't forget it,' she had reminded him.

'Don't let's build our lives on what other people say,' he had retorted grandly.

'One thing more,' she had said, before they finally parted. 'The question of finance.'

Then he had shown himself at his very nicest. He said:

'That's the one subject that I dread because it makes me feel ashamed. You know my position. I earn about a couple of thousand a year when things are going well—and until lately you know what a poor time we stockbrokers have had—and I'm extravagant. My poor old father is still alive—totally crippled, and has only just enough money to pay his own expenses. He lives with a retired nurse who has quite a nice little house in Hampstead. She looks after him and I go and see the poor old chap when I can. Burnt Ash Manor is closed except at week-ends. I've got an old boy there who is a sort of gardener-handyman-cum-groom-cum-caretaker. I know I ought to have sold the place long ago, but it's been in the Pethick family since the reign of Queen Anne and I loathe the idea of selling it. But it really isn't fit for a woman like you to live in. It could be glorious but it wants a lot spent on it.'

Venetia had remained quiet, listening. He ended in a sheepish voice:

'Really, what right have I to propose to a woman like you?'

'I'm not poor, Mike darling.'

'I don't know much about your means, although it is obvious'—he waved a hand around Venetia's elegant drawing-room—full of Queen Anne walnut which Geoffrey Sellingham had loved, the fine rugs, the expensive drapes—'quite obvious that you must be well off. That makes it more awkward for me. It will look as though I am marrying you for your money.'

'You *need* to marry money—you said so.'

He flushed scarlet.

'Venetia, for God's sake, don't insult me by suggesting that it is your money that I want. It

27

is you.'

'Darling,' she had said tenderly. 'You need both. Don't let's be silly and over-sensitive. You openly admitted once that you wanted a rich wife. But I do *not* insult you or myself by presuming that it is my money that you are after. I think it is just lucky that you happen to have fallen in love with a woman who can— and will—help you to restore Burnt Ash Manor. I've often considered moving with Maybelle into the country, but didn't want to break up Geoffrey's home. But I know that one oughtn't to live in the past, and if you have room for it my period furniture will look lovely in your old house.'

Then he had taken her hands and kissed each in turn with a genuine humility.

'I think you are the most wonderful woman in the world. I adore your sincerity and I'll try to be just as sincere as you. I do need money, but I swear that I would still have fallen in love with you even if you hadn't a bean.'

She saw that he spoke the truth.

'I believe you, Mike. So we'll just call it luck on both sides. I'll take my young and handsome husband and you take your older wife with her three thousand a year, which is about all taxation allows me these days.'

He gulped and laughed.

'Three thousand a year *untaxed*—golly—I didn't know you were as rich as all that, my sweet.'

'I have a good bit of capital I can draw on, too—for Burnt Ash Manor.'

'You don't know what that would mean to me—to see that placed restored to its former glory—as it was when I was born. Two world wars and the falling means of the Pethicks have almost wrecked it, but it isn't too late. It's a wonderful example of Queen Anne architecture.'

'My favourite, and such a much better setting for all my walnut pieces than this little house.'

'I'm beginning to be madly excited,' he said. 'I'm luckier than I deserve.'

'Darling, so am I. How many women of my age can boast that they have the love of such a young—' But here he interrupted.

'That angle on our love is forbidden.'

She laughed and kissed him. The face that she saw in her mirror was radiant. She did, indeed, look like a girl.

Venetia was beginning to feel more sure of herself and the rightness of what she was doing. Michael picked up a photograph of Geoffrey in a leather frame which stood on her writing bureau.

'He was a jolly nice-looking chap, your husband.'

'He was one of the sweetest men who ever lived.'

Michael put down the photograph and turned back to her.

'He had brains, I believe. I'm not awfully clever, Venetia. Will I bore you?'

'*Bore* me?' she had repeated and laughed that to scorn. She had never been bored in Mike's presence for a moment. He was far too gay and talkative and energetic. And he assured her that he loved to hear her play and would never let her give up her piano or her singing, and that he would try to read more in order to please her.

'You shall start to educate the boy,' he had laughed.

It had all seemed delightful and full of promise.

He took her out to a late dinner as a private celebration but he had promised to keep quiet until she had heard from her daughter.

Venetia wrote a long long letter to Maybelle and posted it to the school before she went to bed that night.

Two days later she sent for Mike and gave him the reply.

'*You know Joanie Johnstone is my best friend and I asked her what she would feel if she was me and she said just what I feel, so I'll tell you, Mummy. If you love Mr Pethick heaps and heaps and will be frightfully happy of course you must get married. I shall be a bit jealous I expect but I'll try not to because I do love you so much, my own beautiful Mummy, and want you not to feel lonely while I am at school. So*

30

please do get married. I shall be thrilled to have such a handsome stepfather. Do send me his photo to show the girls....'

Mike read this part and skipped the rest—the rather pathetic outpouring of an uninhibited young heart to an adored mother who had always been sympathetic and reasonable. He was a trifle touched by the paragraph concerning his good looks and Maybelle's acceptance of him in general.

'Jolly fine, darling—I'm terrifically glad she has taken it like this,' he said as he handed Venetia back the letter. But he avoided looking at her because he saw tears in those dark almond eyes which sometimes attracted him vitally and at others made him a bit uneasy. Venetia could be just a little too sentimental at times in his opinion and he couldn't quite cope with this intense 'mother-stuff', but of course he had to accept it. Venetia flung her arms round his neck and said:

'Darling, isn't it wonderful—now there is nothing to stand in our way...'

He gave a great sigh of relief.

'Terrific. We'll throw a party on Friday night and announce our engagement.'

CHAPTER THREE

So it was *fait accompli*. The Venetia who lay in bed trying to recover from her slight 'hangover' rejoiced because she was so happy. This morning Mike was taking her to buy the ring. Tomorrow they were going down to Burnt Ash to the Manor House.

'You have perfect taste. You must see what improvements you want made, darling,' he had said.

The burr-burr of the telephone roused Venetia thoroughly. Now she reached a hand out for the ivory instrument and said, 'Hullo!'

At first she thought it might be Mike ringing her, but when she heard the deep voice with a foreign inflection, she sat up and a look of surprised delight came over her face.

'*Herman!*' she exclaimed.

'Ah! So you are there, my dear. I was afraid you might be out of town.'

'Herman!' she repeated. 'You are in London—how marvellous.'

'I have come over to see various people and to give a short recital before my tour of America. And, of course, I cannot leave London until I have seen my Venetia.'

'I should have been heart-broken if you hadn't got in touch with me—more especially as I have some wonderful news for you.'

'Tell it to me.'

'I am going to be married again!' said Venetia and felt the colour warm her face. The 'heavy' sensation had left her. She felt well and bright again. Her heart beat quite quickly as she gave the news to this, her greatest friend; Geoffrey's friend, whom she had not seen for nearly two years.

Herman Weissman was one of the finest of the pianists alive today. A great exponent of Beethoven in particular, he had played before all the crowned heads of Europe—before so many kingdoms had been dissolved and two world wars had laid music-loving Europe in ruins.

An Austrian by birth, with Jewish blood in him, Weissman had sought and found asylum in America during the Second War. Now, nearing sixty, he could still play more beautifully than anybody Venetia had ever heard. The long years of extraordinary hard work which such a pianist must endure before reaching the pinnacle of fame that Weissman had reached had not yet sapped his marvellous vitality. His very voice brought Venetia a quick mental vision of the man—small, with a noble, high brow, a thick mane of silver hair, and deep-set eyes under jutting brows. His thin face suggested delicacy—quite erroneously. Herman was rarely ill. That big curly mouth, as Geoffrey used to say, was the replica of that so familiar one in photograph or sculpture of the great Beethoven himself.

Venetia and Geoffrey had first heard Herman play in Dresden during one of their holidays before Maybelle was born. A mutual friend and impresario had introduced them after the concert. From the moment that Herman had taken one of Venetia's hands in his, kissed it and given her his young yet age-old smile, and from the moment that she had looked into those fine eyes that burned with feeling and intellectual power, she had loved him! With the deep respect and humility that one loves a great *maestro*. Geoffrey had loved him, too. They met whenever Weissman came to play in London, or if the Sellinghams attended one of his concerts, abroad. After Geoffrey's death, Herman had stayed with Venetia in her mother-in-law's house in Richmond. He had comforted her as only he could do; with all the homage an ageing man may with ease pay a young and lovely woman, combined with the most tender paternal interest.

Herman was a philosopher. He, who had lost his own wife and child tragically, and who had seen so many of his people tortured and wrecked, could still believe in a God, and in the existence of goodness in human beings. He also believed implicitly in the Hereafter. He had induced Venetia to take courage to feel that she had not really lost the husband she loved so well.

'Death is the closing of a door, but another will always open. For an interim you will be without him,' Herman had told her. 'Somebody else may even take his place one day, although you will not believe it possible. But you are young and it is not right for the young and warm-hearted to live alone. Geoffrey has not forever gone out of your life. Only out of *this* life as we live it on this particular planet.'

Venetia could remember how she had wept and assured him that she would never replace Geoffrey.

'Ah!' he had said with a sad laugh. 'How many times have I heard such things said in the first sharpness of a great grief. But the day will come when you may think otherwise. My beloved Venetia, were I young and not wedded to my work, I myself might ask you to let me take care of you and Maybelle.'

That had made her smile through her tears. It had seemed so wonderful that the greatest living pianist and dearest of men should pay her such a tribute. But she knew that for Herman Weissman there could be no earthly tie now with another woman.

Naomi, his wife, had been a beautiful Bavarian. He had worshipped her. She was a Jewess. And she had died on that dreadful day in Berlin during the first blood bath promulgated by Hitler against the Jews.

Herman had been playing in Moscow at the

time. He had not been able to get back to Germany in time to save either his lovely Naomi or their little son. It was not that they had been deliberately murdered. Perhaps some kind of mercy might have been shown to the family of a great musician who had been a particular favourite of Goering's. But Naomi and the child, out in the streets on an innocent shopping expedition, had been caught in the crowd when Storm Troopers were pursuing a number of their helpless Semitic prey. A spray of bullets from the machine-gun had caught first the mother and then the child. Herman had never seen them again. He had been advised of their death and warned not to return to Germany.

There had been many such tragedies during those terrible seven years of the war. But to Venetia and Geoffrey Herman Weissman's had been one of the most heart-rending. They knew and loved both him and his family. Added to which, Herman had not been young when he married, and his wife and son had been the apple of his eye. He would certainly never replace Naomi now.

This morning after she told him her news, there was a little silence, then Venetia thought that she heard him chuckle.

'So it has come—as I predicted. Congratulations, my dear!'

'Thank you, and darling Herman, you must meet my Michael. We must all lunch together

36

as soon as it can be arranged. How long will you be in London?'

'A fortnight. Tell me more about your young man.'

Now she gave a slightly embarrassed laugh.

'He *is* young, too—younger than I am—'

'So! But you have no age, Venetia. Geoffrey used to say—and I agree—the old dictum applies more to you than any woman: *"Age cannot wither her"*—and so on.'

'Well, it had better not,' Venetia said joyously, 'because Michael is *much* younger than I am.'

'He is an artist—a musician—tell me?'

Now she bit her lip.

'Neither of those things. In fact he is not in our particular world. No—I am going to marry a man who is the antithesis of our beloved Geoffrey. You may think me mad.'

'Madness can be very delightful,' came from Weissman. 'I shall reserve my criticism till I have met your fiancé. If he is your *beau ideal*—he is sure to appeal to me.'

'What are you doing on Sunday? Where are you staying?' she asked.

'At my usual hotel. You know it. I was going to suggest that you lunch with me in the country somewhere on Sunday. I am jealous, but I must include your wonderful young man.'

'Oh, what fun!' Venetia exclaimed. 'I know Michael will be thrilled, too! He has a car. We will call for you at midday.'

'Not a moment before, and I rely upon you not to put me in the hands of a reckless driver.'

They laughed together. That was one of the perfect things about Herman. Greatest of great men, profound of soul and intellect, he could still laugh at foolish things. He possessed an extraordinary simplicity.

Venetia put down the receiver, sprang out of bed and called for Margaret, the Scots cook-housekeeper who had lived with her for the last two years. She was a middle-aged widow who came from the Lowlands and, as Venetia told her friends, the one person to preserve an even keel when everything else in the place was chaotic. Venetia was lucky to have Margaret, more especially as the woman adored Maybelle.

'Ready for the tea and toast!' she sang out.

Margaret came in with a tray, by which time Venetia had pulled the curtains, opened the windows wider and stood looking up at a blue sky. The green bay trees in their striped tubs in the front garden were gilded by the sunshine. It was going to be warm. She drew in a deep breath and pressed her fingers against her temples.

'Oh, what a wonderful day!' she exclaimed.

'Aye,' said Margaret and set the tray down by the bed. Venetia turned to her and began to braid the long fair hair that made her look so extraordinarily young even although the merciless morning sunshine revealed the lines that no woman of her age could conceal.

Margaret had a disapproving look. It worried Venetia. That look had crossed Margaret's face the first moment Venetia told her that she was going to marry Mr Pethick. Margaret had received the news in stony silence. Her face never betrayed her feelings anyhow. She had the cool reserve of her race; an unemotional exterior which in her case hid a heart of gold.

'Aren't you going to congratulate me, Margaret?' Venetia had asked.

Then Margaret, looking at her apron as though it was much more important than Venetia, said:

'Aye—my congratulations, madam.'

Not another word could Venetia get out of her; not a comment or opinion. It had left her curiously flat, and she had been forced to the conclusion that Margaret was one of the ones who would look askance at the marriage.

Now, suddenly Margaret said:

'Am I to take it that you won't be needing me any more once you become Mrs Pethick and go down to the country?'

Venetia sat on the bed, lifted the teapot, and answered:

'Of course not. I've never heard such nonsense. *Of course* I shall need you—more than ever. How do you think I can run a country house without you? Naturally I'll have a bigger staff there because there'll be more to do, but you must know that Maybelle and I can't do without *you*.'

She looked up, smiling, and saw Margaret's lips twitching. So she really did feel moved by this, did she? But still Margaret did not reveal what she felt about the coming marriage. She said:

'I've *sairtenly* no wish to make a change. And I quite like the country. We'll have to see how it works.'

After she had gone, Venetia drank her tea and ate the thin toast. It was absurd, she reflected, but she was quite disappointed by Margaret's reception of her great news.

Now she waited until she finished her breakfast. She was just about to call Michael and tell him about the arrangement with Herman when he forestalled her.

Michael began:

'Good morning, good morning, my divine Venetia.'

She laughed, lying full length on the bed with the telephone beside her and her eyes shut, savouring the sound of his voice.

'I've fallen in love,' at length she sighed. 'Isn't it *appalling*?'

'Might I enquire the name of the object of this devotion?'

'No—you must guess it for yourself.'

'Godfrey Chello,' he said, mentioning a man whom they both disliked. He was fat, greedy

40

and effeminate

'No!' said Venetia and was ready to giggle like her school-girl daughter.

'Then it must be the little waiter who nearly spilled the minestrone on your lap that night in Soho.'

'No.'

'Chiang Kai-shek?'

'*Darling!* He is married to one of the most beautiful and brilliant women in the world.'

'But he might have visited London and seen you and decided to get rid of Madame Chiang—'

'Darling, stop being so absolutely foolish.'

'Then it's *me*. It's got to be me or I'll raise hell. I'll raise an army, too. I'll attack your house with an armed force. Venetia, my love, is it *me*?'

'You know it,' she said and felt overwhelmingly and madly in love with Michael, more than ever sure that she *had* done the right thing. It was years, years, years, she thought, since she had felt so happy, so released and so excited. The future held such heavenly possibilities. Mike's youth, his schoolboy humour, and his undeniable adoration of her were precious things not to be ignored. She wanted all this gaiety and love— she realized now how much alone she had been; what a hunger she had felt all this time for this sweetness, the joy of loving a man like Michael and being loved by him.

41

She told him about lunch with Herman Weissman. He received the news in a characteristic way.

'Anything you want. But who's Weissman? Sounds Teutonic.'

It gave her quite a shock to realize that Mike did not recognize that exalted name.

'*Mike!* Herman Weissman is the pianist—one of the greatest in the world and—'

'Oh, yes, of course,' he broke in, 'now I know—I didn't quite catch on—I can't exactly say I've heard him play, because you know my knowledge of music is a bit limited. But if he is a friend of yours—he's a friend of mine—'

'He's a very great friend. He's Austrian, not German, and we don't mention Germany because he lost his dearly loved wife and son. They were Jewish.'

'What a damnable thing,' said Mike and was full of sympathy.

But after that he got off the subject of Herman and discussed what time he would meet Venetia this morning in order to go on that hallowed expedition in search of an engagement ring.

'The only thing that worries me,' he added, 'is that I can't afford to give you the sort of ring that you ought to have.'

'You know perfectly well that I don't care,' was her answer. 'I never have been the sort of woman to love expensive jewellery and anyhow I've got all I want. Geoffrey's mother was very generous to me when I first married. You can take me to Woolworth's if you like, darling. It's all the same to me.'

'We'll try and do a bit better than that,' he said and gave his infectious laugh, adding: 'I can't wait to see you. I've had a splitting headache since I woke up because I drank far too much last night. Tony and I started on a second celebration after you'd all left. Ghastly! But I seem to want to go on celebrating—it's so perfectly marvellous being engaged to you.'

CHAPTER FOUR

'The weather,' said Herman Weissman, 'is the worst part of the England I love. But even today cannot really depress me.'

'Well, it does me,' said Michael Pethick and gave his hearty laugh while he chose a cigar from the boxes the waiter handed him.

'Well, I'm perfectly happy—a most lucky woman to be lunching with two such wonderful men,' said Venetia.

The meal had taken place at Claridge's. Not at all what the three of them had arranged, which was a day out in the country. Dawn had broken with a steady downpour of rain and even a mischievous wind which cooled the summer warmth and made the day, as Venetia observed, seem more like March than June. It

43

was no use Michael taking them for a drive. Herman suggested that they lunched with him here in the Grill Room.

Venetia liked Claridge's. It was quiet and they could talk as well as enjoy their food. She had been a little nervous when she first entered the lounge with Michael and introduced him to Herman. How would they get on—the two men who were dearest to her on earth? And how strange that two so temperamentally and fundamentally different should be so dear to her. One as a lover; one as a friend. Yet it was so. Inexplicable but a fact. Within a short time she lost her nervousness. She grew more easy in her mind. Herman was, as ever, courteous, charming, and an entertaining conversationalist. Michael was in a good mood and obviously proud of her. He took her hand and said to Herman:

'You can imagine what it means to me, sir, to be able to come here with Venetia today—as her future husband.'

He said it with sincerity and Venetia, who knew her Herman, was pleased to see the look of pleasure that spread over his fine intellectual face. He shook hands with Mike and said:

'I congratulate you with all my heart. And I do not need to tell you, young man, that you have chosen a pearl among women.'

Venetia laughed at that, but Michael agreed with enthusiasm.

'Don't I know it! I'm a lucky fellow.'

44

'I'm lucky, too,' put in Venetia.

And that was the happy beginning to the lunch party. All seemed to go merrily. She and Herman exchanged news, talked of Maybelle, whom he described as 'my beloved little god-daughter', touched on the subject of his work, his future concerts, and his forthcoming tour of America. Not forgetting to comment on the beautiful ring which Venetia wore on the third finger of her left hand. It was a yellow diamond in an old setting. Venetia adored yellow diamonds. It was not as valuable by half as the pure white Brazilian stone that Geoffrey had given her, but it had cost Mike more than he could strictly afford. He had insisted on buying it because it had been Venetia's choice. She had loved him for his generosity. It fitted her long slender finger perfectly and she was ridiculously pleased with it. Even more so when Herman praised it and she saw a look of boyish satisfaction cross Mike's brown face.

Now Herman turned to Michael, interested in all he had to say—even listened, benevolently, when Michael touched on his pet subject—horses.

'I know nothing about horses,' Herman observed, 'beyond the fact that I think they are excellent creatures and that I would like to be able to ride. It must be a very fine thing and very healthy.'

'That's where Maybelle comes in,' said Venetia. 'She will adore it. But I'm afraid I'm too old to begin, and I've never mounted a horse in my life.'

Herman turned back to her, drawing on his cigar. He looked at her thoughtfully through the wreath of blue smoke.

'Do not touch on this matter of age. You have no need, Venetia,' he said.

'That's what I'm always telling her, sir,' said Michael.

Venetia laughed.

'I should soon have a swollen head if I listened to either of you for long. The fact remains that I *am* too old to start riding. It is the one thing I cannot share with my darling Mike, but we have so much else in common so what matter?'

Herman Weissman continued to smoke thoughtfully. Was that true? Had these two people anything in common? Surely little but passionate love—or might it be called *infatuation*? This idea had not struck Herman immediately; it had been rising gradually to the surface during the meal. Now it took definite shape and would not be banished. He was quite sure that Venetia was not as truly in love with this young man as she had been with Geoffrey, with whom she had had an affinity. Herman had been sincerely attached to Venetia's late husband and mourned his untimely death. But he had thought it right and proper that Venetia, still in her early forties, should marry again. He had wanted it that way so that she

46

should find happiness and have a companion for later years when Maybelle was grown up and married.

Every time he returned to England Herman half expected to hear that Venetia had found another love and was ready to make a new life for herself. But never had he anticipated this: that she should choose a man so much younger than herself and one so *different*.

It was the *difference* between Venetia and Michael that alarmed him. Age was of no account. He had seen several extremely happy marriages where the woman was the older of the two, but in such cases there had been mutual interests and that deep spiritual union which transcends and outlasts the physical side. Passion was necessary but alone it could not endure. Herman Weissman had to confess himself deeply perturbed, when he had had time to consider Venetia's choice and form an opinion of the man.

First impressions had not been bad; on the contrary, he thought Michael Pethick splendid to look at. He could see what had originally drawn Venetia to her Michael.

There was, too, a warmth, a deep strong emotion flowing between Venetia and Michael which Herman found charming. Once he had loved his wife, Naomi, in just that way. Venetia and Michael obviously could think only of the time when they could possess each other wholly. It was all part of the pattern of love and

47

loving, but it frightened Herman. For it was as though they were surrounded by a thick, sweet fog. They could not see through it. They were sequestered in their passionate desire for each other. But for Herman who knew his Venetia so well and loved her so much, the treacherous mist lifted just enough to show him the unhappy truth. A truth which Venetia, herself, must inevitably discover. It would not be pleasant or happy for her. But it existed. She and this young man were totally unsuited. It appalled Herman that she could deceive herself into believing that Michael was the right man to put in Geoffrey's shoes. To Herman, it seemed almost desecration.

Michael Pethick was a 'Peter Pan'. Vain, perhaps egotistical, charming, and at Venetia's feet. But that was not enough for *her*. What madness possessed her, Herman asked himself, while he listened to Michael chattering about his Manor House, the Stock Exchange, the trip he was taking over to Ireland to see a horse that an Irish friend wanted him to buy—and his and Venetia's plans to marry before Maybelle's summer holiday commenced.

Herman's shaggy brows met. He turned to Venetia:

'You plan to marry at once?'

She laid one of her slender and lovely hands on his. She and Mike saw no reason to delay their marriage, she said.

Herman wanted to implore her to wait a

48

little longer; to get to know Michael Pethick much better than she knew him now.

What of the child? Venetia had said how lovely it would be for Maybelle to have a young stepfather and a country home. But to Herman, Michael was too young still and self-centred to be genuinely interested in the growth and development of a fifteen-year-old girl. Truly it was amazing, Herman reflected, that the beloved Venetia, whom he had thought such a wise and intelligent woman, should not behave with greater wisdom. She was like an inexperienced girl in the throes of her first love affair. How deadly was this attraction between the sexes! What a honeyed trap!

The great pianist grew more and more depressed and silent as the moments went by.

'You will be in America and not able to come to my wedding, which grieves me,' added Venetia.

'Me, too,' he said, smiling at her with tenderness.

But he knew that even had it been possible he could not have brought himself to attend the marriage. He could not bear to watch Venetia make such a terrible mistake, for by now no amount of good looks or charm about Michael could alter his opinion that Venetia was about to make a mistake.

He talked to the engaged pair for a few moments and then the party broke up. Herman must have an hour's rest and then was going to see his friend, the young conductor, Herbert Menges.

Once back in her house, Venetia took off her hat and gloves and with a peculiarly young gesture moved towards Michael who threw away his cigarette and caught her in his arms.

'I do love you so much,' she said.

Even as she said it she remembered all the cynical advice she had ever been given or read about: that a woman shouldn't keep telling a man that she loved him; that it's good to keep a man guessing; that men like to make the overtures; bits of advice to be found in heart-throb columns, in women's magazines, in articles for girls. Venetia grimaced, keeping her face hidden against Michael's shoulder. His kisses were warm upon her head. He said:

'I was so proud of you today. There wasn't a woman in Claridge's to touch you.'

She looked up at him, eyes sparkling.

'Did you like my Herman?'

'I thought he was a nice old thing.'

Venetia grimaced again.

'Not so old—only sixty—but I suppose to my young Michael that seems senile.'

He laughed, caught her left hand, and looked at the yellow diamond, head on one side.

'Still like it?'

'Enormously. More so what it symbolizes.'

He let her go and looked around the

charming room. It had stopped raining. The sun slanted through the soft creamy transparent curtains that looped over the windows. He said:

'I think it is going to be fine after all. Shall we run down to Burnt Ash now as well as tomorrow? It won't take more than an hour and a quarter. I'd love to get your opinion of the place.'

She hesitated. She was a little tired. Like Herman, she felt inclined to take a rest after that big lunch. Especially as she had had several late nights in succession, and the days had been so full of excitement and movement, but it never entered her head to reject Michael's idea.

'I think it would be heavenly,' she said. 'Just give me ten minutes to change into a suit and some more countrified shoes.'

'Okay, my sweet.'

Michael sat down, helped himself to a cigarette from a porphyry box and smoked it with lazy contentment while he waited for Venetia to come back. He was thinking:

'This would be rather an attractive house for us to keep as a *pied à terre* in town. I don't see why we shouldn't afford it with Venetia's income added to mine. I think I'm doing rather well for myself. Venetia's a darling and most attractive and I don't think she's the type to get old quickly. The daughter may be a bit of a bore but she'll be away at school for the next few years. Yes—I think I'm quite a lucky chap.'

The telephone bell rang. Michael put out a hand to lift the receiver, then remembered that this was not his house, until he heard Venetia calling out from the bathroom:

'Answer it for me, darling.'

A woman's voice said:

'Oh—have I got the right number—is that Mrs Sellingham's house?'

'Yes, it is,' said Michael.

'Oh—er—is she in?'

'Yes, but she can't come for the moment. Can I give her a message?'

'Oh!' said the voice again, and this time sounded surprised. It was a gentle, elderly voice. Said Michael:

'Who shall I tell her has called?'

'Lady Sellingham—I think my daughter-in-law may have forgotten but she half promised to come down to Richmond to me for tea today. I wondered if I may expect her. That is all.'

'Ah!' thought Michael. *Mother-in-law.* Another slight bind if the old bag means to go on appropriating Venetia.'

But he spoke to Lady Sellingham in his most pleasant voice.

'Do hold on, please, Lady Sellingham. I'll see if Venetia can speak to you now. This, by the way, is Michael Pethick. I have not had the pleasure of meeting you yet, but I expect you

52

know Venetia and I are going to be married.'

There was a silence from the other end of the wire. After he has spoken, Michael felt a bit of a cad—and a tactless one. After all, maybe Venetia had not told Geoffrey's mother yet. It might have been a shock to the old lady. Michael was not unkind at heart. Quickly he added:

'I do so hope to be allowed to come and see you with Venetia, Lady Sellingham. I know Venetia's future must be of great importance to you, so I do assure you I shall do my best to make her very happy.'

That was better. Lady Sellingham said:

'Oh—I am indeed glad to hear that—I—as a matter of fact, I didn't know about this, Mr Pethick. Although, of course, Venetia has spoken of you. I do congratulate you, and *of course* we must meet soon. I'm devoted to my daughter-in-law. And I'm most glad she has found the right man because I know my son would have wished her to marry again.'

Now Michael beamed and felt good. Decent old bag, Lady Sellingham sounded, he thought. He felt quite affectionate towards her.

'I say—thanks awfully!' he exclaimed in his most boyish and charming voice.

'I won't bother Venetia if she is busy—' began Lady Sellingham.

But at that moment Venetia's voice came over the 'phone from the extension in her bedroom.

53

'Hullo—who is it?—Venetia here.'

'Darling, it's Mother—'

Michael put down the receiver. He stretched his long legs in front of him and whistled a little tune under his breath. He had a strong streak of curiosity in his make-up and he would like to have heard the conversation between Venetia and her ex-mother-in-law. 'Ex' was the right word in Michael's opinion. He didn't really want his wife to remain involved with her first husband's relatives. Much better to begin a new life. Lucky for Venetia *she* wouldn't have a mother-in-law when she became Mrs Pethick. There was only poor old Pop, who wouldn't be with them very long anyhow. Relations could be both a tie and a bore—one was better without them. It would, of course, have been a lot better if there hadn't been that daughter, Maybelle. Going on for sixteen! Put years on to Venetia. It would inevitably make her appear older to have a tall girl hanging around calling her 'Mummy'. He did not *mind* the age business all that much ... but Venetia looked so young ... why not try to preserve the illusion, especially as he was only thirty-three?

Michael got up and moved across to the writing bureau. He stared, frowning, at the framed photograph of Geoffrey Sellingham, and beside it the one of Venetia's daughter who looked very shy and sweet in a party dress with frills, and two plaits tied up on top of her head with a ribbon in the American style. It must have been taken when she was a year or two younger, he decided. Pretty kid. But something in the grave, even critical look in the big contemplative eyes made him feel uneasy.

'I must say you're taking something on, Mike, my lad,' he remarked to himself and twisted his lips as he threw his cigarette-end into the empty grate.

CHAPTER FIVE

'I'm glad Mike introduced himself to you, Mother darling, but I didn't mean it to be broken to you quite so abruptly. I was saving it up for when I saw you,' Venetia explained on the telephone alone in her bedroom.

'My darling girl, please don't apologize,' said Lady Sellingham. 'Naturally it was a little bit of a shock, but you know that I am *delighted* for you. Nobody wants you to be happy more than I do.'

'Bless you, darling. I'm glad you spoke to my Mike. Did you like his voice?'

'He sounds quite delightful, dear. Is he the young man you've been telling me about whom you met at the Hunt Ball?'

'Yes.'

An instant's silence as though Lady Sellingham was considering this. Then:

'Well, there's so much for us to talk over,

55

dear—suppose you come down and see me.'

'Look, darling,' said Venetia. 'Would you mind very much if I popped down to see you on Friday instead of today? I'll come to lunch if I may. But Mike wants me so much to drive down to Sussex with him now. We want to go over the Manor House, which is to be my future home.'

Unhesitatingly came Lady Sellingham's reply to this apology.

'Of course, dear. Don't mind about me. I've got plenty to do in the garden now the sun's out.'

Venetia rang off. Then something which she could not quite explain urged her to sit down and telephone Herman before joining Michael again.

Venetia said:

'I just had to know what you thought of my Michael.'

An instant's delay. Then from Herman:

'A most handsome and attractive young man.'

'But did you *like* him?'

'Venetia, my beloved one, must you ask me such an intimate question over the telephone?'

Venetia went quite white.

'Oh, Herman, don't you *like* Michael?'

'Venetia, my child, I hardly know him. I hesitate to form opinions of people so speedily. It would be unfair and wrong to do so, for first meetings can be most deceptive. But if you wish me to tell you whether I think he is right for you or not, then I will be honest, since he who flatters for the sake of flattery, or expresses an opinion only because he thinks it will give pleasure, is no true friend.'

That was enough for Venetia. The colour did not return to her face. She said:

'Then you think I am making a mistake?'

'Tush, I have said nothing so definite. I do not know about Michael yet, nor can I guess what lies in his heart. But this I *will* say. The question of your age is of no matter. He might be twenty years younger and still right for you. But you and he are temperamentally different. You are physically very much in love. There is a very strong magnetism between you. These things may be sufficient for an *affaire d'amour*, but not always for marriage.'

Now the colour surged into Venetia's face, burning and distressful.

'But, Herman, it doesn't matter just because *he* hunts and *I* play the piano, or that *he* doesn't read and *I* do. We *have* a great deal else in common.'

'I did not think so, but if you tell me so—I must accept it.'

'A lot in common,' she repeated as though reassuring herself.

'My dearest Venetia—you love him very much. If he truly loves you—maybe the differences that I can see can be bridged. As I have just said—I do not know him well enough

57

yet to be able to judge. On the surface he seems a charming young man greatly enamoured of you.'

'Well, it's not just a question of money—he would marry me if I lost everything tomorrow,' exclaimed Venetia.

'I devoutly hope so. He would be totally unworthy to touch your hand were that not so.'

'We love each other so much that I am sure that the fact that we have different interests won't matter.'

'Then do not let anything I think or say deter you.'

'Nothing will, but Herman, I did *want* you to like him.'

'If he makes you happy, I shall like him, my Venetia.'

'You're a wonderful friend,' she said huskily.

'And did your young friend like your old Herman?' came the question in a lighter vein.

'Of *course*.'

She thought of what Michael had said about Herman being 'a nice old thing'. She felt suddenly that she wanted to cry for no reason at all. She told herself that she must remember that people like her mother-in-law and Herman Weissman, who had known and loved Geoffrey, could not be expected to accept Michael at once, with full appreciation and understanding. But he would soon gain their trust and regard.

'Are you there, my dear?' asked Herman.

'Yes. But I must go. Mike's waiting for me. I just wanted to feel that you will give me your blessing.'

'I have already given it, but please, dearest, give me time to get to know your young man better. You must remember that he is very different from Geoffrey.'

'I suppose that is why you think I'm being unwise.'

Silence. Then said Herman:

'Passionate love is often reckless. Please do not rush into marriage. Make quite sure.'

'I *am sure, now,*' she said proudly.

But after she had put down the receiver she felt depressed. She realized that Herman did not think that she was doing the right thing. Yet every set-back of this kind only made her feel more tenderly towards Mike and more determined to prove to her critics that it was they who were wrong; that she and Michael were justified in their decision to marry.

She forgot about Herman during the drive to Lewes. The country was fresh and sparkling after the summer rain. Michael was in high spirits and she was very happy. She put one hand lightly on his knee and he covered it with his. It made her feel youthful and much in love.

He chattered of the future and all they would do together. She felt excited at the prospect of seeing the place that was to be her future home. And she was not disappointed, even though, as

59

Michael had warned her, the house was rapidly deteriorating through the lack of necessary repairs. The interior had not been touched since his mother's lifetime. It was very shabby. Paint was peeling and wallpaper stained. Only the two rooms that Michael occupied when he came down for the week-end looked at all comfortable and lived in. But her first impression of Burnt Ash Manor drew an exclamation of delight from her.

'Oh, it's absolute heaven, Mike!'

He was justifiably proud of his home. It was one of those small manor houses built during the reign of Queen Anne. One came upon it suddenly at the bottom of a hill. It nestled under the shadow of the Downs, and there it had stood for the last two hundred years protected from the wind. On a June day like this, it dreamed in the sun, warm and welcoming with its beautiful small bricks, the lovely roof and the dignified white portico over which tumbled a profusion of purple clematis intertwined with yellow roses. There was a walled garden in which espalier peaches spread green arms against the rosy bricks. There was an orchard, and one approached the house through white gates down a pleasant drive flanked by chestnuts gay at this season with the white candles in full bloom. One of the features of the place was the huge cedar on the front lawn—a truly magnificent old tree spreading its dark silky shade over grass that had been baked to a yellowish tinge by the mid-summer sun. Today's rain was the first for many weeks. Venetia liked the fact that the estate was isolated yet only two miles from Burnt Ash village and five from Lewes.

'I could not have imagined a more enchanting spot,' said Venetia, and felt her heart beat quite fast with pleasure.

The lawns were fairly well kept and some attempt had been made to weed the flower beds, although there was plenty to be done in that huge long herbaceous border, and Venetia wished that her mother-in-law could come here and give good advice. How much she would love the place—she being a great gardener and full of the knowledge of herbs and flowers.

There was a small cottage in the grounds occupied at the moment by the groom, who looked after Michael's hunter and acted as caretaker in the house while his master was up in town.

'And now for the stables,' he said eagerly and pulled her towards a wrought-iron gate which led into a courtyard behind the house. 'You must make the acquaintance of my beloved Red Prince.'

'The stables before the house?' Venetia laughed.

He laughed with her.

'Am I being selfish or shall we inspect your domain first?'

'Darling, the inside of the house is going to

be *yours* as well as *mine*,' she protested, laughing again.

But first she went with him to inspect the stables, joined by the groom, Bennett, a dried-up little man who looked as though he might have been a jockey in his youth, and whom Venetia thought quite a pleasant type, with his small twinkling eyes and skin like wrinkled leather. He touched his checked cap to her and called her 'Milady', which amused her.

Michael informed her, afterwards, that Bennett had once been in the service of titled people and never liked to forget it.

The stable occupied by Mike's hunter was, Venetia noted with some amusement, quite the best kept building in the place. It had been modernized. No expense had been spared. Red Prince himself lived up to his name—a truly royal animal. Venetia knew nothing about horses but could understand that those who did must love them very much. She stroked the roan's satin nose while she listened to Mike extolling his perfections.

'You know I weigh about fourteen stone. Well, Red Prince is sixteen and a half hands. Look at that head, darling—and what a chest—terrific depth. He isn't too long in the back, either. Nice clean legs. Look!'

It was all Greek to Venetia but she tried earnestly to understand and appreciate what she was being told. Red Prince nuzzled her hand, then with a flick of his long lashes turned his liquid and beautiful eyes upon his master, tossed his whitish mane, and whinnied softly.

'He really is a darling—Maybelle will adore him,' said Venetia.

'We'll have to buy something for Maybelle,' said Mike carelessly. 'But she won't want anything as big as Red Prince.'

'Would you like me to saddle him, sir,' asked Bennett, 'and let her ladyship see you up?'

'I'd love to see you mounted,' said Venetia.

Michael was wiping his face and neck with a silk handkerchief. After the heavy rain the earth was steaming. He felt hot. He shook his head at the groom.

'Not now. And look here, Bennett, Prince is too fat. Look at that belly. Cut down his oats and give him more exercise, you lazy little swine.'

Bennett touched his cap and grinned.

'Very good, sir.'

'Now for the house,' said Venetia eagerly.

As they walked back through the orchard and round on to the front lawn again, Michael said:

'I honestly don't see why you shouldn't learn to ride, Venetia darling. You'd look terrific in a well-cut habit and bowler—just the type.'

She was just about to say 'Too old' but desisted.

'I don't honestly think that I should like it. I have no sense of balance. Even as a child I

63

could never ride a bike without falling off,' she laughed. 'You'll have to concentrate on your step-daughter.'

The name 'step-daughter' rendered Michael speechless.

He rubbed his curls. They were damp with sweat and glistened like a raven's wing in the sun. He was tremendously handsome and buoyant, she thought, and regretted that she could not drop her ten years and be thirty again for *him*. Yet that very thought seemed disloyal to the dead. At thirty she had been Geoffrey's wife and love. There could be no regretting.

Now they began their tour of the Manor House. It was all and more than Venetia needed to make her entirely happy. The kitchen was old-fashioned. There were too many draughty passages and she knew at once that she would never keep a maid here unless all this was altered. But it would be easy to do. Geoffrey's great friend, Jack Fuller, who was an architect, would be just the ideal person. She would enlist his help. Eagerly she pointed out to Michael how this wall could come down, and that room be thrown into the next, and a modern cooker replace the old-fashioned stove and, of course, the whole hot-water system must be modernized. They must have central heating. *That* she couldn't live without.

'You shall be as warm as you wish, my Madame Orchid,' he said and pressed her arm to his side. She was not quite sure that he had listened very carefully to her plans but he expressed full agreement with anything suggested. Neither of them mentioned the cost nor that it would be *she* who would pay the bill.

She was enchanted by the long, lovely drawing-room with its three windows overlooking the wide lawn and the dark tranquil cedar. Then there was that queer little room at the back of the house which would make a perfect study for Michael. It had a view of the gentle green slopes of the Downs. And the dining-room was 'heaven' she said. She adored those alcoves for her special china. Upstairs there were many bedrooms, one big one in particular which had an uninterrupted view of the Downs and pastureland across to the rooftops of Burnt Ash village; the square grey tower of the old church.

'Truly, it is glorious, Mike,' she said, in a moved voice, as they stood at one of the windows in this bedroom which they had planned should be theirs (the little room next door should be turned into a bathroom).

'This was my parents' room. I believe the infant Michael actually opened his blue eyes in here and yelled to the rooftops as he has been doing ever since,' said Michael and gave his rollicking laugh.

Venetia did not know whether she felt like his mother or his future wife in that moment, but she was full of tenderness for him. She hugged him close to her.

'Oh, what an abominable child you must have been, and what a noise you must have made and how much I love you!'

He hugged her in return.

'I'm damned glad you like the old place so much. I was afraid you might find it depressing.'

'It's the very reverse. It has charm and dignity and it's sunny and sweet.'

He released her and pulled out a cigarette.

'With your taste you'll make it perfect. You can clear out everything you don't like.'

She was relieved. Most of the furniture was Victorian and ugly and carpets and curtains were worn out. Quite wrong for the period. Obviously Michael's mother had been no artist, but Venetia would never have said so. It was Michael who said it first.

'Poor old Mamma had *ghastly* taste and Pop never cared about anything but hunting and shooting—a bit like myself.'

Venetia felt sorry for her Michael. Little wonder he was not like Geoffrey. Geoffrey had had Lady Sellingham's training. Children grow up accustomed to the type of *décor* and furnishing enjoyed by their parents. Mike had never had a chance. But *she* would re-educate him.

Michael made it all delightfully easy for her when he flung her that careless permission to 'scrap' anything that she did not care for!

'We'll have to send a lot to the Sale Room if

you really don't mind, darling,' she said.

'I couldn't care less,' he said.

'But you will be interested in all that *I* am going to do?'

His gay blue eyes smiled at her.

'But of course, sweet.'

How easy he was, she thought, and how charming he would be to live with. He was so amenable that she could see that there would be little argument between them. In her life with Geoffrey, dear and sweet though he was, she had had to tread more carefully, for he had held very decided views on the little things that laced their lives together. Mike seemed delightfully unconcerned about the house. All his thoughts turned to the out-of-doors. Did that cause her a pang of regret? Not in this moment when she was so wholly in love. There were so many things she wanted to ask Geoffrey's mother, but she supposed *that* would hardly be tactful. She regretted the fact that from now on dear Mother must play a much less active part in her life. One could hardly intrude a former mother-in-law into the existence of one's second husband.

'Well, I suppose we ought to get cracking on the homeward journey. I've got a date this evening with a chap who is on the Stock Exchange and who Tony and I are meeting at the Club,' said Michael.

Just before they went downstairs Venetia glanced into a small room at the end of the passage.

'That would make an ideal sitting-room for Maybelle.'

'You mean in the holidays?'

'Yes.'

'I suppose she'll go to her grandmother sometimes, though, won't she?'

'Yes, of course,' said Venetia.

Michael looked relieved. Venetia came up to him, gave him a quizzical look and then put her tongue in her cheek.

'Do you know, darling, sometimes I feel you're quite jealous of my young daughter.'

He caught one of her hands and put it against his cheek.

'I think I'm jealous of anybody in the world that wants any of your time. I'm absolutely crazily in love with you, you know, darling.'

Now for a moment passion was alight, flaming through them both. They clung together in a long embrace that left Venetia pale and shaken. She had never felt more in love. To know that he cared about her as much as that was tremendously exhilarating. The memory of Maybelle faded. They seemed to be in perfect harmony as they drove back to London. Only when they reached town and her house and she was about to step out of the car the perfection was marred by a jarring note. Michael looked at her with some slight expression of awkwardness.

'You know, sweet, all this business about

getting an architect for Burnt Ash and embarking on these improvements—it's going to cost a hell of a lot, isn't it?'

'I dare say it is, Mike.'

He pulled the lobe of his ear and avoided her gaze.

'Darling, I hate saying this, but you know my position. I'm damned short of capital.'

Now it was her turn to feel awkward. She took his hand and squeezed it.

'That's all right, darling. I've got some capital and I can spend it. *I want to*—on making our home beautiful. Don't feel badly about it. We're going to be married and from now on what's mine is *yours.*'

His face grew hot. He looked at her with genuine love and gratitude.

'You're divinely generous, Venetia. I thank you from the bottom of my heart. I only wish I had more money to spend on *you.*'

'I know, but I don't in the least mind that the shoe is on the other foot. You give me so much else.'

'Do I really, Venetia?'

'Yes, darling, I'm just as much in love with you as you are with me; perhaps more so.'

That was foolish of her, she thought immediately. A thing that a woman oughtn't to say to a man, but Mike answered it with sincerity and an endearing warmth.

'You couldn't be. But we won't argue about *that.* Just go on loving me. When I see you tomorrow we shall fix that date for our wedding and it's got to be early next month. Agreed?'

'I expect so,' she said and her eyes were luminous with happiness. The thought of marriage with Michael was quite intoxicating. So far their love-making had been conventionally curtailed. She felt that Michael, like herself, was sensitive to her wish not to spoil things by a careless and too previous intimacy. But her very knees seemed to shake at the thought of their future possession of one another.

There was no more talk about money. Mike drove off and she walked into the house. She had much to think about. She was going to have an early night because she felt suddenly extremely tired. She wanted to write another letter to Maybelle and tell the child about Burnt Ash, then try to contact Jack Fuller on the 'phone and make an appointment for him to drive down with her and survey the Manor House.

CHAPTER SIX

On the following Friday a very strange thought struck Venetia as she drove the small car, which she used as a 'taxi', down to Richmond. She had arranged to lunch with Geoffrey's mother and at four o'clock Mike was going to get away early from the Stock Exchange and join them there in order to be introduced to Lady Sellingham. And Venetia suddenly reflected that every time she introduced Mike to her old friends it was with the query in her mind: '*Will they like him?*' But it should really have been: '*Will he like them?*' *His* opinion should be the only one to matter to her from now onward. There should be no cause for any nervousness when she made these introductions.

Threading in and out of the traffic on this busy morning—it was fine and warm—she considered that matter and decided that it was all because of the difference in ages and because most people were bound to think the marriage 'unsuitable'.

She must be strong-minded enough not to let it worry her at all. If Mike did not mind—why should she?

She found Lady Sellingham, as usual on a summer's day, working in her garden.

Geoffrey's mother was a small woman of fragile physique with the rather sweet expression and large clear eyes which always reminded Venetia of her late husband. She was in her late sixties but looked younger. There was scarcely a thread of grey in the fair hair although its once bright gold had faded. She invariably wore a hat—both outside and inside the house—a rather unbecoming straw hat

71

with a wreath of cherries on it. Somehow Venetia always connected with her mother-in-law with that hat and when little Maybelle could first speak she used to talk about '*Granny's chelly hat*'. Geoffrey used to laugh about it and forbid his mother ever to discard it. It was an heirloom, he said.

Today the sight of that cherry hat gave Venetia quite a pang. She meant to maintain the old ties with Geoffrey's mother but her re-marriage and new life would be bound to put a certain gulf between them. She kissed Lady Sellingham. The older woman was serene and welcoming. She dropped trowel and trug, wiped her hands with a handkerchief, and said:

'Come in, my dear, and let us have a sherry and a cigarette.' If she had a fault it was one that she could not break herself of. The habit of smoking. It was a vice with her, she declared.

They walked into the cool pretty drawing-room. The Venetian blinds were down, keeping out the strong sunlight in order to save a valuable Aubusson carpet. This little period house in Richmond was lovely both inside and out.

There were only three photographs in the drawing-room, which was furnished in exquisite taste. Venetia and Geoffrey in a double frame and one of Maybelle.

Lady Sellingham did not mention Venetia's engagement until sherry had been poured out, cigarettes lighted and the two of them were seated side by side on the Chesterfield. The room was full of the scent of roses which Lady Sellingham grew in profusion and which were her pride and joy.

It was Venetia who broke out with:

'Well, Mother—tell me what you think about it.'

'Your engagement, you mean, dear?'

'Yes.'

'Well, as I said on the 'phone, it was a little bit of a shock but I most heartily congratulate you. I know Geoffrey would have wanted you to find love and happiness again, and I feel the same.'

'You would,' said Venetia and put out a hand and pressed one of Lady Sellingham's, which were still as firm and youthful as a girl's.

'Of course I shall be able to give you a more considered opinion after I have met your fiancé,' added Lady Sellingham.

Venetia bit her lip.

'He's twelve years younger than I am, Mother.'

'You look so young for your years, my dear, I don't see that it matters. It's what you have in common that is important.'

Venetia's teeth pressed harder into her lower lip.

'We have different pursuits—but we are very much in love. I *adore* Mike and I'm sure you'll find him irresistible.'

'If he makes you a good husband and is good

to Maybelle what more could I ask?'

'I know he will be,' said Venetia with enthusiasm.

'Has Maybelle met him?'

'Not yet, but any young schoolgirl would fall for Mike, he's so full of charm and vitality and she'll share his love of riding. You know yesterday we went down to see his home— Burnt Ash Manor.'

Venetia launched into a glowing account of the old house and the grounds and ended:

'It is just your cup of tea, Mother darling, and I wish you could help us do it up.'

'I would like nothing more but I don't suppose your young man will want me around interfering.'

'Oh, Mother, I don't want my marriage to divide us at all,' broke out Venetia impulsively.

It was on the tip of the older woman's tongue to answer: *'But it will. It's bound to. I'm losing you, my beautiful, kind daughter-in-law, just as my Geoffrey will be losing his widow. It is right and proper, but I shall miss you dreadfully.'*

But she said:

'Nothing shall come between us, if that is how you want it, darling. You will always find me here, just as you have done for the last twenty-two years.'

Venetia felt the tears sting her eyelids.

'It's been a long time,' she said in a low voice.

'Now you're not to get morbid,' said Lady Sellingham briskly and rose and called out to

74

the old housekeeper who had been with her since Geoffrey was a boy:

'We're ready for lunch when you are, Minnie.'

Later that afternoon Lady Sellingham knew beyond doubt that Michael Pethick was not right for Venetia. She learned it to her bitter disappointment and anxiety. She had known and loved Geoffrey's wife long enough to be fully aware of what Venetia needed in her life. She should have chosen an older man with some of Geoffrey's wisdom and tranquillity if not all his love of art and music. But this 'Mike' as she called him—oh, what a *terrible* mistake! She felt it as soon as she saw him; when first he walked up to them in the garden where they were sitting on the hammock seat by the rockery. Handsome, yes! Quite a young god with his thick dark curls, his fine figure and gay blue eyes. A handsome, healthy young animal. And 'all there', the old lady thought shrewdly. No flies on Mr Mike. Quite a lot of common sense and horse sense ('horse' was the word). She could picture him mounted and he'd ride superbly. Charming manners, too. Kissed her hand in Continental fashion and showed a suitable humility when he said:

'Do you hate me for taking Venetia away?'

Yet that somehow had jarred and Lady Sellingham had answered quietly:

'I don't think anybody will ever really take Venetia away from me, Mr Pethick. She is like

75

my own daughter, you know.'

To which Michael had been quick to add the diplomatic remark that he had no mother alive, therefore she, Lady Sellingham, would be the only mother he would have. He hoped they would see a lot of each other and that she must come down to Burnt Ash and give her opinion because he had heard that she was such an artist at interior decoration. And of course, he could see from her own lovely little house that she was! *Etcetera, etcetera!* Very nice and flattering and glib, thought Lady Sellingham dryly. But as she said to her dear old confidential maid afterwards:

'I just didn't take to him, Minnie. Nobody can deny that he is attractive, but he is not good enough for Mrs Sellingham.'

Minnie, white-haired, bespectacled, and that rare thing in modern days, a devoted (and contented) servant—replied briefly:

'You've said it for me, my lady. He is handsome enough but only a boy with his ways. Not what Mrs Sellingham needs, and after Mr Geoffrey—'

'We won't go into that,' said Lady Sellingham gently but firmly.

She had a hard task before her. She knew that the moment her daughter-in-law got home, Venetia would telephone to ask her opinion. And Venetia would expect an honest one. Never before in her life had Lady Sellingham told a deliberate lie; but in this case

76

it seemed that she could not help it. She would not have the heart to decry Michael in the face of this joyous love which Venetia made no effort to conceal. She was so obviously in love ... how, Lady Sellingham asked herself, could anybody risk destroying that faith? So when Venetia telephoned the older woman compromised:

'He is most attractive; rather young for his age of course, but you look much of a muchness together, my dear, so don't worry about that.'

'But you do approve?' demanded Venetia's voice with its husky underlying note of excitement.

Lady Sellingham closed her eyes and prayed to be forgiven.

'I believe that if two people are truly in love they will make a happy pair, my dear.'

'And you will give me your blessing?'

'Oh, of course.'

'I know he isn't a bit like Geoffrey,' added Venetia.

The note of apology in Venetia's voice hurt Lady Sellingham.

'Dear girl, comparisons are odious. The two men are not in any way comparable. I don't pretend there isn't an element of risk about your marrying a young sportsman of Michael Pethick's type, but the decision must rest with you.'

There the conversation ended.

But Venetia's friend, Barbara Keen, remained obstinately against the whole thing. That same evening after Venetia's lunch with Lady Sellingham, Barbara came to the house for a drink and in her blunt, remorseless fashion tried flagrantly to dissuade Venetia from making this marriage.

'You know me—I am not going to pamper you over this just because you seem blissful,' she declared.

The two women were sitting opposite each other in Venetia's drawing-room. Barbara, slinky, ultra-smart, looking more American than English with her long legs and the beautiful clothes which had come from New York like the little *Hattie Carnegie* hat—small, flat as a pancake and perched on her cropped black head. She wore many bangles and rings and had a nervous habit of flicking the ash from her cigarette with her little finger: Venetia wore a house-coat and looked a trifle tired. There was an unusually resentful look in her soft dark eyes.

'I really can't think what you've got against Mike,' she said, 'but it's obvious that you don't like him.'

'Darling, don't be a fool. I'm not just doing the jealous bitch because you've got the chance to marry a handsome young thing and I haven't. I love you and you know it. But I am not going to sit back and watch you make a mess of your life.'

'I refuse to accept the fact that I'm doing so,' said Venetia coldly.

Barbara's brutal and destructive statements came as ice-cold blows after the friendly tolerance from Herman and Lady Sellingham's sweet acceptance of the situation.

But Barbara was not to be snubbed.

'Don't go all haughty with me, ducky. Face facts.'

'I'm rather tired of being told to face facts. I'm aware of the whole situation. I am twelve years older than Michael and we have nothing basically in common, except that we are very much in love. But there *are* a lot of things we *do* like doing together. And he's just as keen about making a lovely house out of Burnt Ash as I am and ...'

'*And?*' repeated Barbara as Venetia broke off.

Venetia crimsoned.

'Are you trying to make me believe that this, is only an infatuation on his part and mine which won't last, and that I shall regret it bitterly and that Mike will be unfaithful to me with some girl and that he will be cruel to Maybelle?'

'Venetia, ducky, you're being terribly touchy and not awfully sensible tonight.'

Venetia looked at Barbara's haggard yet handsome face and almost hated her old friend.

'You're just a bitter, cynical, suspicious

woman, Barbara,' she said in a muffled voice.

'Right each count,' said Barbara and laughed harshly. 'That's what life has made me. And *you* don't want it to make you the same. So far you have had all the sweetness and romance that any woman could extract from this dreary existence. I admit you lost it when poor Geoff died, but you're still young enough to be able to get it back and you've got an adorable young daughter who worships you. What else do you want?'

'Are you telling me that I don't need a man in the house?'

'In the house! In your *bed*—wherever you want him, ducky. But do pick the right kind, if it's going to be a "till death us do part" affair.'

'You have yet to prove why Michael is wrong for me.'

'Have you lost your mind that you can't see it for yourself?'

'I do not see it.'

'Preserve me from falling in love,' groaned Barbara. 'But then I never was a romantic creature. You're a darling, Venetia. I don't want to upset you and I'd give anything to be able to embrace you and say I'm delighted that you're getting married again. I'm not ruling out marriage for you, *but why Michael Pethick?*'

Venetia's hot colour deepened. She rose and, walking across the room, stood looking through the filmy curtains. The summer sun was still shining, but her eyes stung with tears.

'You're trying to spoil my wonderful happiness,' she said in a choked voice.

Barbara shut one eye and with the open one threw a sardonic look at the straight youthful back.

'I refuse to soften and say I'm sorry for being so frank, although you know damn well that I wouldn't hurt a hair of your head. I'm so damned fond of you, Venetia, that I'd do anything for you. You're the nicest and most sincere woman I've ever known. I've an enormous admiration for you, too. It's because of all that that I refuse to behave like the others and say "How marvellous it all is" to your face and then go away and mutter behind your back.'

Venetia swung round.

'And pray what are my other friends muttering?'

'Ducky, I'm not out to repeat gossip. But you know damn well how hypocritical most people are—they just adore flattering one to one's face and then sneering behind one's back. I, personally, am *persona grata* in all the most amusing houses but am quite aware that behind my back I get torn to shreds. Well—if there is any tearing for *me* to do—I do it in people's faces. Now don't I?'

'Yes, I admit you're not a hypocrite, but I think you've got to do more than just tell me that I ought not to marry Michael. Why not?'

Barbara's plucked brows drew together in a scowl. She jammed her cigarette-end into an ashtray.

'Oh, God, you do put me in a spot.'

'Well, if you like being so honest—out with it—what have you got against Mike?'

'I don't know him awfully well.'

'Then you aren't fit to judge,' said Venetia triumphantly.

'Oh, I know him enough.'

'Do you really dislike him?'

'Not at all. One couldn't. He's great fun. He dances like a dream and I've been to one or two very good parties with him and think he's most stimulating. He looks divine, too.'

'Those don't seem good reasons for *not* marrying a man.'

Barbara looked her friend straight in the eyes.

'Listen, honey—you've asked for it and you shall have it. I don't mind about him being so young, although I think in ten years' time you might be beginning to feel a bit worn out with that dynamo dragging you round the universe. You're as lovely as a picture and you still look like you're thirty, and I know you're physically strong. I don't even doubt he'll stay in love with you for a long time. But if I know men— Mike Pethick is an egotist of the first water and as shallow as a brook. He'll think first of Mike Pethick and second of Venetia, and he won't settle down for years. That's my opinion. You

82

say he's thirty-three. Well, he still acts just as though he had just left Oxford. Oh, he may be a good stockbroker and I dare say you can rake up all kinds of things to prove to me that he is steady and industrious. But he is *not* serious-minded. Without being at all effeminate (and I grant you he is the reverse of pansy) he's a playboy by nature. Playboys make attractive companions and divine dance partners but not good husbands. Especially not for *you*, who are really a very serious-minded woman under that social strata and the party spirit. There—now I've said it all. The lot!'

Venetia had grown pale during this speech. She stood nervously twisting a chiffon handkerchief between her long fine fingers. Then she said:

'Well, you certainly haven't minced words.'

'Don't hold it against me. I'm the best friend you'll ever have, ducky.'

Venetia said:

'It would be pretty depressing if I were for a moment to believe all you say.'

Barbara shrugged her shoulders.

'There's plenty of time for you to break the engagement—it's only a few days old.'

'Thank you,' said Venetia, 'but I don't propose to break the engagement.'

Barbara shrugged her shoulders again, dived into her bag for a cigarette, put it between her bright red lips and lit it with a small gold lighter.

83

'Then there's nothing more to be said. I've done what I think my duty as your true friend. I may be wrong. I hope so. Naturally I'll stand by you whatever you do.'

'If I didn't know you so well, Barbara, I'd really think you rather impertinent,' said Venetia.

Barbara groaned.

'Oh, Venetia darling, get off it—*don't* start taking offence with me. We've known each other far too long.'

'All the same—I don't know that *anybody* has the right to be quite so—so *cruel*.'

'I disagree,' said Barbara bluntly. 'But have it your own way. I apologize.'

Then Venetia sat down and lit a cigarette for herself and Barbara saw that her fingers were trembling, and that her face was quite white.

'I don't want apologies from you,' she said.

'Honey, I really am sorry if I have distressed you,' Barbara added in a voice more gentle than most women heard from her. 'Marry your Michael and be happy if you really think it's wise. Maybe it will work out and I'll have to eat my words.'

'I believe it will. Mike is not a playboy, and not such an egotist. He's marvellously considerate of my feelings. You misjudge him! He adores life and he may, perhaps, be young for his age, but just because he's gay and enthusiastic about his hunting and all the things he does, that does not make him a

84

playboy. I find that a most offensive description.'

'Sorry!'

'And he is much steadier than you would think and has a very serious side,' added Venetia.

Barbara sighed.

'Naturally you think he is perfect.'

'Nobody is perfect. I'm not such an idiot as to think so. But Mike is a much nicer person than *you've* made out.'

'You don't think there'll be trouble with your daughter?'

'What sort of trouble?'

'Well, in a couple of years' time or so you'll be bringing her out. I should not think Michael Pethick is the type to make a suitable stepfather.'

If it were within Venetia's heart to agree with that, she was not going to let Barbara know it. As if to shut out the warning voice deep down in her own consciousness, she argued:

'He'll be sweet with her. Mike's friendly and nice to everybody and I shall never ask him to do the heavy father. That would be ridiculous.'

'Okay. What about the financial side?'

'Oh—there of course you are bound to think that he is attracted by the fact that I'm well off. (At least, as well off as anyone can be in these days of tax-paying.) I don't deny everybody will imagine that.'

Barbara sighed again.

'Well, that's your pigeon. I dare say Mike is in love with both you *and* your income. A handsome alliance.'

The colour came back to Venetia's cheeks.

'You really are a detestable woman, Barbara. I don't know why I let you into my house.'

''Phone up for a taxi,' said Barbara.

'Oh, don't be silly.'

Barbara smiled.

'Are we still friends?'

'Yes, of course, but I do wish you really liked Mike. I assure you he is *not* marrying me for money. I can swear to it. I told him, myself, I'm quite sure the fact that I have an income must be a relief to him because the Pethicks are not well off. I can help him restore that perfectly wonderful old house of his. But it isn't the money he's after—honestly, Ba, I'd *know* if it was. I'm not such an infatuated fool as to fall for *that*.'

Here Barbara was inclined to agree. Whatever she thought about Mike Pethick she did not regard him solely as a fortune hunter. In these days it was an accepted fact that women should pay their share—and sometimes more, if they had more than their husbands. No—it wasn't the money that troubled Barbara. But as she had just said, she was not of the romantic type and she had a horrid way of seeing things as they were rather than through rose-coloured spectacles. With

86

all her heart she hoped that Venetia would be happy if she married Michael Pethick, but she continued to doubt it. She sat listening patiently for the next half hour to Venetia's rhapsodies about him and thought: 'Venetia's got it badly! He, maybe, is just as mad about her. But she's too good for him. It just won't work!'

CHAPTER SEVEN

'It's a damned nuisance,' said Michael Pethick, 'about this currency. I would like to have stayed here another month.'

He was in the bathroom shaving. Venetia, at her dressing table, touching her lashes with mascara, heard this and before she could comment, Michael's voice added:

'Wouldn't you?'

Venetia put down the tiny black brush and hesitated before she answered.

This was her honeymoon. The end of a glorious fortnight which had commenced in Paris, continued down South and finally they came North and were ending up in Deauville.

They had taken their car over from England by air. The new car that had been Venetia's wedding present to Mike; a handsome Lagonda—open, because Mike liked open cars although he was willing enough to put the hood up when Venetia asked. Venetia did not so much like being blown about. But it didn't seem to matter in France, this warm luscious fortnight of golden summer. Nothing seemed to matter except the idyllic beauty of the Côte d'Azur, the warm grip of Michael's hands, and the touch of his lips.

It was still a wonder and a delight to wake and find the sun-brown vital youth of him lying at her side, to see the boyish head of dark curling hair burrowed into a pillow; the gay blue eyes opening, smiling. All the ecstatic passion which, unashamed and splendid, they shared. No age difference could spoil that perfection.

But it had all been a little strenuous for Venetia because Mike never wanted to stay anywhere for more than a night or two. He adored change. He was fundamentally restless. He drove at a cracking pace that sometimes had made her gasp although she had been unwilling to admit it or ask him to slow down. Under the blazing sun, with the car hood down, Venetia with a scarf tied over her hair and Mike like a young Frenchman, wearing white shorts and shirt, and with a beret on the side of his head, they had raced along the *Routes Nationales*. They ate wonderful food. They drank the finest wines. They stayed at half a dozen luxury hotels and spent a lot of time lying on the beaches and swimming in water that glittered like blue oil. It was never too hot for Mike, who, as he remarked, speedily burned to the brown of one of his saddles. Where it was possible he hired a horse and went riding in the cool of the early morning. Then Venetia was glad to lie quiet and store up some of the wasted vitality in order to meet the long strenuous day ahead of her. She, too, grew brown and was not afraid of sun and fresh air. But she did feel fatigued by the evening. Even after two weeks of marriage with Mike, the disparity in their ages showed itself in that one marked fashion. In physical strength. Sometimes Venetia told herself that even a girl of his own age would find it difficult to keep up with Mike. But she was happy, not only for her own sake but because she could see that she made him equally so. No woman could have had a more appreciative or attentive lover.

They stayed in Cannes and in Monte Carlo. The Lagonda roaring along was watched with admiration by the little French boys as it passed by. Here, in Deauville, it was cooler, for which Venetia was thankful, and she was allowed three days' rest. They had a beautiful suite in the *Hôtel Normandie* where their windows overlooked the charming apple trees in a quiet courtyard. Mike found a willing 'pro' to play tennis with him. Venetia sat on a chair by the hard court, proud of the fact that on several occasions her husband beat the young Frenchman and beat him thoroughly. The 'pro', mopping his forehead, announced to *Madame* that *Monsieur* should enter for a tennis championship. His game was '*par excellence!*' Venetia looked at Mike's perspiring brown face and smiled benevolently because of the look of pleased vanity which she read upon it. Another thing she was fast learning through intimate association with Mike was that he had no great modesty. But she was still at a stage to find it charming and amusing when he lapped up flattery instead of receiving it with the average Englishman's attitude of '*Oh, I'm not really so good*'. After all, why shouldn't one be honest? And Mike was certainly *that* in his conceit.

But did she wish to prolong this hectic and feverish fortnight? That was the question. She hesitated to answer it, because she was aware of the feeling deep down in her heart that she would be glad to get back home and 'settle down'.

Mike appeared in her room now, wiping the soapsuds from his face with a hand-towel. He wore a thin foulard dressing-gown. His hair stood up on end, rough and unbrushed. How young he looked like that, she thought. She, herself, was already dressed in a white and green cotton frock, her hair brushed silkily into its usual sedate twist at the nape of her neck. She had just clipped on some long gold earrings—costume jewellery—that Mike had bought her in the Casino last night. She had

90

seen the ear-rings in one of the cases and wanted them.

They had played '*Chemmy*' until two this morning. Venetia was in luck, she had won fifteen thousand francs. She had meant to spend it on presents but Mike had come up behind her—they had been sitting at different tables—seen the pile of *plaques* in front of her and reached out his brown fingers.

'Lend me those, sweet. I'm cleaned out.'

She had given him the *plaques* at once. She could not yet see that warm intimate look in his eyes without thrilling and after the mad rush of the last twelve days still could not believe that she really was Mrs Michael Pethick; that Geoffrey Sellingham's widow had undergone such a complete metamorphosis. In the Casino, Mike promised to return the borrowed francs but he lost again. Walking back to the hotel under a blaze of stars, he had grumbled a bit. Bad luck had pursued him at the 'tables'. But he didn't really like gambling. Anyhow it was too infernally hot and stuffy in the Casino; a frightful lot of Jews and dagoes there, he said. The nuisance was that he had pretty well spent all his traveller's cheques. Venetia would have to wait until they got home before he could pay back all that he had borrowed (and he had been borrowing for the last two days).

'That's all right, darling,' she had said and hugged his arm to her side, 'What's mine is yours.'

'You're an angel,' he said, and dropped a kiss on the top of her head.

She did not mind about the money. She had plenty in the bank in London. The trouble was that she hadn't the francs here with which to buy all the presents she wanted to take home; especially for her young daughter and Geoffrey's mother.

She had twice heard from Maybelle since she came abroad. The child's letters had followed her round and finally caught up with her here. One of Maybelle's she had read aloud to Mike. He was amused and guffawed with laughter.

'Do hope you're having a wizard time, Mummy. We're having a heat-wave at school so I bet it's hot in France. I have started my Five Years' Diary that Granny gave me for my birthday and wrote a description of your wedding. I've said that you looked super and that there was a frightful crush of people and that it was absolutely marvellous being your sort of bridesmaid even though you weren't really a bride.....'

'I would like to know what she thinks you were,' Michael laughed.

'I'm not quite sure,' Venetia had laughed back, 'except that I suppose she thinks a bride ought to wear a white veil and orange blossom. She quotes a bit more of what she wrote about us:

92

'My mother looked tall and elegant in a silky sort of dress the colour of pale tobacco with three rows of pearls round her neck and a huge transparent black hat on her golden head...'

'I like the "golden head",' Mike commented.

'Maybelle is at the romantic age,' said her mother and continued to read:

'Mummy's husband whom I'm going to call Uncle Mike looked terribly handsome in a pale grey sort of suit and wore a white carnation. All the girls here think he is terrific, and I'm longing to ride with him in the summer hols. I forgot to say that Mummy had the most gorgeous orchids which Uncle Mike sent her. The reception was terrific at Claridge's. Auntie Barbara came and talked to me and was quite decent to me although I don't usually like her. Everyone was decent and the best man, Tony Winters, brought me an ice and made me blush because he said I looked jolly nice. I wore very pale pink and had roses. Uncle Mike sent them to me, too, and gave me a wrist-watch which is super...'

All this seemed to Venetia very sweet and naïve but at least it had satisfied her that Maybelle bore her no resentment for putting somebody in her father's place. Michael continued to laugh over the letter, and said that Maybelle sounded 'a nice child' but he 'drew the line', he added, at '*Uncle Mike*'. Whose idea was that?

Venetia said:

'Mine, darling. What else could she call you?'

Then he said that Maybelle ought to call him just 'Mike' because after all she was fifteen, and he was only just over twice her age; hardly the 'uncle' type.

So Venetia wrote and told Maybelle to drop the 'uncle'. If she felt a bit embarrassed about it that feeling soon wore off. No awkward moments; no brief instants of apprehension because of Mike's youth could linger when they were so much in love. Every one of the wonderful nights of the honeymoon lying in her husband's arms, Venetia felt fulfilled and content; certain that she had taken the right step.

But now she wanted to get home and see Maybelle again, especially as the child was not to spend the whole summer holiday with her. Venetia had promised to send her to her grandmother for at least three weeks. The first time they would have spent school holidays apart for so long.

Michael did not seem anxious to have Maybelle at Burnt Ash Manor when they first got back.

'Maybelle's had you for fifteen years. Now it's my turn. Let us be alone as much as we can at the start of our married life,' he said.

If Venetia did not agree, she certainly could

not resent such flattering jealousy. It was good to know that he wanted her to himself.

But just how much they would ever in fact be alone, or whether it was just a deep-seated antipathy that Mike felt towards the daughter of Venetia's first marriage, she had yet to learn.

Michael came up to her as she sat looking at him through the mirror, and he placed his hands on her shoulders.

'Can't we rake up a few more francs and stay on?' he sighed.

'Darling, *I* can't. And I do think we ought to go home now.'

'Then we'll have to get cracking early tomorrow morning and press on for Le Touquet and the air-ferry. A pity!'

She leaned her cheek with a fond gesture against one of his hands.

'We get another allowance at the end of the year. Then we can come over again.'

'I'm dead keen on making up a party and going to winter sports,' he said.

Venetia remained silent. This was one of her embarrassing moments. She detested skiing. She did not like the life one leads at a winter-sports hotel and she only really liked Switzerland in the summer. After Geoffrey's death she had felt she never wanted to go back to a country where she had spent one or two happy and lovely summer holidays in the mountains with him. Silently she began to tidy her dressing-table and put make-up away in the drawer. Michael said:

'I don't believe I've ever asked you if you ski, darling?'

'I've tried, but I don't really care for it, although I daresay Switzerland would be a very good holiday for Maybelle. Perhaps we could take her out for Christmas. She ought, at her age, to learn to ski and skate.'

Venetia, still watching Mike's face in the mirror, saw the good humour leave it and the corners of his mouth go down. Only for an instant. Then he was smiling again.

'Oh, well—we'll see.'

She thought:

'He really doesn't want Maybelle. And I suppose Barbara would say I was mad to try and push it when we are so newly married. I must just be patient and accustom him to things gradually.'

But she knew that she would be disappointed and miserable if Mike raised any serious or lasting objection to the inclusion of her beloved daughter in their holiday plans.

'What shall we do today?' she asked him.

'Well, you know that chap I was talking to in the bar last night?'

'The rather nice American?'

'Yes. He happens to share my hobby.'

'Horses?'

Mike smiled and reached out for Venetia's enamel cigarette-case and helped himself to a cigarette.

'Yes. He's got racehorses at his place in Virginia. We've a standing invitation, by the way, to stay with him and his wife if we ever go to the U.S.A. He's over on business in Paris and is just snatching a long week-end in Deauville. He and I thought we might nip along to La Rivière—that place not far from Arromanches. Do you remember, darling, we passed it when I took you to see the D-Day beaches.'

'Yes, I remember.'

'What do you want to do?'

She had risen now. He slipped an arm around her waist. He was proud of Venetia's slenderness. Nobody would ever think she was twelve years older than himself, he thought, with that small waist, but, of course, it was not to be expected that a woman of over forty would be perfect. Especially when she had had a child. A pity about the slack muscles, and Venetia had complained last night she was putting on weight because of the rich food— and her happiness. Nothing like contentment for making a woman plump. She would have to go on a strict diet when she got back if she wanted to keep that girlish waistline. But she was very beautiful he considered, an enchanting wife, and in many ways a wonderful companion. It was enormously pleasant, too, to feel that there was no need to economize—with Venetia's bank balance to augment his; and she couldn't be more generous. There were just moments when Michael was afraid that he fatigued her, and last thing at night, sometimes, she didn't look quite so young after all. Still—he adored her.

He explained that the American, Randolph Sutton, had an introduction to a French *Conte de* Something-or-Other, and he had this château in Lamarche and fine stables.

'I suggested I might take Sutton along to La Rivière in the Lagonda, if you don't mind, sweet. We'll only be gone a couple of hours and I don't suppose you want to come.'

She did not. He was quite right. It was going to be another very warm morning and she intended to write letters and find some presents—even if not expensive ones—for those at home.

Yet she felt a tiny spurt of resentment because, without consulting her first, Mike seemed already to have arranged to drive the American to La Rivière.

'Would you like to come with us, sweet?' Mike put in quickly. But she answered:

'Not in the least, darling. Besides, the Lagonda's only really comfortable for two.'

He dropped a kiss on her cheek.

'*And* my Venetia is not keen on talking horses by the hour.'

He walked back into the bathroom, whistling. She slipped on her rings, then moved to one of the long windows and looked down at the sun-gilded tops of the apple trees. The fruit was ripening. In two more months they would be shaken on to the ground, put into great sacks and turned into cider, or the Calvados that Venetia had learned to drink and found quite attractive although she preferred ordinary cognac. She liked Normandy. It was, in fact, her first visit to this fashionable watering-place. She liked the charming tree-shaded streets, the beautiful flowers and the tempting Parisian shops. Mike had been here before. He thoroughly enjoyed the place. He had a dual nature that she was beginning to recognize. The half that was the lover of sport, the other that was the London 'playboy'. She had yet to see signs of Mike *wanting* to work; of enjoying his job on the Stock Exchange. It was quite obvious that he only did the job because he needed to earn his living. But he had no real interest in it. She found that a pity. It is not really good for a man to work only because he must. Geoffrey had loved his job. But then he had been a publisher and enormously interested in books. Geoffrey used to say that no matter how much money he had, he would always want to do *something*. He used to say, too, that he had no use for the 'idle rich'.

Venetia pulled herself up with a jolt. The last thing she must do was to start making comparisons between her two husbands, the dead and the living. Anyhow, there could be no comparison, because they were so totally different.

Even about the car ... she and Geoff used to share a preference for a closed car and comfort. One in which there was room so that they could take his mother out or, later, their little girl. When Venetia had asked Mike what kind of car he wanted (he had been utterly thrilled and grateful for the handsome wedding present) he had chosen the sports Lagonda saying that it was what he had always wanted but had never been able to afford. When she suggested something more spacious (thinking of Maybelle) he had grinned and said:

'*Not* a family car, sweet. *Please!* I couldn't take it!'

And she, in a state of mind that wanted him to have the earth, allowed him to choose the sports Lagonda. After all, there was a tiny back seat into which Maybelle could be huddled at a pinch, and Venetia had to admit the car had lovely long lines and a powerful engine.

Just before they left the bedroom ready for this new day Venetia (who had decided to go down on the sands and sit under one of the striped umbrellas) put her arms around her husband's neck.

She said:

'Do you realize, darling, that this will be the first time that we have been separated for two or three hours since we were married? And I don't expect you back for lunch either.'

Mike, looking his best as usual in an open-neck sports shirt and grey flannels, hugged her in return. He was not by nature a romantic man although if he chose he could say the right thing at the right moment. And he was capable of an ardour that knew no inhibitions. But he was apt to feel a little nervous of Venetia in her moments of extreme *tendresse*. Perhaps it was because she was older, he mused; but he found her very sentimental; more so than girls like Jix, who were enthusiastic in bed but pretty casual out of it. That was really the way Mike liked them. He had to get used to living with a sentimental woman. However, he was still so much enamoured of Venetia that he found it easy just now to respond. He kissed her long and ardently and told her that he would 'get back to her as soon as he could,' to which Venetia, perversely, replied that he was not to hurry on her account.

'Enjoy yourself with your horsey friend and all the horses,' she smiled.

She watched him drive away from the hotel. He waved and smiled at her. As the Lagonda disappeared in a cloud of dust she thought:

'What a boy he is at heart! I'll certainly have to keep young for him.'

The morning passed pleasantly and quickly. There were all the 'thank you' letters for wedding presents to be written as well as personal ones (a special note for Barbara Keen):

Having the most divine honeymoon. Mike is a perfect husband. You were all wrong, darling.

She sent that off triumphantly in a glow of amorous contentment as she thought about Michael. She wrote to Herman, too, and told him how happy she was.

Did a voice say to her—*early days*?

Did her inner self reason that if she was not happy during this fortnight of honeymoon with a young ardent man she never would be, but that she should *wait*? ... Perhaps, but she shut out the reasoning voice.

After a light lunch on the terrace of the beautiful and elegant restaurant, she went to her shuttered room and lay down for a *siesta* which she found she sorely needed. It was not until she woke at half past four and discovered that Mike had still not come back that she was somehow jolted out of her smug contentment.

She had expected him to stay at La Rivière for lunch. No doubt the *Conte* (whose name she had not gathered) had offered the uttermost hospitality to his two visitors. And it would not have taken much to get Mike up on to a fine horse, Venetia reflected. On the other hand, he had been away from her nearly five hours now. That was a long time.

She went out to the shops, spent an hour looking at lovely things, some of which she longed to buy for Maybelle but could not because of the lack of wretched francs. She contented herself with choosing a little bracelet with dangling coloured glass ornaments which the child could wear for parties.

When Venetia got back to the *Normandie* she was quite sure she would find the Lagonda parked outside the front entrance of the hotel. She was astonished that it was not there. Suddenly her heart sank. The first real anxiety shot through her. It was not, of course, that Mike was just being casual about coming home, but that he had had an accident. He would drive so fast; it terrified her. Under the delicate coating of rouge her face paled suddenly. She asked at the Reception if there had been any telephone message. The answer was '*Non, Madame!*'

All the lounges were full of people. Some just about to go into the bright sunshine; others coming in from a late bathe. Everybody looked happy. But Venetia felt cold with nerves and an indescribable feeling of apprehension came over her.

She went up to her own room again. She looked at a coat of Mike's hanging over a chair; at a newly bought box of Havanas lying on the table. He had chosen them yesterday. She closed her eyes and thought:

'If anything happened to Mike I would die. I love him so much I am part of him now and he of me.'

Why didn't he come back?

By six o'clock she was sure there had been an accident. She went downstairs and spoke to the

103

head porter. She felt rather absurdly naïve as she told him her troubles. Did he think *Monsieur* had had an accident? Would he have heard by now? Would the police communicate with the hotel? But how would they know where *Monsieur* was staying? The courteous and sympathetic porter tried to reassure *Madame*. There had been no accident—no, of a certainty there had not—it was just that *Monsieur* had been detained. Or maybe the car had let him down and he had to have a reparation made. After a moment, Venetia went away. Why should the Lagonda let Michael down—a brand-new car of such excellence? She was not consoled. Then she tried to feel angry and to believe that it was just that Mike had been thoughtless. He had enjoyed himself and not bothered to 'phone.

With nervous fingers she peeled off her clothes and lay in a hot scented bath, struggling against the doubts and anxieties that circled like bats around her mind.

'Don't flap, Venetia,' she kept telling herself. 'You know you hate fussy women.'

Over an hour later she was ready for dinner, except for her actual dress, sitting on the edge of her bed in a dressing-gown, smoking, when the door opened and Michael came in.

She stood up jabbing the half-smoked cigarette in the ashtray on the bedside table. Her whole body was trembling. She had been smoking one cigarette after another and her

104

nerves were raw. She looked at her husband. Her first impulse was to throw herself into his arms and say '*Thank God!*' He was alive. His shattered remains were not lying under an overturned Lagonda. Her relief was enormous; but so was her reactionary fury. She said through clenched teeth:

'How dared you frighten me like that! *How dared* you!'

Michael closed the door and stood with his back to it. His sunburnt face was fiery red, his eyes a little bloodshot. He grinned sheepishly.

'Venetia—my poppet, terribly sorry. I know it's late! Honestly, sweet, I had no idea how late until I got into the hotel.'

She gulped. No idea that it was so late … and it was half past seven. She said in an icy voice:

'You've been gone eight whole hours—practically the whole day.'

Michael scratched the back of his head and laughed. It was a laugh with a touch of nervousness to it. He eyed her cautiously. He could see how angry she was and how pale. He had never seen that hard look in those soft, slanting eyes before.

'Oh, God,' he muttered. 'I suppose I've put up the hell of a black!'

He was so like a truant schoolboy facing maternal accusation that Venetia's heart sank. She did not want him to feel that way. He was … no, not drunk … that was too strong. But

105

he had been drinking. His breath was definitely alcoholic. Now he was throwing off his coat, still laughing.

'I don't know whether it's me or the room but I find it damned hot in here,' he said.

He walked to the window and stood breathing in the air, deeply. She looked at his back in a scared way. She had not wanted things to be like this when he came back, and the last thing she must do was to act the suspicious, nagging wife. She believed in husband and wife having independence of mind and action ... up to a point. If Michael wanted to stay away from her all day with his friends she had no right to criticize even though it was their honeymoon. Admirably she controlled herself. She said in a quiet voice:

'I didn't mean to fly at you just now, but I was rather nervous when you didn't come home. I was petrified that you had had a smash. You drive so fast.'

At once his brow cleared. He could not cope with an angry Venetia because he had no experience of her anger. She had always been gentle and sweet with him. Now he came up to her and took her right hand and kissed it humbly.

'Venetia, my sweet, I can't apologize enough. Honestly, it was damnable of me. I *ought* to have 'phoned. It never struck me you would think of an accident. The truth is Jean— that's the Count—persuaded both Rand

Sutton and myself to go out with him after lunch. We had a look at his stables and then he particularly wanted us to drive on—twenty miles or so beyond Arromanches to see a pal of his who is a trainer. It took up time and in the general excitement I forgot to 'phone. I wasn't near one, anyhow, most of the time. I have never seen such superb animals. Jean's entering one of his for the next Grand National...'

He chattered on with enthusiasm on his pet subject but it trailed off a trifle lamely. He kept pressing Venetia's hand but looked away from her steady gaze. His breath reeked. Suddenly she turned her head away when he tried to kiss her.

'I quite understand,' she said. 'Don't bother to explain any more. I'm glad you enjoyed yourself. I was a bit worried, I admit, but it was foolish of me. I am sure it was a lot of fun. You certainly seem to have celebrated.'

'Darling, you're still cross with me.'

'Not at all,' she said with her back to him. 'But I think you had better hurry up and bath and change. It's half past seven.'

'I'll be quick—I promise you.'

He slid his shirt over his head as he spoke. He looked strong and muscular with the dark hair curling on his chest. But Venetia was undergoing an unpleasant reaction in general. She hated the fact that he had stayed away so long and not thought about her. She hated the

107

signs that he had done some heavy drinking. She felt a distaste for his appearance in spite of his exceeding good looks. He was just selfish—and callous about her feelings. A typical egotistical male without delicacy or tact. She was terrified that she was going to burst into tears and in consequence snapped at him:

'I'll go down, if you don't mind. I'd better start on the gin. You're several up on me.'

'You *are* cross—' he began.

She interrupted:

'Not because you enjoyed yourself, I assure you. I had a quiet and pleasant day by myself, but I do think you might have troubled to let me know you were going to be so late.'

She regretted the words as soon as she had said them. There she was, being exactly what she despised in other women—the nagging wife. She had been frightened by his prolonged absence. Her love for him had made her frightened. And it was rather humiliating to know that she had been so little in his mind all through this long summer's day—the last of their honeymoon.

Michael decided that if Venetia was going to be angry—so was he. He was not afraid of her—damned if he was afraid of any woman, even Venetia. His mind was a little inflamed by the considerable number of drinks he had had with the American, Randolph Sutton. They had stopped at rather an amusing little bar coming through Deauville. He had sat on a high stool next to an exceedingly attractive French girl whom Sutton seemed to know. A *'poule'*, he called her, but 'terrific'. Red curls and the most seductive legs Michael had seen for a long time. She had taken care that he saw plenty of them, too, and asked if he was 'beezy' tonight. Well, of course he had told her that he was.

'I'm a married man,' he had laughed.

'Mal fortune', she giggled, and her immense eyes with their heavily blacked lashes sparkled wickedly at him. He had left Rand Sutton there with her, a little regretful that he had had to come away. Of course, he had *wanted* to come back to Venetia. He could have told the little *poule* with all sincerity that he did not consider it *'mal fortune'* to be Venetia's husband. But he had not expected this cool welcome.

'Damn it, I did apologize for being late, Venetia,' he said in a surly voice.

She walked to the door in silence. Then he changed his tune again. He prevented her from opening the door and caught her round the waist. Venetia in that cool, grey chiffon off-the-shoulder dress with a twisted gold and pearl necklace around her long throat, the slender elegance of her and that sorrowful look in her eyes, completely melted his anger. It was all his fault and he began to tell her so generously. He couldn't be more sorry. It wasn't lack of love—he adored her—it was just that the day had been one long rush and later, he admitted, too many drinks. These Americans sink the gin and one had to keep up or appear 'pansy'.

'I really am upset if I've annoyed you, darling,' he ended. And his very blue eyes pleaded with her. 'Don't go on being angry. Stay up here with me and tell me I'm forgiven.'

It was only a matter of seconds before she surrendered to that appeal and was in his arms with her cool, perfumed cheek against his hot brown one. The alcoholic breath was excused; and the long hours of waiting for him forgotten. She was still very much in love.

'I'm a cross beast. Forgive me, too, darling,' she said, and locked her fine fingers behind his head and pulled it down to hers.

Now his ardour was for her and her alone. He was ashamed of ever having thought the little French *poule* attractive. That had just been animal instinct. This was where his true love—and his true heaven—lay, in this cool, fair-haired woman so much older than himself—so much wiser and better—so adorable.

*   *   *

He could not stop asking for forgiveness in between the long kisses. She was wholly convinced that he had, indeed, just been like a thoughtless boy who had done no real wrong and with whom one could not go on being cross. His passion excited her own. The colour returned to her face and the sparkle to her eyes. She was happy again.

It was half past nine that night before they appeared in the restaurant together, a handsome elegant English couple at whom many interested glances were thrown. And not a soul said of the beautiful radiant woman:

'She looks older than he does.'

PART TWO

PART TWO

CHAPTER ONE

One morning towards the end of the first week in December, Venetia sat at a walnut bureau sorting bills and receipts which were piling up. It was Michael's desk in this small room with windows opening on to the garden which she had designed as a 'study' for him—not that Michael ever did any studying but the walls had already been lined with bookcases and it had given Venetia an excuse to bring down most of her own books—and Geoffrey's. She was keeping Geoffrey's really beautiful collection of classics and modern first editions for Maybelle.

Like all the other rooms of Burnt Ash Manor this one now bore the unmistakable stamp of perfect taste. Throughout the summer Venetia had been working hard to make her husband's old place as beautiful as it should be. She had not failed. Friends of Michael's, coming here after some long absence, declared that they could not recognize the old 'relic'. It was a job that Venetia had thoroughly enjoyed doing during the early months of her marriage. She had abandoned everything else and driven down from town daily to supervise the work.

Paint had been removed to reveal genuine panelling. Charming wallpapers with the right design and the right curtains to match now replaced the former colours and ill-chosen draperies. Some antique furniture had been brought down from Venetia's little town house. She had disposed of her old home itself, despite Michael's hint that it might be 'useful'. It was too big and expensive to keep up if she was going to do all she wanted to do with Burnt Ash Manor, and as Michael was such an enthusiast about his horses and hunting she felt he would prefer to live in the country, especially during the winter. Later, if they wished, they could find a tiny flat. Michael had agreed.

Michael agreed to most things, Venetia thought, as she began what seemed like a formidable task upon the pile of letters—most of them unopened and tossed idly into pigeon-holes. She had learned that on principle he rarely opened bills and paid them only after receiving a lawyer's letter.

'Keep them waiting,' was his motto. 'They charge enough for everything these days.'

But that had never been Venetia's policy. She detested bills and disliked the idea of debts hanging over her head. If she could not afford a thing she did not buy it. That also had been Geoffrey's way of life—and his mother's.

Venetia had not yet found it possible to clamp down on the many memories that brought comparison between the two men she had married. Lately she had begun to feel a little afraid that she allowed such comparisons to arise too often. It was, she tried to tell herself, merely because Geoffrey and Michael were so completely different and she had not yet adjusted herself to this new way of life.

She began to open up the bills and lay them in front of her. Quite a few from Michael's tailors—many for hunting outfits. *To one swallow tail scarlet coat £65. White breeches £20.* From the the bootmakers, *hunting boots £30.* All very expensive but that did not particularly shake Venetia, who ran up her own high bills at various houses of *haute couture.* But hers were always *paid.* She continued to sort. Harrods—a really alarmingly high bill for silk underwear for Mr Michael Pethick. Then local accounts; fodder for the stables, repairs done to Bennett's cottage ... *and* the rest.

Venetia had learned many things about her young and charming husband since their marriage. That amiability of his, for instance, could be annoying. Whatever she suggested he would fling up a hand and say:

'Anything you like, sweet.'

But he would rarely discuss the matter unless it was an expenditure which really interested him. He left everything to Venetia. That was the antithesis of her former married life, when Geoffrey had taken such good care of her and been master of his household. Despite the fact that she had money of her own, Geoffrey used to keep all financial worries from her. He said it was a man's duty to do so.

But Michael tossed these duties over to her as lightly as he tossed an order over the shop counter for something he could not afford.

If things became urgent, he gave Venetia one of his most delightful smiles and said:

'Settle it for me, Light of my Life. I've got a bit of extra money coming in at the end of the quarter—then I'll pay you back.'

She was always quite willing to pay and content to please him. Whatever one did for Michael he was grateful and it was nice to be kissed and told you were the most generous woman in the world and that 'all the lovely presents made life terrific.' '*Terrific*', that favourite word of Michael's. Life was terrific. She was. Everything was. She was beginning to be aware that he had little sense of discrimination and exaggerated values. If things weren't '*terrific*' they were '*bloody*'. Michael did not indulge in half-measures.

Venetia did not always find it easy to understand or adjust her own mental outlook to his. All she could do was to continue to humour him and (although she had sworn not to do so) spoil him. When he wanted something he wanted it so madly. She felt delighted to give it to him and felt warmed by his rapturous reception of her gifts.

Sometimes he made Venetia feel dull. She had never previously imagined herself so. She used always to feel very much alert and certainly, before Geoffrey died, full of enthusiasm. She had been heart-whole over the delight of restoring and furnishing Michael's own home and making it hers, too.

But these six months with Michael had shown her how reserved and cautious a person she was; she had so much more common sense than he had and the only times she had ever really forsaken caution and rushed blindly over a precipice was when she first joined her life with his.

Now that the honeymoon was over and they were leading a normal married life, propinquity and habit disclosed to her this tendency of Michael's to push her into the background. He made her feel that she held the reins, but that he could and would at any moment take the bit between his teeth and bolt. It was not altogether a pleasant sensation and had the effect also of making her feel her age. That was the main trouble; whenever she disagreed with his viewpoint or appeared too cautious, she immediately felt those twelve years that lay between them. And if she had not been aware of it in the first stages of her tremendous passion for him, she knew now very well indeed that he had never really grown up. At times he was almost absurdly immature. The stockbroker, the master of Burnt Ash Manor, the hunting man who could master a difficult horse well, became at times a stubborn and rather stupid boy.

That touch of stupidity had not made itself apparent until recently. Venetia had known that Michael never opened a book and accepted the fact, but during one or two discussions lately he had betrayed the fact that he was not merely allergic to any form of art but that he belonged to that maddening sect of people—especially those who made a god of sport—who found something always to deride or despise in the world of art.

He liked to hear her play her piano but he preferred her to play sentimental sob stuff from musical comedy, or revue, or the latest dance tunes. If she ever sat down when he was at home to practise her Beethoven or Bach, which she could play well, he would come over to the piano, lift her hands from the keys and laugh:

'Give over, ducky—sounds like a schoolgirl practising. Play me something from *Pal Joey!*'

And she would play it because she could read anything at sight. Then he would beam at her and say that it was '*terrific*'.

Once Maybelle, when she was here during the summer holidays, gave her mother quite a shock when, at the end of one of these performances, she suddenly asked in her grave way:

'*Mummy*, what *would* my godfather say if he could hear you playing *that*?'

Venetia had blushed and risen abruptly from

the piano stool, whereupon Mike, who was humming the tune as she played it, cocked an eyebrow at Maybelle and said:

'Who's your godfather?'

'Herman Weissman,' she had answered.

Then Michael had laughed in his good-natured way and said:

'Oh! Well, I don't personally care what your long-haired musician says. I think they're an awful lot of hypocrites, these musician chaps. They really only say they like Beethoven to make an effect or because they are after a career.'

'That's not true...' Venetia had begun hotly, and felt ashamed of him suddenly because she saw the look of shocked astonishment on her young daughter's face. Maybelle, like her parents, was genuinely musical and thought the great pianist, Weissman, a hero to be worshipped. Venetia sent the child out of the room on some pretext before she continued the argument. On principle she did not encourage debates with Mike in front of Maybelle. Mainly because she could not bear Maybelle to think for a moment that the man her mother had married was ignorant either about great music or any of the arts.

Once Maybelle vanished Venetia was still not allowed to carry on the discussion. Michael had a way of avoiding the issue—perhaps because he knew that he did not come out of such arguments very well. Venetia was his mental superior. He had a cunning way of putting an end to any possible difference of opinion by making love to her. He would catch hold of her, stroke the fair gleaming hair which always fascinated him, and say:

'Are you beautiful? Don't let's worry about Mr Beetroot-Hoven.'

And although Venetia could have hit him for using that foolish belittling nickname, she had to laugh and surrender to his kiss. He was still so much in love with her and her body responded eagerly to the ardour of his. She did not want to feel ashamed of that body's urge, nor of the weakness that arose from it. But at times she was ashamed. Those were the moments which she found peculiarly embittering.

Maybelle had spent the best part of a month at the Manor and the rest of a long vacation with her grandmother, who had been glad to have her. Lady Sellingham never really complained but Venetia deduced from the old lady's letters that she missed the old companionship with her daughter-in-law sadly. The month here with Maybelle had by no means been an unqualified success. For the first time in her life Venetia had been quite glad when the child returned to school. Venetia had seen her off by the school train. She had looked into the big clear eyes that were so like Geoffrey's and which always held the glimmer of tears on these occasions, and said:

'You did enjoy yourself at Burnt Ash, didn't you, darling?'

It had been more of an appeal than a question. Both of them had known it. Maybelle had blushed with that bright pink colour that came only when she was emotionally disturbed. She answered:

'Yes, thanks, Mummy darling. It's always super being with you, and Burnt Ash is a super place and I'll write and thank Mike for taking me out to ride.'

So much he had done for her, certainly, Venetia reflected this December morning. Where horseflesh was concerned Michael could be relied upon to give any amount of help and enthusiasm. He had insisted on choosing a sturdy pony for Maybelle (for her mother to buy) and gone to a lot of trouble to find the right one. Maybelle had looked starry-eyed at her acquisition. And Mike had spent quite a bit of time instructing her—once even taking her out to follow the hounds. She had come back full of pride and praise for Mike. But apart from that bond between them, it was easy to be seen that Mike and Maybelle had nothing in common.

Gradually Venetia was being forced to realize that her husband and her daughter, far from being friends, were antipathetic. He discouraged the young girl's musical ability and love of reading. She resented it. He said she spent too long with her books and ought to be out more. He complained because Venetia wanted to include Maybelle in many of their parties. Her place was in a schoolroom, he said. It was a bore having her 'hanging around'. Venetia remarked that Maybelle had never been the slightest nuisance in the past and that it would be hard on the child if she were banished. She was used to being constantly with her mother. Mike shrugged his shoulders and sulked.

That was another phase that soon showed itself—Mike's fits of sulking when he did not immediately get his own way.

When Barbara Keen came down for the week-end her ruthless and penetrating eye saw everything. She was not to be deceived by Venetia's surface happiness and the general spirit of goodwill and gaiety at Burnt Ash.

In her blunt way she attacked Venetia.

'Mike's jealous of Maybelle—that's the trouble, and she cramps his style. He can't do quite as much swearing or tell as many bawdy stories as he would if she weren't present.'

Venetia laughed this off. But Barbara twisted her lips and added:

'You're not looking so well. You're getting puffy under the eyes, my sweet. Country life doesn't seem to be agreeing with you.'

'Oh, it's just that I'm tired—too many late nights—don't be such a raven,' Venetia laughed back.

124

But it was not really a laughing matter and she knew it. Barbara was right. Michael *was* jealous of Maybelle and there was nothing she could do about it. And not even her ardent passion for him would induce her to give Maybelle a raw deal and make her feel 'out of things'.

Another of Barbara's remarks rankled:

'I think Michael would have taken this step-child better if she had been seven or seventeen. But Maybelle's at the awkward age and he doesn't know how to deal with her.'

That also Venetia knew to be true and she did not like the truth. It was too unpalatable.

It was astonishing how Michael's general humour improved as soon as Maybelle left the house and Venetia and Mike were alone again.

That very first night she left he had taken Venetia in his arms and told her, with the boyish charm that was so irresistible, that he was sorry if he had been irritable at times but that he *did* like having his lovely Venetia all to himself.

'I slipped Maybelle a quid to add to her pocket money,' he added magnificently.

'That was sweet of you,' Venetia answered but wondered how she could make Michael understand that the pound note would not mean as much to the young girl as sympathetic understanding—apart from sitting astride a horse.

Neither could she tell him that much as she

loved him, she had missed Maybelle this evening; and passed the little bedroom that would be unoccupied for three long months with a foolish lump in her throat. No, he wouldn't understand that.

Then at the end of November Michael's father had a heart attack and died. Venetia had only visited the old invalid once or twice and could not honestly grieve for him. But Michael's attitude was one of frank relief.

The poor old man, he said, was no pleasure to himself or anyone else.

'And the whole thing was such an expense,' he had ended.

That had seemed to Venetia a little shocking but she was gradually becoming inoculated against this sort of remark from Michael. One couldn't go on being shocked or surprised by his apparent total lack of sensibility.

Once his father was buried and the old man's affairs wound up Michael launched into new extravagances to which he had little right. It seemed as though the knowledge that he now possessed a rich wife went to his head. Nearly every night the Pethicks gave a party, or went to one in the district, or drove up to town for a theatre or dance. Down here they were never without week-end guests. And the guests were rarely friends of Venetia's. They were Mike's hunting friends.

She liked a few of them. The M.F.H. and his wife were charming. And there was one elderly

126

bachelor whom she particularly favoured, Colonel Woollacombe, who had the red face, silver hair and monocle of the old-fashioned English gentleman—and the courtly manner that went with it. His hobby was sailing and Mike, when he was a bachelor, used to spend odd holidays on his yacht. It was not that Venetia had anything in common with the Colonel but that she appreciated a certain touch of gallantry and sympathetic charm in old 'Woolly', as he was called by his friends. When she thought about the rest of Michael's close associates who were not members of the hunt she shuddered. Mamie and Ted Linnell, film stars, both of whom drank like fishes and hung on—the last to leave any party—until no more drink was forthcoming. The Hon. Agatha Bellathorp, too, who according to Mike was a demon shot and owned the finest pheasant shooting in the district. She strode like a man, had short-cropped hair and a flow of language that would have found approval in the lower deck of any ship. The things she said in front of the rest of the company appalled Venetia although she had never hitherto thought of herself as a prig. But Mike found 'old Aggie' highly amusing and always insisted that she should be included in their parties.

The same thing applied to many others of his friends whom Venetia tried to like and just could not. And she could see that it was equally hopeless for her to expect Mike to entertain

127

with any cordiality the friends of her own choosing. She soon saw that she could not even begin to invite a man like Herman Weissman to spend more than an hour or two at Burnt Ash Manor.

But so far there had been no disputes between Michael and herself—not a breath to indicate that this marriage was any other than a brilliant success.

'I find life *terrific* with you, darling,' he continually assured her.

She believed it. But that was because he was not forced to lead the life that she personally would have chosen but was allowed to continue following the course he had always taken.

But how were things with her?

That was a question she had never dared honestly and openly to ask herself.

Almost in a queer state of panic she carried on—snatching oblivion in her husband's arms—and in the many moments when he was so charming and tender and at her feet. Then he was the Michael with whom she had first fallen in love.

CHAPTER TWO

That night Venetia and Michael dined alone, which was a pleasant change from Venetia's point of view. They had had a succession of late parties.

Michael was in his usual amiable mood—more amiable than ever perhaps because he had had an excellent day on the Stock Exchange. He and 'old Tony', he told Venetia, were busier than they had been for years.

'It's a bore being quite so rushed but at least it means a few more shekels,' he grinned.

Dinner was over. It had been cooked by the faithful Margaret who, despite the fact that she had never quite thawed towards Mike, had settled down at Burnt Ash. The meal had been served by a young Spanish girl named Pippa, one of the new necessary importations from the Continent. Venetia had found it difficult to induce English maids to live so far out in the country as this. Pippa was gay and the English that she spoke so badly amused everybody. Nothing was too much trouble for her. But old Margaret barely 'suffered her'. She did not like foreigners.

'We'll have coffee in the drawing-room, Pippa,' Venetia smiled at the girl. Pippa answered her but her big black eyes sparkled at the *señor*.

'*Sí señora,*' she nodded.

As Michael followed his wife into the drawing-room he said:

'That little thing has got quite a good figure, hasn't she?'

'Yes—perfect,' said Venetia in her frank and

129

generous way.

'So have you,' said Michael as an afterthought; and slipped an arm around her waist.

Venetia would not have dreamt of being jealous of one of her staff but somehow Michael had made a comparison by adding that word of praise. She found it odious. She moved away from him to the fire-place and kicked a log in the big basket grate. It sent the sparks shooting up the chimney. She made no further comment but lit a cigarette while Pippa brought in the coffee-tray and set it on the pie-crust table in front of the Chesterfield.

Venetia had her back turned to both Michael and the Spanish maid. She heard Michael say in a jocular voice, using the pidgin English that he always did for Pippa:

'You—ride—gee-gee—horse—yes—no—?'

Pippa giggled.

'Ride horse? Yes...'

'No—no—' Pippa protested. 'No like horse—me!'

Venetia turned and saw Michael making the movements of a person riding a horse. Pippa was rocking with laughter. She shook her head, threw Venetia a somewhat scandalized look and hurried out of the room.

Michael flung himself into an armchair, stretched his legs and lit a cigar.

'Jolly nice here this evening,' he murmured. 'It's cold out tonight. What have you been doing all day, sweet?'

For a moment she did not reply, but started to pour the coffee into small Minto cups which had belonged to Michael's mother and were one of the few tasteful things she had found in this house. She did not quite know why, but she resented Michael's familiarity with the Spanish girl.

'I am not a snob,' she told herself. 'It isn't that I mind that Pippa is a paid domestic and he jokes with her so often. It's just the free and easy way he treats all women of all classes. He has no dignity—absolutely none at all—and no delicacy of feeling. Yet one can't be cross. He is so *amiable*.'

Queer, but now that very amiability of Michael's which she had at first thought one of his greatest assets had become at times an irritant. She even felt that she wanted to wipe that perpetual smile off that handsome young face; to *make* him be serious.

She ought not to be thinking this way, she told herself, and tried to induce a cheerful note into her voice as she gave Michael a *résumé* of the day's activities. She had been into Lewes this afternoon and done some shopping. But she had spent most of the morning writing letters—and paying bills. (Here she threw Michael a significant look but he was flipping idly through the pages of a *Tatler*.) He looked up and said:

'Good lord—have you seen this, Venetia?'

131

He gave her the magazine. She saw that he referred to a photograph taken last week of the Hon. Agatha Bellathorp with a gun under her arm. Standing beside her was Miss Jix Lawson. Michael laughed:

'So Jix got herself into the *Tatler*. That'll please her. Marvellous legs, that girl, you know. She looks her best in those...' and he leaned forward and tapped a thumbnail against the picture. Jix wore boy's breeches and pullover.

Venetia handed him back the magazine.

'I thought you said Jix wasn't at Agatha's shooting party and that you haven't seen her lately.'

'Did I? I don't think so, darling. She nearly always turns up when there's a spot of shooting or hunting.'

Again Venetia was silent. She kept a check on her innermost feelings. It was true that Jix Lawson was Michael's former 'girl friend' and perhaps she did not altogether like him being seen regularly with a girl with whom he had actually lived. But she supposed that if she were to voice such sentiments, Michael would roar with laughter and tell her not to be old-fashioned. That was a little dart he liked to jab at her sometimes.

She said coolly:

'How is Jix these days?'

'Oh, she was telling me that she had just had an affair with some man much older than

herself who wants to marry her but she's
through with him now. I doubt if Jix will ever
get married.'

'Perhaps she is still in love with you,' said
Venetia.

'I wouldn't wonder,' said Michael and
yawned.

'How hateful you can be at times!' Venetia
said in a low voice.

He burst out laughing. It nearly always
seemed to amuse him when he said anything to
shock Venetia's susceptibilities.

'I'm honest if nothing else, my angel.'

'I think I'm rather sorry for Jix.'

'Well, I may say she doesn't like *you*.'

'I don't suppose she does,' said Venetia
coldly.

'You've always avoided her since we've been
down here and it was pretty marked when you
didn't ask her to our house-warming.'

Now Venetia's fair skin coloured. She
opened her eyes wide at him.

'But, Michael, you *agreed* that we shouldn't
include her.'

Michael was looking at the *Tatler* again. She
could not see his expression.

'Well, you didn't seem keen, darling, and I
suppose you had a "thing" about it because of
the old days so I didn't press it. All the same I
think perhaps it was a bit unkind. Jix has lived
in these parts all her life and she goes
everywhere except to us, which is a bit marked,
really.'

Venetia started to speak, then closed her lips. Her heart beat quickly. The flush remained on her cheeks. Michael was carrying his lack of tact a little too far. She could see that he resented the fact that she had never asked Jix Lawson here. After a moment she said:

'I am sorry, Mike, but I thought we had agreed that it wasn't possible for me to make a friend of Jix. After all—everybody in the place knows—' She broke off and bit her lower lip.

Michael, although he had lived with Venetia for six months, had never been able to understand or appreciate her acutely sensitive nature. It was too extreme for him. He was, perhaps, used to women of coarser fibre. Without really meaning to be unkind he now said exactly the wrong thing:

'Well, there is no need for you to be jealous of Jix. But if you are—leave things as they are and don't ask her round. I just thought it might be more pleasant if you made friends.'

Then Venetia was moved to anger.

'Kindly understand that I am *not* jealous of Jix Lawson, and I think it's insulting of you even to suggest it.'

He glanced up at Venetia in mild astonishment.

'Oh, lord! Have I said the wrong thing? Sorry! Keep calm—my sweet. You don't have to have Jix here if you don't want to. I just thought it would be nice. She's great fun when she wants to be, the little devil!'

Venetia poured out a second cup of coffee. She was quite ashamed to find her hand shaking.

'If you want to have Jix here and you find her such fun I'll ask her to our Christmas dance.'

'Please yourself, darling. I don't really mind.'

She turned away from him, feeling exasperated. That was so typical of Michael. What *did* he mind? How could anybody be so shallow? Yet she had imagined him a man with deep and sincere feelings under the 'gay boy's' façade. The long months of familiarity with him had left her wondering if she had been right and terrified that she had been wrong.

She had no cause to be jealous of Jix Lawson. Of that she was sure; and just as sure that Michael was still wholly her lover. A provocative glance thrown at Pippa or the egotistical desire to see more of an old mistress who still cared about him—what did that mean to Michael? Nothing much. Yet Venetia would have vastly preferred to know that because of *her* feelings he would not wish to bring Jix to this house. It did not place Venetia in a good position, knowing that the whole crowd in or around Burnt Ash knew of the former liaison between Michael and Jix. Yet she could see that Michael had no strong feelings about the situation either way.

He did not even realize that she was upset,

she thought ironically. He changed the subject and held out a hand to her with one of his sunniest smiles.

'Come and sit down by me and let's talk.'

Deliberately she stopped thinking and allowed him to draw her down on to the arm of the chair. She sat there, with her arm around his shoulders.

The room was beautiful. She had invested it with her own natural dignity, and a tranquil charm. It was not recognizable as the badly-furnished, gaunt room which had been a painful reminder of the days when Michael's mother was mistress of Burnt Ash Manor. Now it was perfectly lighted by tall standard lamps with deep satin-fringed shades. There were three long windows facing the front lawn framed by curtains of thick yellow satin brocade; and Venetia had put the loveliest of her own rugs in here on the polished parquet. The furnishings were a combination of yellow and deep claret. The Chesterfield was piled with small velvet cushions. Her beloved piano was here at the far end and on it Venetia kept a huge vase of flowers—at this time of the year full of red and yellow chrysanthemums. At the opposite end on either side of the door stood a pair of Georgian bookcases which had belonged to Geoffrey. Lady Sellingham's wedding present had been that Queen Anne escritoire. Upon it stood two magnificent Sèvres jars. Over the carved wood mantelpiece, which Venetia had stripped of its ugly Victorian paint, hung a flower painting in oils in an exquisite Florentine frame. There was one other beautiful picture in the room—a Cézanne which Herman Weissman had given her. It was the most valuable thing he had had in his possession. It had been stored for years. He had insisted on bringing it out and presenting it to Venetia when she married Michael.

'One day it would have been left to my god-daughter,' he had said. 'But her mother might just as well have the pleasure of it now.'

It was a superb painting—a study of trees fringing a river. Venetia had received it with pride and pleasure. As her gaze fell on it now she remembered what Michael had said when she showed it to him with delight.

'*Terrific!*' he had exclaimed.

That monotonous adjective fell so continuously from Michael's lips. She was glad he had liked the painting but afterwards he had spoiled even his own word of praise by adding:

'Worth something, too, I imagine, if it's an original.'

The monetary value of things meant so much less to Venetia than the glorious fact that such a masterpiece as this was hers and that she and Maybelle could look at it every day.

Michael was nudging her arm.

'Did you say you had been paying bills this morning?'

'Yes. A good many. Mostly yours, darling. I do wish you'd get down to looking through those accounts. You can't keep people waiting for ever.'

'I can,' said Michael and laughed.

She ruffled his hair.

'Sweetie—please do pay some of them.'

'Darling, I would,' he said and drew her hand against his lips with one of his most affectionate gestures. 'But I'm overdrawn at the moment.'

She was silent. She knew why Michael was overdrawn. The one thing he had to pay for in cash was drink, and last month he had bought up an entire wine cellar, from a house near Lewes which had been sold and the wine with it. He had also bought that second and expensive hunter which he had seen in Ireland and coveted. And he had engaged a regular boy to help Bennett and do odd gardening jobs. Things like that which Venetia insisted he himself should pay for. He was quite willing to do so and with a grand gesture had even ordered his bank to pay a regular amount every month to Venetia. He intended to 'keep his own wife', he had said. She accepted the money not because she really needed it but because she felt it was good for his morale. He should be allowed to feel that he was doing his share. The trouble was that he spent so much money on things that were not essentials, and were merely for his amusement. He was perpetually short of ready cash if and when she asked for it.

'Tomorrow's the week-end, thank the lord—and I'll get down to some bill-paying in the morning,' he added.

'And with only three weeks to Christmas we ought to think about presents,' she said.

'My first Christmas as a married man, eh?' he murmured and pulled her down on to his lap and began to caress her.

She kissed him back with all the warmth in her heart and wished that that heart did not ache a little because she was losing—*no, had already lost*—the wonderful, satisfying sensation of close contact with him. Nowadays she felt that she was married to an elusive Michael whose inner thoughts she could never catch, and whom she could not understand. But the physical intimacy with him was still new, desirable and sweet. She stayed in his arms for a moment, then with a little laugh slid on to her feet and smoothed back her disordered hair.

'How undignified,' she said.

'Oh, all this dignity!' he mocked her.

'You don't like it, do you?' She stood looking down at him thoughtfully.

He yawned and laughed.

'In its place.'

'Would you like Pippa to find me sitting on your knee?'

He shrugged his shoulders. An impish look gleamed in his eyes.

139

'She might envy you—who knows?'

Venetia was nonplussed. She sighed and tidied her hair.

'Impossible person!'

But she leaned down to him, pressed her cheek against his and kissed him with the utmost tenderness.

It was dear and sweet of him, she thought, to want to pull her on to his lap as though she were a young girl, and perhaps he was right— why all this dignity?

There was a performance of *Tristan und Isolde* on the Third Programme tonight. It was her favourite opera but she knew better than to suggest tuning-in to it. Instead, to please Michael she said:

'You want a television set, don't you?'

'When I last suggested having one you said you thought they were a waste of money and that there wasn't anything you ever wanted to see or hear except on rare occasions,' he reminded her.

'But you want one, don't you?'

'I think it might be fun on a winter's evening when there's nothing else to do.'

'Then I shall give you one for your birthday next week.'

His eyes brightened. He threw down the *Tatler* and reached up a hand to her.

'Venetia, you *are* a darling. I've never met such a generous person. And fancy you remembering my birthday—I'd forgotten.'

'It's the first I shall have spent as your wife,' she smiled and pressed the hand he gave her.

'Let's meet in town on Monday and choose the set,' he said with the enthusiasm that Michael always showed for new toys.

She was warmed by his pleasure but she thought:

'It will put an end to all good music for me. I dare say Maybelle and Mike will be glued to it through the holidays when we're at home.'

But that was just another sacrifice that she was prepared to make for the two she loved. And in a queer way she had begun to bracket Maybelle and Michael. They were her 'children'. But of the two, the grown up 'child' was far and away the most difficult to manage if he did not get his own way. Maybelle had her bad moments but was on the whole sweetly reasonable and always had been so as a baby.

'Thinking of Maybelle,' Venetia said aloud, 'she'll be home on the seventeenth, only another fortnight.'

Even as she spoke she had the uncomfortable sensation that the announcement would not be received with any cordiality by her young husband. She was right.

The gaiety faded from Michael's eyes. He grumbled:

'Oh, lord, the end of the term already!'

Venetia's spirits fell, but she tried to cajole him.

141

'Maybelle doesn't interfere much and you like taking her out riding, don't you? You said she was shaping well.'

'Not bad. She's rather too nervous. I wouldn't say she was born to the saddle.'

'Like her mother,' said Venetia wryly.

'I certainly shouldn't say it's in her blood.'

'No, Geoffrey didn't ride, either.'

'Incidentally,' added Michael, as he rose and bent down to throw a fresh log on the fire, 'I haven't had time to tell you before but I've had a letter from Monica Tellever asking if we'd join her party for St Moritz for the New Year. I'm dead keen to go if you'll just give it the okay, darling.'

Venetia's heart sank. She had been wondering how long it would be before Michael carried out the threat in those words he had spoken on their honeymoon. The last thing she wanted to do was to go to Switzerland and kill time in a luxury hotel while Michael went ski-ing with his party. He saw her expression and walking to her, slid an arm around her waist.

'Do let's go,' he coaxed. 'It will be a lot of fun, I promise you.'

'I don't even know who Monica Tellever is.'

'Oh, she's very gay. Lady Tellever, when she's at home. George, her husband, was a client of Tony's and mine. Bags of gold, but he died about a year ago in an air accident near Frankfurt, poor chap. Monica's now the merry widow—about my age, I suppose, and damn good-looking. Her voice spoils her—she's a bit of a parakeet and screams at you—but I'm rather fond of old Monica.'

Venetia remained silent. She had so often in the last few months heard Mike say he was 'fond of old so and so'. It never meant much. He never, in fact, produced really serious or close friends. But he knew a vast number of people who swarmed in and out of his life like bees in search of honey. And he seemed to find it satisfactory so long as their hives were open to him in return. He generally saw to it that he was at the receiving end of the surplus honey. Venetia had once openly accused him of never entertaining anybody for long if he did not find the contact a 'useful one'. He was continuing to tell her about 'old Monica', who appeared to be the very type of woman whom Venetia had avoided in the past. She liked smart and amusing women like Barbara Keen who worked or had a motive in life. But Monica appeared to be another of the motiveless women who spent their days in pursuit of sensation and little else. Monica was also obviously amoral. Michael affirmed with a grin that she had 'lived with' two men since old George died and was just beginning a third affair. She was not in a hurry to get married because she had money and because of surtax demands it didn't suit her to make a marriage which would only put up the rates.

'Really,' Michael ended lightly, 'there's something to be said for living in sin these days. I'm surprised that the religious body of gentlemen who govern us should put such a tax on the holy state of matrimony.'

Venetia moved away from her husband's encircling arm. She faced him with a smile but her heart-beats quickened and her colour was high.

'Your friend, Monica, sounds most amusing, darling, if that sort of woman does amuse you.'

'It does,' said Michael and guffawed. 'You would have met Monica before only she has been in Bermuda.'

'No doubt if she's all that rich she can afford to go on to St Moritz in the New Year but I don't really think we can.'

'Oh, we can rake up the odd pound between us, can't we, sweet?'

'You don't think it might be a good thing if we settled some of those outstanding accounts of yours first, darling?'

It was on the tip of Michael's tongue to reproach Venetia—to call her a 'schoolmarm' and accuse her of preaching. He refrained only because he knew that she was absolutely justified. But he was accustomed to complete liberty of movement and to doing what he called 'a wangle' and getting what he wanted out of life. He could not submit easily to the restraining hand of this newly-made wife of

144

his. Venetia had always led an orderly and scrupulously honest existence. He was aware of that. He even admired it but he did not want his fun spoiled.

He launched into a further description of the good time they would have in St Moritz and of Monica Tellever's assets. As hostess of the party she would see to it they were in an amusing crowd—all ski-ing experts—and why shouldn't Venetia put on a pair of skis, anyhow, and make a further effort to take part in the sport?

Then Venetia on her part launched her own attack.

'I'll only come on one condition, Mike, that we take Maybelle. She spent most of the summer holidays with her grandmother. I want her with me this Christmas.'

Silence. A stony expression replaced the cheerful twinkle in Michael's eyes. He said slowly:

'I don't think it would be a good idea. She's a bit young for that sort of party.'

'What sort of party?'

'You know what I mean. There'll be Monica and this new boy-friend of hers, and she suggested in her letter that her cousin, Robin Gunter, would go with us and—'

'You mean the Major Robin Gunter who has just been divorced and is marrying that Hollywood film star, Vicki Dorn?'

'Yes,' nodded Michael, 'that's the chap. He's

145

in the Grenadier Guards.'

'You mean he *was*.'

Michael shrugged his shoulders.

'Oh, I dare say some of the narrow-minded fellows will soon have him out.'

'Michael,' said Venetia slowly. 'Do you really think it's narrow-minded to look down on a man who leaves a very nice wife—and I knew Mary Gunter as a matter of fact—she's one in a million—and three young children, just when they most need him? Three sons, too. And all for a bit of nonsense like Vicki Dorn who has nothing to commend her except a fabulous pair of legs?'

Michael scowled.

'Darling, you do bring a note of grave propriety into the home, I must say.'

Now the temper that was deep-seated in Venetia and which needed a lot of rousing, spurted into life.

'Well, don't sneer at it, Michael. We just don't speak the same language. I happen to have moved always in quite another set from yours. You may like people who continually change husbands and wives and live with other people, and never pay their bills and think it's rather clever. But I don't. I never did and I'm not going to start now.'

She saw the red burn his face and knew that he, too, was angry. But she did not care. She added:

'You're quite right when you say that it

146

wouldn't do to take Maybelle out with that crowd. So I withdraw my suggestion. Don't even bother to make a protest. I shan't join the party either.'

'I see,' said Michael in an icy voice. 'So because my friends aren't good enough for you and your daughter, I am to be robbed of the pleasure of my ski-ing holiday with old friends.'

'Don't be ridiculous,' exclaimed Venetia. 'Those people aren't your real friends and you know it.'

'My dear Venetia, that's for me to say. And when I married I didn't bargain for this sort of thing—I am not prepared to be told by my wife whom I may or may not know, or where I may or may not go.'

Venetia went dead white. There was an ugly note in Michael's voice that she had never heard before. It filled her with dismay—with a sick fear that unless they were both careful this was liable to develop into a row that would leave an ineradicable mark. Things said in hot temper would not easily be forgotten. And the glamour of their love for each other might be torn away like a veil and reveal something which she, for one, would not care to see.

She made an effort to control her annoyance and to be reasonable.

'Mike,' she said. 'I don't want to dictate to you—honestly I don't. But I just can't agree that it is a good thing for us to—to mix our friends in this way. We have such very nice ones. Surely a woman like Monica Tellever and a man like Major Gunter wouldn't be welcome in a lot of houses?'

'Victorian twaddle, my dear.'

'Very well, then, I'm Victorian and proud of it!'

'Now look here, Venetia, don't be childish. You've always been friendly and entertained a lot, and you're quite broad-minded. What's this all about?'

'Just that I'm broad-minded only up to a point and I *don't* want to know either of the people you've mentioned and that is *that*.'

He eyed her covertly.

'Are you sure this isn't all just the outcome of your maternal anxiety for little Maybelle?'

Venetia flushed hotly. His voice was hatefully sarcastic.

'I *have* her to consider.'

Michael flung himself down on to the Chesterfield again.

'I always knew that kid would be a bore.'

'How *dare* you!' Venetia exclaimed, and now there was rage in her heart and a deep resentment in her eyes.

'Oh, come off it, darling. Don't ride the high horse with me. I can't take it.'

'How dare you,' she repeated, 'call my daughter a bore? It's not deserved and I think it's both rude and unkind of you.'

He avoided her gaze.

148

'Oh, I'm sorry if I've hurt your feelings.'

He has done more than that, she reflected. He has destroyed something ... something that was sweet and precious to me.

'Michael,' she said in a low voice, 'for God's sake don't let's talk to each other this way—it's *terrible*.'

'Well, you started it. You insulted my friends.'

'Can they be insulted?'

'There you are again,' he said and spread out a hand.

'Is a woman like Monica Tellever of more importance to you than my own child?' Venetia went on.

'I didn't say she was.'

'In fact, she seems to be even more important to you than I am.'

'That's ridiculous.'

'Yet you're prepared to hurt me and call my daughter a bore—just because I won't accept Lady Tellever's invitation.'

'Well it's rather selfish of you to turn it down out of hand when you know how much I want to go.'

She stared at him as though she could not believe her sight; his own selfishness was so incredible.

He flung her a sulky look.

'Oh, hell,' he muttered. 'Have it your own way. I'll write and tell her that it's not on.'

'You can always go alone if you want to,'

said Venetia, and picking up a library book which lay on the table she started to walk across the drawing-room to the door. She was shaking and she felt slightly sick. She was shocked by the speed with which the argument with Michael had developed into a brawl. Yes, it was nothing but a brawl—a senseless hateful quarrel between two people who could not see one another's points of view and were trying to 'get at each other' by fruitless recrimination.

Michael now stood up. He, on the one hand, was furiously angry because Venetia had turned down the plan for the ski-ing holiday. On the other, he had no wish to upset her to any extent. In his own way he still loved her. He was anxious to keep her affection. He hurried after her and caught her by both arms.

'Look, darling, wait ... Don't sweep out in this state. I'm sorry if I've said anything to offend you—honestly. It was just that I am disappointed about St Moritz—that's all.'

She could still only stare at him unbelievingly. The longer she lived with Michael the more was she astonished by his extraordinary immaturity. That he could risk losing her affection by slighting Maybelle just because he was 'disappointed' seemed to her monstrous—yet, at the same time, pathetic. She shook her head. He continued—using the old caressing voice:

'Come back and talk, sweet—don't let's fight. I don't really care a damn about Monica

150

and you needn't ask her or Gunter to the house if you don't want them.'

It was a bit late, she thought. The harm had been done but Michael did not seem aware of that.

'Come back and talk,' he repeated cajolingly. 'Don't be cross with me.'

But for a moment she was stiff and unbending. He took her wholly in his arms and tried to kiss her. She dodged his lips.

'It was what you said about Maybelle that upset me,' she said. 'Why do you find her a bore? She tried to keep out of your way last summer. I didn't think she interfered with your life at all and you seemed to enjoy quite a lot of jokes together and the horses. Everybody loves Maybelle. I can't understand you not liking her.'

'I do, I *do*,' he said. He was concerned now because he could see how deeply he had upset Venetia. 'She is a nice little girl and of course I like her. It's just that I want you to myself, I suppose. I'm afraid I'm not cut out to be a good stepfather—not the type—you know that.'

She did know it. She had known it before she married him. She had been warned by both Geoffrey's mother, by Herman and by Barbara that the existence of her daughter might be the stumbling-block in this marriage. But in the flush of her crazy passion for the gay handsome young man she had put her head in the sand

151

and tried to believe that all was well—that she could circumvent any of the difficulties.

Now Michael was warming to his act of contrition. He seemed truly sorry that he had offended her. He was as extravagant in his declarations of love and of goodwill towards Maybelle as he had been the reverse earlier this evening.

'I assure you I don't want to go to St Moritz and it was just a whim,' he said.

Venetia relented. She was tired and depressed, but he held her so closely and kissed her with such passion that she could no longer refuse to thaw in that embrace. But *'forget it'*—that wasn't going to be easy.

Mike had an astonishing and incomprehensible nature, she thought, when later that night they lay side by side and he slept, quite happy again, like a child who has been forgiven his misdeeds. But she, restless and wakeful, considered the thorny path that lay ahead of her. There was bound to be a repetition of this evening and she knew it. Mike swung so easily from one mood to another. Before sleeping he had made a dozen promises about what he would do for Maybelle this Christmas. But it was Venetia's private opinion that the less he was called on to do anything for Maybelle, the better.

CHAPTER THREE

For Maybelle Sellingham it was not at all the sort of Christmas she wanted and had been accustomed to all her life. Like most young people she woke early. She found the usual stocking packed with little surprises with an exquisite Italian marionette peeping over the top—she had coveted one of these after going to the marionette show with her mother. She was delighted with that and with all the little presents that had been so carefully chosen to delight her. Mummy knew her taste exactly—in fact they both liked the same things.

The young girl had drawn the curtains. It was still dark and very cold but there was no snow, which was a disappointment to Maybelle, who had wanted a 'white Christmas'. The house was centrally heated so she did not feel cold. She wore the warm pyjamas which were a legacy from school. She hoped to be allowed to wear really pretty nightgowns. She liked pretty clothes, and particularly the beautiful things that her mother wore. However, Venetia had had a new party dress made for her and it was there in the wardrobe ready for the dance which was to be given at Burnt Ash tonight.

Maybelle knew that she ought to be looking

forward to this dance but it wasn't really the kind that she was likely to find amusing. The guests were all 'grown-ups'—mostly Mike's friends; a few of Mummy's. The trouble was that there were not many teenagers in this district who could have been invited and the only 'possible'—a boy named Peter Willet, son of one of Mike's hunting friends—had annoyingly gone down with measles. That meant that Maybelle would have no companion of her own age this evening. No, she wasn't really looking forward to the dance much and she didn't like Mike's friends much either. They drank too much and then they got horrid. At a cocktail party in the summer, one of Mike's contemporaries had taken Maybelle into a corner, pulled her plaits and told her she was a very pretty little girl, then asked her to give him a kiss. His alcoholic breath had disgusted the child. She had run out of the room and made an excuse not to return. She hoped that there would not be a repetition of that this evening. She hoped, too, that Mummy would enjoy the dance, because although she hadn't said a word, Maybelle was ready to swear that Mummy didn't like Mike's friends much either ... with a few exceptions.

In the middle of unpacking her stocking, reading all the funny little messages which Venetia attached to the parcels, Maybelle suddenly stopped and sat motionless, thinking. In the light of the table lamp her round girlish face looked serious. She felt suddenly sad; not at all what one should feel on Christmas morning. But unfortunately Maybelle was imaginative—acutely sensitive to atmosphere. Despite all the beauty and luxury of Burnt Ash—her beloved pony—all the material things that she had in life (she never had to ask Mummy twice for anything within reason)— Maybelle did not feel really gay and content as she used to do in the little Kensington house alone with Mummy; or as she felt in Richmond with her grandmother. She had 'phoned Ganny last night. They had exchanged all the old jokes and pleasantries. Maybelle had asked after the health of the 'chelly hat'. Gan had answered gaily that the 'chellies' were still wobbling and the straw standing up to wear and that it was in its winter box, hibernating, waiting for next spring. Maybelle added that she had seen a big parcel waiting with Ganny's handwriting on it, and was most excited. Lady Sellingham replied that she looked forward to Maybelle spending a day and even a night with her soon. Then she had ended by asking after Mummy. Maybelle had answered: 'Fine, thanks, Ganny!'

But was that true? Maybelle asked herself on this winter's morning. She stared at the little pile of Christmas paper and tinsel ribbon spread over her bed. Her serious grey eyes then turned to the double-framed photograph on the mantelpiece. Mummy in evening dress, and the one of Daddy. All the girls at school said he looked like a knight—a sort of crusader with his fine features and his intellectual brow and so much goodness and kindliness shining from his eyes.

Maybelle remembered Daddy so well. What friends they had always been! And she remembered the other Christmases; the happiest of all those when Daddy was still alive and they would all three open their parcels together and say:

'*Just* what I wanted!'

She and Mummy had missed him dreadfully at first but they had still had each other and it was an accepted thing that as soon as she woke on a Christmas morning Maybelle should rush into her mother's room, climb into her bed and then they would start delving into their stockings. The bigger presents waited till after breakfast.

It was always such *fun*. Maybelle and Mummy would go to church for the Christmas service, and then on to Richmond for lunch with Ganny.

It was once a ritual. Now it belonged to the past. There had been a great change in all their lives and this morning Maybelle felt that change profoundly.

When she had first learned that her mother was going to marry again and she had been introduced to Mike, she had been glad. He had seemed so handsome, so gay and such fun. But last 'hols' she had seen the other side of Mike. And at fifteen she was quite old enough to size up a human being and even analyse character. She was, in fact, at the age when a young girl becomes serious and contemplative—apart from all the giggles. It had not taken Maybelle long to discover that other, less attractive side to Mummy's new husband. The extreme egotism, the fits of bad temper when he did not get what he wanted, the slight tendency to be coarse in his jocular moods. She no longer altogether trusted the gay smile or winning word, because she had learned that although Michael was the most easy-going man in the world when things were going his way—he was appalling when they were not. In fact he was what Daddy used to call 'a poor loser'. This to Maybelle was almost as bad as being a coward.

Neither was she blind to the fact that her stepfather was jealous of her. This had made her nervous and withdrawn. By nature she was frank and uninhibited. She was so used to rushing to Mummy any odd time she wished and telling her what lay in her mind. Now she had to wait for Mummy to be alone. She had learned to be cautious of Mike. And even though he said nothing, she was aware that he usually wanted her out of the way. Not to be wanted was something that Maybelle had never experienced before and Mike on several occasions had wounded her childish feelings deeply. At the same time she would not have dreamed of expressing these feelings to Mummy. Mummy loved Mike. Maybelle was still very young—but with the dawning knowledge and instinct of her womanhood she felt it her duty to help Mummy keep her illusion. If there was one thing Maybelle could not endure it was to see her beloved mother unhappy. It had been terrible after Daddy died but since then Mummy had seemed to have recovered and the two of them had been very happy during the holidays.

But lately Maybelle had heard and seen things—just little things—that troubled her exceedingly. Mike sulking, for instance, or Mike drinking. Mummy looking rather pale and harassed and once Maybelle had surprised her seated on the edge of her bed in tears. That had been awful; although Mummy had assured Maybelle that it was just that she had a bad headache. But Maybelle believed it was because Mike had done something to upset her.

Maybelle had thought a lot about this situation during the school term, but she had not confided in anybody, even her Best Friend. She was a loyal child and she would have felt it disloyal to Mummy to discuss Michael adversely. But Maybelle had come to the definite conclusion *that she did not like Mummy's husband.* At times he was wonderful—he could not have been more patient with her when he was teaching her to ride. Yet in the next five minutes he would turn his back on her and seemed to want her out of the room.

But there was one big thing that she would not have told her mother even, as she put it to herself, if she had been tortured.

On the last day of the summer holidays she had taken a walk with Poppet, the spaniel bitch which was the latest addition to Burnt Ash. They had turned into Ash Forest.

Through the green lace of leaves Maybelle had suddenly seen two figures lying in the bracken. They were clutched in a hot embrace which left nothing to the imagination. It was there undeniably and horridly for the young, innocent girl—the act of sex between two people which she understood only because of her vague 'farmyard' knowledge of any child who has kept animals.

It was not a pretty sight. For her, it was a revelation of such astonishment and disgust that it seared across her mind like a branding iron. For she recognized the man as her young stepfather. The girl she had seen occasionally in Burnt Ash and at the Meets. Maybelle did not remember her name. She had certainly never come to Burnt Ash Manor and been included in Mummy's list of friends. All that was visible to Maybelle in that shocking moment was the girl's red, passionate face and disordered shirt—half torn from her shoulders—and her arms twined around

159

Michael. Then her gaze sped to the two horses tethered close by the pathway. Michael and this girl had obviously been hacking.

A sensation of panic seized Maybelle. Her one terror was that either of those two lying there in that dreadful abandon to sex might see her—that Poppet might scent them and bark. She turned, seizing Poppet's collar, and dragged her away. With a pounding heart Maybelle rushed then through the woods and stopped when she felt herself secure. Then she was suddenly violently sick.

The full implication was lost on her—but she was not stupid. She knew that Michael was doing something awful to *Mummy*. And that if Mummy knew, she would be terribly upset. So when Maybelle finally got home, only one thing stuck in her outraged mind. She must never tell Mummy.

For Maybelle, the revelation of such deceit, such hatefulness on her stepfather's part spoiled the whole of the holiday and filled her with confusion and disgust. It turned her completely against him—especially when at dinner that same night Mummy asked him if he had seen anyone that they knew when he was out exercising Red Prince, and he had answered 'not a soul'. Then Maybelle had had to add the word '*liar*' to the unpleasant names she could now apply to the handsome young man Mummy had married. The young girl returned to school with the secret but confirmed conviction that Mummy had made a mistake and that Michael Pethick was not worthy to be in Daddy's place.

Maybelle had spent her mid-term holiday at Richmond with her grandmother. On the Sunday, Mummy and Mike had gone down there to lunch. Mike had been most amusing and pleasant and teased her in a brotherly way. But she could not forget what she had seen and what she felt about him. After he had gone, Maybelle's grandmother had said:

'Michael really is very jolly, I'm sure he'll keep your mother young and she seems to be so happy, bless her.'

It was then that the memory of what she had seen in the forest returned to Maybelle. Unable to bear this burden alone any longer, she had burst out with the story to the one person whom she knew she could trust.

'Don't you think it was ghastly, Gan? And he told Mummy a lie and said he hadn't seen anybody, too,' she ended.

It had taken Lady Sellingham quite a little time to reply. She had grown quite pink and turned her face quickly away from Maybelle. She busied herself by picking dead leaves off a pot of azaleas. Then she said in her quiet voice:

'I don't quite understand, darling. But I think you did quite right not to mention it to Mummy. One has to learn to be diplomatic in this life. Try hard to forget it, my dear child, and don't let it worry you.'

Her voice had trailed off rather lamely. Maybelle was too intelligent to be so easily put off. But she took the hint from her grandmother and said no more about the incident. Nevertheless it remained in her mind. Now she knew who the girl was. She had seen her at the Meet last Saturday. They called her Jix Lawson. A Miss Lawson was coming to the dance tonight, so Mummy had said. So Jix would be here and that fact depressed Maybelle.

On this Christmas morning she was deeply conscious that this new life with Mummy married again was far from being the happy and united one they had both hoped for. She would not have dared run down the corridor and knock on Mummy's door with Mike in there. In fact, it made the young girl rather hot and embarrassed to think of him in that intimate relationship with her mother. So she felt lonely as she unwrapped her stocking presents. She wondered if Mummy was awake, or feeling the same sadness, and wanting to come in to her.

Maybelle suddenly whispered to her father's photograph:

'Daddy, I wish you were back again, and I bet Mummy does sometimes.'

With this sinister thought she continued the unwrapping of her presents. Mummy always had such amusing ideas. There was even a fountain pen with a quill on the end of it 'with

162

love from Poppet'. At this moment Pippa, according to instructions, opened the señorita's door, and Poppet rushed in.

Maybelle hugged the little dog, who wagged her tail furiously and licked her cheek, while she pulled Poppet's floppy ears.

'Thank you, Poppet, for spending all your pocket money on me!' she said, and felt less lonely for the spaniel's company.

It seemed a very long time to her before her mother finally came in to see her. In fact, Maybelle by that time was up and dressed and beginning to tidy torn Christmas paper, ribbons and string. There was no longer need for artificial light. The grey morning was growing brighter. One dim shaft of sunlight pierced the gloom of the sky and glistened on the red berries and glossy leaves of the hedge just below Maybelle's window. It was going to be a fine day, after all.

Maybelle remembered that Mike, last night, had said he would take her out riding before lunch.

Her mother walked into the room and the young girl immediately flung herself into Venetia's arms in her joyous and friendly way.

'Oh, merry Christmas, Mummy darling.'

'And merry Christmas to you, darling,' was the rejoinder.

But now Maybelle looked at her mother and was quite shocked by what she saw. For all Venetia's efforts to disguise her appearance had not achieved the object. Her face looked pale and drawn and her eyes shadowed. The lids were pink. She looked, in fact, suspiciously as if she had been crying.

'Why, Mummy, what on *earth's* the matter!' exclaimed Maybelle.

'Nothing, just that wretched head again,' said Venetia in a light tone. 'Nothing, really, Maybelle. Now come and sit down and tell me what you found in your stocking. By the way, thank you for the *beautiful* handkerchiefs I found in mine.'

'I missed us not opening our stockings together,' said Maybelle.

'So did I,' said her mother, and this time there was no lightness in her voice. But she sat down on the edge of the bed and averting her face from her young daughter's searching gaze, began to pick up the little presents one by one, and read the labels.

Nobody must know what an anguish of feeling weighed down Venetia's spirit this Christmas morning. The bad headache must remain the excuse. And during the day she must put on a lot of make-up and make strenuous efforts to appear as if she had not a care in the world. For Maybelle's sake, not for anybody else's. Certainly not for Mike's. For at this early hour Venetia, with the most bitter resentment and anger, felt that she did not care what Michael thought—either now or ever again.

It was an unhappy and dreadful thing for her to feel. Deep down inside her she was aghast because of it. And it had all arisen from nothing—so it seemed, now, when she looked back on it. But it is out of the 'nothing' that the biggest misunderstandings arise.

It had all begun when she first woke up—about half past seven, which was her usual time for stirring and having a cup of tea. Margaret used to bring the tea to her when she lived alone. But because Michael disliked being disturbed before eight she had arranged that a Thermos should be left on the table beside her bed and she could drink her tea quietly without waking him.

This morning of all mornings Venetia was determined to go and see Maybelle for the ritual of 'stocking-opening', since the child could not very well come in to her, now that Venetia shared a room with a husband.

She had tried cautiously to slip from the bed but Michael had opened an eye, given her his most engaging smile and grabbed her wrist.

'Oh, no you don't, my angel. It's much too early. Let's have another hour's shut-eye!'

She had started to laugh and played with his hair for a moment, then, kissing him, murmured:

'Let me go, darling. I'm late as it is.'

'Late for what?' he grunted. Both eyes were shut again. How long and curly his lashes were against his brown cheeks and how

165

devastatingly good-looking he was, she thought.

'I've got a date with Maybelle,' she explained. 'It's one we have always kept since she was a small child. We always open our Christmas stockings together.'

He grunted again and kept a firm hold on her.

'Nonsense! She can open her own stocking in her own room.'

Venetia started to argue gently, still kissing him. Then he grew cross.

'Oh, do stop trying to get out of bed and letting all the cold air in. And don't be so damn sentimental about that kid of yours. Anybody would think she was a baby.'

Then it had been Venetia's turn to change from good humour to annoyance.

'It may seem "damn sentimental" to you, but it's just something we've always done and we enjoy it and I'm sorry for you if you can't enter into the Christmas spirit with us.'

Then both Michael's blue handsome eyes opened. He positively glared at her.

'Look, Venetia—this *isn't* your old family life. It's your life with me. You're always trying to lead the one you used to lead with your former husband and it's beginning to irritate me. That and all this business about Maybelle. Anybody would think the house centred around her. It happens to be *my* house.'

'*And* mine, if it comes to that!' flashed

Venetia, who had lost all her colour and begun to shiver as the cool morning air pierced through her gossamer nightgown. But she could not reach her dressing-gown because Michael had pinned her down with one strong arm. She added hotly:

'I never try to lead my former life. And I assure you this one bears no resemblance to it.'

'But you do a lot of hinting that the old times were so much more to your taste.'

'That is an absolute lie, Mike. It's abominable of you to say such a thing. You know how much I've tried to fit in with all your plans and tastes.'

The wrangle continued in earnest. Now and again Michael caved in and admitted that the things he said were unjustified only to lash out at her again about the unfortunate Maybelle, who seemed to be a bone of contention. Venetia tried to remember Barbara's warning that this was all the result of jealousy on Michael's part and to make allowances for it. She was so appalled by the fact that discord should have arisen on Christmas morning that she lowered her pride and made an appeal to him:

'Darling—really—this is childish. Let's be rational, and behave like adult people. And don't let's forget about "peace on earth—goodwill to men",' she had tried to end on a laugh.

But the spirit of cruelty, latent in Michael,

entered into him now.

'Okay, I'll remember the peace and goodwill but I'm not letting you go in to that girl. You can see her at breakfast. Now, please, darling, settle down and have another snooze with me.'

Venetia was by nature a tranquil woman but this determination of Mike's to prevent her from visiting her fifteen-year-old daughter in accordance with old Christmas traditions seemed to her not only grossly selfish on his part but slightly sadistic. She lost her temper.

'Let go of me, Mike, and stop being so absurd,' she snapped.

He laughed and pulled her closer to him, imprisoning her now with both arms.

'Not on your life. If it's a question of who gets you—Maybelle or me—it's going to be me.'

Crimson and half suffocated she fought with him.

It was an ignominious fight and because of his physical strength she was bound to be the loser and to get nothing for her pains except a few bruises. Between his teeth, Michael said a lot of things which made unpleasant hearing and which left her considerably shaken.

It was time, he declared, that she learned that she had a husband to consider now; that he refused to take second place to Miss Maybelle Sellingham, and that if the said Miss Sellingham was still such an infant that she must open her toys with *someone*, she had better spend next Christmas with her grandmother and open the presents with an old lady who was as 'gaga' as herself.

Venetia gasped:

'Neither of them is "gaga" and you're a damned fool, Mike, just making this all appear so serious. It just happens to be a thing that Maybelle and I have always done, this visiting each other on a Christmas morning, and we enjoy it, and it's loathsome of you to make a scene about it.'

He had started to kiss her passionately, thus muffling her protests.

'I rather like you when you look so angry— enjoy a woman with spirit—I'm still mad about you, you know. Stop talking about that damned girl and kiss me back. This is *our* Christmas in *our* house. Come on—kiss me!'

For a moment he defeated her—by sheer physical force. But in every other way he lost that battle and the thing that he lost for good was her respect. Impossible now not to compare him with Geoffrey. Such a humiliating scene with *him* would have been quite impossible. He had too much respect for *her*. Their mutual love had been tender. He had given her homage as well as passion. But Michael's was a love which had neither gentleness nor understanding—which would not allow him to see her point of view—or treat her feelings with deference. The fact that she cared so deeply for her child was not to be

169

tolerated by him. It had become a festering sore—a black spot of jealousy—even after the six brief months of marriage.

He kept her a prisoner for another hour out of a sheer despotic determination not to give her up to Maybelle. When, at nine o'clock, she was still there beside him, she lay spent and white, every nerve in her jarred and quivering. She looked at him and saw that he was actually asleep—he looked pleased with himself— because of his rotten victory, she thought, and her love for him trembled perilously on the verge of hatred.

With blind eyes she turned towards the light that filtered through a chink in the heavy ivory satin curtains still drawn across the windows. She did not see the beautiful figured wallpaper which she had chosen with such care and pleasure for this room; nor her favourite spinet which had been converted into a dressing-table, with its triple mirror; and the crystal vase—reflected in the glass—full of scarlet carnations which Michael had brought her down from London yesterday. She could not bear to look at those flowers either, but she had received them with joy. Mike had few such spontaneous generous moments and she delighted in them. And certainly she could not complain that he was no longer physically her lover. But his passion of this morning had left her disgusted and furious. For the first time she had not responded to it. It was not possible for

Venetia to enjoy love-making under such conditions. Especially as she knew now that what Mike felt for her was desire, it could not be love. No man, who loved a woman, would have tried to prevent her from enjoying that silly little tryst with her own child on Christmas morning.

It was half past nine before Mike let Venetia go. Then she at once put on her dressing-gown and went in to Maybelle's bedroom. She felt sick to the depths of her being. For her this Christmas could have no further meaning. She felt the memory would spoil every Christmas for her in the future.

The worst part was the fact that the scene had left no mark on him. She was beginning to wonder if he had such a thing as a heart. She had been amazed when he woke up, smiled at her quite gaily, released her, and said:

'Afraid I was a bit rough just now, sweet. Sorry! You shouldn't be so attractive! Go along to your precious baby and tell her I'll kiss her under the mistletoe later if she's good.'

Speechless and with a rigid look, Venetia walked out of the bedroom. It just was not possible to deal with a man like Michael. But this time he had gone too far and she was not ready to forgive or forget.

She stayed only a short time with Maybelle because she felt ill—mentally overwrought— she was afraid she might betray herself to the young girl. But as she looked into Maybelle's clear bright eyes and watched her playing with Poppet and listened to her rapturous comments on the stocking presents, the mother thought:

'Thank God I've got *her*!'

And following that thought came another which she could not restrain but which seemed to her both terrible and tragic.

'*I wish we were still alone. I wish I'd never married again.*'

So soon to feel that way! So quickly to have been disillusioned! So surely to be forced into facing the grim truth that Barbara, Herman and Geoffrey's mother had all been right. She should have waited—waited till she got to know Michael better. For she would never have linked her life with the Michael she knew today. Now there was nothing left save for her to make the best of things. Not if she died, she reflected, would she allow anybody in her set to guess that she had reached this pitch. And the last person who must know was Maybelle, who would be so terribly upset if she thought her mother was unhappy.

The most difficult thing to Venetia would be the necessity to act a part from now onwards. Imprisoned in Michael's arms this morning, she had felt that she would like nothing better than to get up and dress, walk out of Burnt Ash Manor—with Maybelle—and never return.

She was laughing gaily, however, as she kissed the girl, patted Poppet's silken head and returned to her own bedroom.

'Thanks awfully, Mummy, for all the things. And merry Christmas,' the girl's voice followed her.

'Merry Christmas,' thought Venetia bitterly. *'My God!'*

CHAPTER FOUR

Venetia returned to her own bedroom to find Mike up and in his bath. His cheerful whistle sounded through the door which was ajar. The sound increased her resentment against him. How *could* he behave so vilely then forget it— treat it as though it had been only a mild dispute between them?

She was, herself, fully dressed by the time he sauntered into the bedroom again—wearing a black satin dressing-gown with a red cravat. He looked theatrically handsome and his grin was as boyish, as charming as ever. He rubbed his hands together.

'Hullo, sweet! Quite a nip in the air. What's for breakfast this Noel morn? ... I could do with a kipper. Is there a hope?'

Venetia busied herself tidying the cream jars and bottles on the dressing-table. She had made up her face so that she appeared quite normal, but the artificial pink colour was deepened now by a dark flush. She almost

173

hated Mike and the fact terrified her. She said:

'No—I ordered boiled eggs. You'd better go down, Mike—I told Margaret nine for us all and it's nearer ten.'

She nearly added: 'Thanks to your abominable behaviour—refusing to let me get up and go to Maybelle—just to spite us both.' But she refrained. Then she felt his hands on her shoulders. He pulled her round so that she was forced to face him. He looked with genuine surprise into the soft velvet brown eyes that were so attractively set in the pure oval of her face. But even her make-up could not deceive Michael this morning—he could see in the morning light the cruel network of lines and the violet stain beginning to underline those beautiful eyes. Her lids looked puffy, too.

But he bent to kiss her.

'Happy Christmas, Mrs Pethick,' he said gaily.

To his still further astonishment she pushed him away.

'Don't—please,' she said sharply.

'Why ever not? What's bitten you?' he began sulkily.

She gave him a steady look which spoke all that she could not put into words. His gaze wavered before hers. He flushed.

'Oh, hell,' he muttered, 'you aren't still going to keep up our little difference of opinion?'

'It may have been little to you. It meant more to me. You were quite ruthless.'

174

He shrugged and turned from her, hands in pockets.

'Well, I don't want to fight all Christmas Day. I'm going down; and to hell with Margaret, that sour old bitch, if she's cross because I'm late. She gets me down—the old-fashioned so-and-so—I do loathe routine. Must be here at *this* time or *there* at that. Give me Pippa. She wouldn't care if we were a day late. The Spanish have no sense of time. I like them. They know how to enjoy life.'

He began to whistle again and walked out, closing the door behind him.

Venetia found herself trembling violently. The agitation she had felt earlier over his unpardonable conduct began to disturb her again. The inclination to give way and cry was so strong that she had to cover her face with her hands and stand motionless, trying to recover her control. It was quite obvious to her that Mike wanted to go on as though nothing had happened. It suited him, of course. He hated unpleasantness. So did she. But she was the one whose susceptibilities had been outraged. He had none to outrage, she told herself bitterly. He had apparently no comprehension of how he had hurt and offended her.

She was not of the nature to bear malice. She did not want a row any more than he did. She certainly did not want Maybelle's Christmas to be ruined. And if she allowed Mike to be upset he might vent his ill-humour on the girl.

So desperately Venetia fought to stamp upon her resentment and misery, and when she was able she walked down to the dining-room and greeted both her husband and daughter with every display of gaiety. She forced her brightest smile.

'Sorry I'm so late, darlings. Hope you two have started.'

'Yes, we have, Mummy,' said Maybelle. 'Will you have an egg? Maggie's done you one—you always have one on Christmas morning.'

'Another—er—tradition?' drawled Michael, who was spreading butter thickly on his toast. He looked at Venetia as he spoke and she was reduced to speechlessness by the sarcasm of that remark. But Maybelle, innocent of what was going on between the two, laughed.

'Yes, Mummy and I are full of traditions, aren't we, Mike?'

'Quite charming,' he said. 'Don't include me, folks.'

Then Venetia, determined not to give him the satisfaction of seeing how he had upset her, joined in the laughter.

'You can be sure we will, all the same. No egg for me. I'm not going to spoil what's coming—an enormous Christmas dinner.'

'Oh, that's tonight—ages away, Mum,' said Maybelle and added happily: 'I say, Mike's given me a wonderful present.'

Venetia seated herself at the end of the table facing Michael. The dining-room was so charming with its grey-blue paint and the alcoves on either side of of the Adam fireplace, full of exquisite china—and all the Christmas decorations to make it gay and seasonable. The breakfast set was an old one—cream with pink roses. The Georgian silver coffee-pot and spoons gleamed. Pippa had polished them well for this occasion. It was warm and luxurious with the central heating full on this cold morning; a log-fire to add to the attraction, and the high mantelpiece crammed with Christmas cards. It should all have been such *fun*, Venetia thought. It always used to be. She had never known a Christmas like this one—ruined by ill-feeling and the undercurrent of sarcasm and jealousy that was flowing from Michael. She knew, of course, that she had only to give him his own way—flatter him and ignore her young daughter's merry chatter—pay him most of the attention, and he would beam again and everything would be all right. But she felt a distinct distaste for pandering so to his ego— for letting him think he could treat her as he had done—and get away with it.

She therefore avoided looking in his direction, sipped her coffee and addressed herself exclusively to Maybelle.

'Looking forward to the dance tonight, pet?'

'Terrifically!' Maybelle replied.

'Shall we go to church as usual?'

'Another old tradition?' put in Michael.

Venetia looked at him across the table steadily although her face was pale under the rouge.

'Rather a good one, don't you think?'

He pushed his plate away.

'I'm not a church-goer myself. And I didn't know you were.'

'I can't say I go regularly, Mike—in fact I'm rather ashamed to say I don't. One gets out of the habit but—Maybelle and I generally try to attend the Christmas and Easter services.'

'Maybelle and you—the inseparables!' he sneered.

Silence. Maybelle glanced sharply at her stepfather then read the misery in her mother's eyes and was shocked. Her astonishment was only exceeded by her alarm—in the knowledge that all was not well between these two grown-ups.

She tried, in her immature way, to be tactful. Hastily she said:

'Maybe this morning I'll ride with Mike instead of going to church.'

'Maybe Mike will decide not to take you,' he snapped.

The young girl coloured.

'Oh!' she said lamely.

Venetia forced herself to say:

'Do take her, Mike. She'd like it.'

'Well, Miss Sellingham's likes and dislikes are not the only ones to be considered at Burnt

Ash,' he said.

Venetia met the antagonism in his eyes. Her heart sank to the depths. But still she tried to steer the ship off the rocks.

'Oh, of course she'll do whatever you want, Mike.'

'Of course I will,' put in Maybelle. But her lashes flickered nervously. She wondered what this was all about.

Venetia added:

'By the way, what was it that Mike gave you, Maybelle? I haven't been shown yet.'

Before Maybelle could reply, Michael rose and stuck his thumbs in the yellow sporting waistcoat he had put on. He smiled—without any humour.

'Just a nice framed photo of yours truly.'

Maybelle produced it. It was Michael in hunting pink with a crop over his knees, and a gay smile on his lips. The handsome young man who had fascinated Venetia Sellingham into marriage. Stonily Venetia regarded this photograph which was in a new-looking red leather frame. Michael grinned impishly.

'I had it done specially for my little step-daughter. I thought it might create a stir in the dovecot at school. You didn't want one—did you, sweet? You see enough of the original. Too much!'

Venetia stood up. Her hands shook so that she had to grip the back of her chair. She had asked Mike to have a new photograph taken

179

for her. This framed copy was to have been one of her Christmas 'surprises'. Apparently he had decided to give it to Maybelle instead; out of a kind of childish spite, she supposed. She was furious that Maybelle should have been brought, even unconsciously, into the fracas. But with admirable restraint she now spoke to Michael.

'I'm sure Maybelle is delighted and that it will do more than create a stir at her school. You're so very good-looking, aren't you, darling?'

Suddenly it seemed that Michael experienced some remorse for the way in which he was behaving. He changed his whole tone. Addressing the young girl who stood there awkwardly, he said:

'Okay—I'll take you riding, Maybelle. Be ready by eleven, will you? Venetia darling—come into the study a sec. I've got a special surprise there for you.'

Venetia, ice-cold and still shaking, followed him without a word.

Once in there alone with her—he could not do or say enough to make up for his offensiveness. He took her hands, kissed them repeatedly and asked her pardon with the utmost sincerity.

'It came over me like a flash just now that I was behaving like an absolute bastard. Darling—please forgive me. I can't think why I said all those b—y awful things. Forgive me

180

and forget it, please. I do get these moods. I suppose it's all jealousy. I am so much in love with you and I know how much you love that girl. She's angelic and I couldn't be more fond of her, I swear it. I'll prove it—I'll do anything to prove it. But I suppose it's because she's another man's child and not mine—I'm just frankly jealous. But I'm a swine to vent it on you. I was ghastly this morning when we woke up. Did I hurt you terribly? My God, I can't bear to see you looking at me like that. Don't, Venetia—please—be generous and forgive me, sweet.'

She stood still, listening to the apologies that poured from his lips. She was as pale and rigid as a marble statue. His kisses seemed to have lost their power to stir her physically, and his protests of love; neither had his admission of jealousy any potency. She almost felt that she had lost the power to *feel*. He had drained her of it—this morning.

But at last she had to speak, to say something, and it was her nature to be generous. She gave a long deep sigh.

'Don't go on apologizing, Mike—please. I won't say any more about it. I don't want to.'

'Do you understand what got at me? Why I sometimes feel so anti-Maybelle?'

'I'll try to understand even if I don't.'

'Haven't you ever been jealous?'

'No, I don't think so.'

'Then you've never really been in love,' he

said grandly.

'Oh, Mike—it isn't as though there's another man involved. Maybelle is my daughter—the love one gives a child can't be compared with the love one gives a husband. I ... I love you *both* ... in totally different ways.'

She stammered on the last sentence. Did she love him any more? *Did she?* Or had all that rapturous feeling been wiped out by a lightning flash—by the revelation of Michael Pethick as an arrogant, selfish, unsympathetic person—unworthy of her deep love?

'I'll try to shut up about Maybelle from now on,' he said. He seemed truly eager to be reinstated in her favour. He adored her, he added in the most convincing voice. He could not tell her how much he regretted having been such a swine. She must forgive him and love him again as she used to.

'You do—don't you, darling?' he asked quite pathetically.

Like this—his blue eyes contrite, so full of devotion, and with his humble kisses on her hands—how could she hold out against him? This was the old irresistible Michael—her young, adoring husband—and no woman of her age could want to lose *that* Michael.

The ice round Venetia's heart thawed. She burst into tears which she could not control and sobbed in his arms. At her request he locked the study door in case Maybelle or Pippa should come in. He caressed and soothed her and reiterated all the apologies, excusing himself again and again on the grounds that he was jealous. Until at length Venetia was half convinced that she had no right to be angry; that if she really loved him she would try to see his side of it and not judge him too harshly. The withering scorn she had felt when she left his bed this morning, died. She allowed him to kiss and comfort her and wipe away her tears. She was even happy once more when she finally regained her control, powdered her face, and listened to his plans for the day. He was charming—he belittled himself and tried to turn the whole thing into a foolish misunderstanding—'a lovers' tiff', he called it. Now it was all right and he was going to show how much he loved her, and be awfully sweet to Maybelle all day.

He then added that he was deeply sorry he had been childish enough to give that framed photograph to Maybelle when it had been meant for her, his wife. Venetia smiled and exonerated him.

'I know—you were just being a silly idiot, trying to get one back on me. Never mind. I'm sure Maybelle will adore taking it back to school and showing you off—her handsome stepfather.'

Michael, himself again, grimaced and laughed.

'God, that makes me feel old.'

Venetia winced but echoed the laugh. He

promised to have another and very special photograph taken for her and framed as soon as he could take himself to the photographer's again. He then unlocked a drawer in his bureau and took from it a small case.

With his sweetest expression, he pressed the little case into her hand.

'Merry Christmas, angel—with all my love. And we'll never fight again,' he said solemnly.

She clung to his arm and opened her present. It was certainly unexpected. It was a black and gilt twisted necklace—costume jewellery of no particular value but quite attractive. The fact that it had only cost a few pounds could not spoil Venetia's pleasure in what she thought to be a spontaneous gift chosen by Mike alone. It took so little to make her happy, she thought wryly. Here she was hugging him, thanking him for the necklace as though he had given her a diamond tiara.

'It's absolutely *sweet* of you, darling, and I think you've got very good taste,' she said merrily and put on the necklace and then admired the effect in the Queen Anne mirror that hung over the bureau.

Michael admired it, too. His remorse increased as he realized how charming Venetia was being to him. He felt a real tenderness for her—she looked so pale and there were such circles round her eyes. And he had done this to her—made her cry bitterly on their first Christmas together.

'I am not good enough for her,' he thought, which was unusual for Michael Pethick. And such humility was new to Michael Pethick, too. There followed a regret that Venetia should make him feel this way. He was beginning to wonder whether a really virtuous woman suited his taste. He also had other thoughts in which Jix Lawson centred. Now there wasn't an ounce of sentimentality in Jix. She not only rode to hounds like a man but she loved like one. Love with her was an appetite. When it was satisfied it was over and then it was time for a drink and a cigarette. The high mental plane on which Venetia moved was *too* high for Michael. He felt unable to breathe easily in such rarefied atmosphere. But he had not the slightest wish seriously to antagonize his wife. There were a great many reasons for that as well as sentimental ones. He not only needed Venetia to put a check on his turbulence and his sometimes unwise impulsive action but he needed all the material benefits of this marriage.

He made perfectly sure that he and Venetia were good friends again before he left the study.

'We're going to be absolutely happy from now on and you'll never cry again because of me,' he said. 'I mean it.'

When she left him she was content—if exhausted. She felt as though she had been through an emotional cyclone. But it had left her young husband quite unscathed. He had kissed the purple bruises on her arms—bruises which he in his ruthless violence this morning had made on the delicate flesh.

'It makes me shudder to see them. I really am not fit to breathe!' he had said.

The bruises would disappear, she had told him. And so they would. But what about the memories? She was not at all sure that she could keep the promise he had extracted from her to forget this morning. It just wasn't a thing that a woman *could* forget.

However, the air had been cleared and Venetia's spirits were rising rapidly as she went to look for her daughter. A quarter of an hour later, Michael, still in the study, saw the two of them walking down to the stables. Venetia, with her short fur jacket and well-cut tweed skirt looked, as always, elegant and fashionable. She was a woman to be proud of. He knew it. There were times when he really hated his own nature.

'My tastes are low,' he thought, 'and I suppose it is because they are, that I was originally fascinated by a woman like Venetia and all that she stands for.'

He certainly had not the slightest interest in the child with the fair plaits who walked beside the tall graceful woman. Maybelle was quite pretty, good figure in that riding outfit and with the little velvet jockey cap on her golden head. But she was another 'nice' person.

Niceness was not really appreciated by Mr Michael Pethick.

The moment mother and daughter were out of sight he picked up the telephone and got through to the Lawsons' house. As he hoped, Jix answered.

As soon as she knew who was on the line she began to curse him for waking her up. But he knew by the underlying note in her voice that she was pleased to get his call.

'Merry Christmas, you basket,' she said sleepily. 'How come that you are off the leash? Has your pious household gone to the kirk?'

Michael laughed and explained that there had been the 'hell of a row' about something that he would tell her about when he saw her and that he had had to toe the line and was going to take the kid hacking.

'My *dear* Mike, don't tell me you've been playing Santa Claus, too. You're stepping right out of character.'

'To hell with that!' said Michael, laughed again and added that he looked forward to seeing her tonight.

'I don't know that I ought to come,' said Jix. 'I think I ought to be proud and stay away.'

'Oh, for God's sake there's enough pride around here. Don't let's have any more.'

'You sound as though you're a bit het-up.'

'I was but never mind about that now. What I have rung you up to tell you is that I'm afraid I won't be able to give you the Christmas present I had all ready for you, which is a b—y nuisance.'

'Why not? You haven't given me a present for years.'

'Well, I got you that necklace you wanted but unfortunately I've had to give it to Venetia.'

A very masculine oath came over the line from Jix.

'There's a thing! And may I ask why? Didn't she like what you bought her?'

'I had to give that to Maybelle,' said Michael, and suddenly guffawed with laughter as though the whole thing were a tremendous joke.

Jix grumbled but Michael persisted that the thing had its funny side. He had made an ass of himself, he said, and offended Venetia, so he *had* to pretend that he'd got a special surprise for her in order to put things right, and so produced the necklace. (Just what he had done to offend his wife he had no intention of telling Jix or anyone else.) Finally he promised Jix a much better present.

'And for the love of your Mike, come early tonight and stay late.'

'I don't see that it's going to be much fun with your wife's chilly eye on us the whole time.'

'Oh, she'll be busy with our guests,' said Michael easily. 'But I dare say we'll snatch a moment. A discreet moment, mark you.'

Then said Jix in a caustic voice:

'I wouldn't wonder if you aren't already regretting this marriage for money. You might have been better off with your poverty-stricken Jix.'

Michael glanced uneasily out of the window as though he expected Venetia to appear.

'Oh, it hasn't quite reached that pitch,' he grunted. 'As I told you the other day, Jix, there's nothing to stop us having fun together. But in my way, you know, I'm quite devoted to Venetia. She is quite terrific.'

'And you are a—' Jix whispered a word that made even Michael protest.

'Really, Jix—over a public 'phone—'

But she laughed and rang off.

Michael chuckled as he walked out of the room, and ran up the stairs two at a time to change into riding breeches. A discourse with Jix always refreshed him. She made him laugh. And if she thought him a 'basket', at least she didn't make him feel one. It was such a pity that Venetia, and all women of her kind, had the unfortunate knack of giving a chap like himself a guilt complex. It didn't exactly inspire one to joyous passion.

But the unfortunate Venetia had nothing but smiles for him when he finally joined her and Maybelle at the stables.

Bennett had saddled Red Prince and Jock, Maybelle's pony. When Venetia saw the two of them—her husband and her daughter—wheel about and ride out of the stable yard side by side on this fine frosty morning, she was not sad any more. She was proud and pleased. And it was as though this morning had been a nightmare which now had passed. She loved those two—Maybelle and Michael—each in their own way, with all her heart. She felt that it might be a happy Christmas after all.

CHAPTER FIVE

'Are we going to see you at the Meet tomorrow, Mrs Pethick?'

'I shall come and see you all start off, but I shan't follow.'

Venetia smiled at Colonel Woollacombe, who had put the question to her.

They stood in the dining-room drinking champagne. It was the end of the buffet supper. Margaret and Pippa and a hired butler were busy clearing away the remains of the excellent repast. Most of the guests had drifted back to the drawing-room. Somebody had put a samba record on the big electric gramophone. Burnt Ash Manor was gay with the sound of music and dancing, full of laughter, and the chatter of voices.

Through the open door Venetia could see some of the dancers; an attractive sight; the men wearing white tie and tails (Venetia approved of bringing this custom back after the lethargy of not dressing during the War), and there were some lovely dresses here tonight. Mamie Linnell was of course the 'star turn' with all her film glamour, her bare brown back, strapless silver dress, red curls, and mauve-tinted eyelids. She and Ted—who had actually been at school with Mike—danced this particular samba with vitality and professional skill. And Venetia could see 'old Agatha Bellathorp' in her purple taffeta, which as Maybelle had whispered to her mother with a giggle 'matched her downy cheeks'. She was striding rather than dancing around the room determined, but out of time, with the M.F.H.

So far the party had been a big success. Michael had behaved beautifully and claimed the first dance from his wife, and even the first meeting with Jix Lawson had gone off well. Out of deference to Mike, Venetia had been her most charming to Jix. The girl had seemed to Venetia a bit subdued but had muttered a 'thanks for asking me'. She was dancing with Mike now. Venetia eyed the slim boyish figure thoughtfully. An out-of-date model, that red velvet dress, which did not really suit Jix. It made her skin look sallow. And she wore cheap silver sandals. She did not look particularly happy, either, although Mike was doing his samba strenuously and trying to whirl her under his arm in imitation of the Linnells. Venetia could almost find it in her to be sorry for Jix. It must be a tragedy to have her expensive tastes and be so hard up—and more so to have been in love with a man who was so indifferent to her that he could go on seeing her even after he was married—although at one time he had been her lover.

'I should loathe it,' Venetia thought, 'but she can't have my sort of feelings, so why be sorry for her?'

'Can't we ever induce you to follow hounds?' she heard old 'Woolly' asking. His fierce blue eyes were looking down into hers with kindliness. He was always especially nice to her. She responded warmly.

'Thanks for bothering about me, Woolly, but I don't really like it. Maybelle will go, of course.'

Colonel Woollacombe eyed her a moment in silence, then let his monocle drop. There was not a woman in the room to touch her, he thought. Twelve years older than Mike she might be, but by God, what a lot of dignity and grace! That fair, ashen hair with her pearly skin, wonderful. It was a treat to look at her. She wore a white silk jersey dress, draped in classic Greek lines, and showing one bare shoulder. Thinking to please Mike, Venetia had put on the new gilt necklace instead of the diamond and sapphire one which was in the collection of fine jewellery which Geoffrey had given her. But Mike had not seemed particularly flattered, and said:

192

'That thing isn't good enough for our dance. Wear one of your own good ones.'

She had smiled and argued that she was quite satisfied with her husband's Christmas gift and intended to wear his necklace. Yet it hadn't seemed to please him at all, which she found odd.

'May I say,' the Colonel spoke again, 'how handsome you're looking tonight, Mrs Pethick?'

'Thank you, you are sweet! Don't you think my daughter looks adorable? Here she is!'

Maybelle had just come into the supper-room room with a fair-haired, red-faced young man who seemed to be perspiring profusely and was vigorously mopping face and neck.

Venetia hardly knew him. He was one of Mike's business friends, but he seemed nice and young enough to be enjoying himself. Maybelle had also obviously enjoyed her samba, too. She was flushed and triumphant.

'I've been teaching Dick some new steps, Mummy,' she announced.

'She's a wizard dancer but we both need a long drink,' put in the young man.

Truly, thought Venetia, Maybelle looked radiant in her frilly party dress and with those wide shining eyes. How proud Geoffrey would have been of her. But the thought of Geoffrey mustn't be allowed to haunt Venetia tonight. She made up her mind to try and see this marriage more from Mike's point of view than her own. That is—more than she had already done. After all, she had linked her life with his knowing that he was '*different*'. She must not try to cling to the remnants of the past. It was unfair to him. She felt glad that she had asked Jix here tonight to show her goodwill.

'I hear you're coming out with us, young woman,' the Colonel addressed Maybelle.

'Yes, won't it be fun,' said Maybelle, gulping down a lemon squash and still panting from her recent exertions.

'I haven't missed a Boxing Day Meet for thirty-five years,' announced Woollacombe.

'And I intend to echo those words when I am your age, sir,' put in Michael, who now entered the room with Jix.

'Hello, darling,' he added, turning to Venetia. 'Champagne forward. It's a thirsty job, the samba. Did you see old Ted Linnell?— these experts move as though they're on roller skates.'

'Oh, Mike, you are funny,' giggled Maybelle, with a schoolgirl appreciation of her stepfather's humour.

He was sufficiently full of champagne and *bonhomie* to include her in the joke and began to pull her pigtails until she yelled for mercy. Venetia stood by smiling. Jix Lawson turned away and bit viciously at a sandwich. Old Wilfred Woollacombe was suddenly and rather peculiarly aware that this horseplay from a stepfather was not exactly in keeping

194

with the dignity of Maybelle's mother. Neither did it seem to him right at all that Pethick should be stepfather to the pretty fifteen-year-old girl. But then, right from the start, he had thought this marriage a mistake. It had been much discussed in the district. A lot of people upheld it because Venetia was so young-looking, and of course she had money! But Colonel Woollacombe belonged to the old school. He did not like to see an elegant woman, well over forty, as the wife of a young chap like Pethick. He had nothing against Pethick, of course. Damn good on a horse; stockbroker, good family and so on. But not the type for Venetia. Incongruous pair. The Colonel was a bit doubtful as to how it would work out.

As for that little trollop, Jix Lawson—he wouldn't have had her in the house, and it was colossal cheek of young Pethick bringing her here. After all, *everybody knew* ... Here the Colonel coughed and searched in his pocket for his cigar-case. He didn't hold with this modern free-and-easy conduct. He supposed he was an old fool. But she was a sweet woman, Venetia Pethick, and her daughter just as sweet. He hoped the marriage would be a success.

Another member of the Hunt hailed him. He moved off, chewing the end of his cigar. Maybelle and her escort busied themselves with sandwiches. Venetia smiled at her husband.

195

'Enjoying it, darling?'

'It's terrific!' he said in his heartiest manner.

She could see that he was flushed, full of champagne and in a 'party mood'. Determined that he should go on feeling gay and happy and not be allowed to regard her as a wet blanket, Venetia smiled at him then walked over to Jix Lawson.

'Has my husband been looking after you, Miss Lawson?'

The girl turned and looked at the older woman through her lashes and looked away in what might have been called a furtive manner.

'Oh, yes thanks, it's a lovely dance,' she muttered.

Michael glanced from one to the other. Rather grandly, he surveyed his mistress and his wife. He felt rather a grand fellow; women were always 'so easy' for him. He knew how to deal with them, he decided. Rather interesting, also, to note the difference between the two— 'that little devil Jix' and good old Venetia. Damned attractive, Venetia, in her beautiful Greek model dress. She really was supremely elegant but a bit of a handful for him. However, one need have no inhibitions with Jix. He was glad he wasn't letting her go right out of his life. He knew perfectly well that Venetia would carp at Jix's frightful red dress, but *he knew* what lay underneath it. Now it didn't matter, reflected Michael, how well a woman kept her youth. Well into the forties Venetia couldn't begin to have quite such a perfect or exciting body as a young girl like Jix, who was built on the lines of a slender boy and yet had the most impertinent breasts. As for her big sensuous mouth—oh, what a thousand pities that Jix had been penniless!

Venetia continued to talk to Jix, wanting to show Michael that she was willing to be friendly and to forget the past relationship. And that was stretching a point for Venetia with her rigid moral outlook.

'You must come and eat with us one night when there isn't this crowd,' she said. And added, 'Are you at all fond of music?'

'No,' said Jix in rather a rude blunt voice, and her face reddened. She dug her teeth fiercely into a smoked salmon sandwich. Michael cocked an eyebrow and guffawed.

'My God, Venetia, you ought to hear Jix try to sing! She's tone-deaf. She only knows it's "*God Save the Queen*" when everybody else stands up.'

Maybelle giggled. Jix curled her lips. She was not particularly happy. When Michael first brought his wife down to Sussex she had bitterly resented the fact that she had been cold-shouldered by her. She had loathed Venetia without having met her because she had taken Mike away from her. She had buried her pride and come to this dance because she had been so infuriated by the numberless

197

people who asked whether she had met Mrs Michael Pethick and what a perfect place she had made of Burnt Ash. Being seen here tonight by everybody had restored Jix's *amour-propre*. Yet she was not happy. Perhaps it was because she had a guilt complex. That was only since she had met Venetia here. Before, she had been perfectly ready and felt quite conscienceless about recommencing the old affair with the one man with whom she had ever really been in love. She loved Mike knowing all his faults. He was a go-getter. He had no scruples. But she was still mad about him. Physically it had always been 'a thing' between them. In the interim, following their break, she had suffered abominably and found no consolation in any other affair. And Jix was never without a follower. On the other hand, she could not pretend to like the present situation. It was worse because *she* was so nice. Oh, what a grim appellation to give anyone—a *nice woman*! The very words bristled with boredom and dreariness. and yet, thought Jix, now that she was face to face with Venetia, she had to admit Mike's wife was neither boring nor dreary but the very epitome of charm and elegance and kindliness. In fact if she had not been Mrs Michael Pethick, Jix would have been the first to say that Venetia was one hundred per cent attractive. She could not even triumph because Venetia was 'old'—older than Jix, herself. She belonged to that type of woman who is ageless.

Jix thought:

'Damn her elegance and her charm and her being so decent to me. I wish she'd drop dead at my feet.'

She went on scowling, shifting from one foot to the other and hoping that she could make a 'get-away' and end all this. While Venetia on her part was thinking what a sad thing it must be for a girl to have lost Mike, and she wasn't so attractive although no doubt she was wonderful on a horse. But she lacked all the social graces.

Venetia turned to her husband.

'Do you know you haven't danced with me since our first? Come on, you shirker. Let me introduce myself. I am your wife.'

Michael struck an attitude.

'At your service, madame.'

She put an arm through his and they walked into the ballroom. Maybelle and her partner followed. A samba lured them back to the floor. Jix was left alone except for the waiter who was still clearing away plates and empty glasses.

'Oh, *damn* her.' She said the words between her teeth. 'I'll never come to this house again. I can't stand it. Michael's a bastard if ever there was one. Why have I got to go on being so fond of him? But I have. I can't help myself. *Damn it, damn it*.'

About an hour later, Venetia hailed her

daughter and said:

'Bed for you, darling. You've stayed up quite late enough.' Maybelle, who had enjoyed herself a lot more than she had expected to do at this Christmas dance, answered as all young people of her age are expected to do:

'Oh, can't I say up a little longer?'

But Venetia kissed the hot flushed young face and was obdurate. Maybelle was still a child and some of Mike's friends were beginning to get rowdy. They had started a chain dance through the ground-floor rooms; hands on each other's shoulders.

Mother and daughter beamed at each other. The dance had been a great success and even Jix Lawson's presence had not spoiled it for either of them—although each had come to it with secret misgivings.

Maybelle said good night to those people whom she knew. She was in high spirits. Now there was the Boxing Day Meet to look forward to. She stretched her arms and yawned. She really was tired. That last samba with nice Dick Shelby had been very energetic—even for Maybelle.

It was hot in the centrally-heated house, and with the huge log-fire burning in the hall, which was gay with the holly behind the picture frames, and the beautiful flowers that Mummy arranged so well.

Maybelle, fanning herself, decided rather naughtily to wander outside and get a breath of that fresh crystalline air. She and Dick had already peeped out and found the sky ablaze with stars and quite clear, which was remarkable. Not a vestige of fog.

Maybelle slipped into the front yard and shivered as the cold air struck through her thin party frock. She knew that Mummy would be cross because she had no coat on. She decided to run, just once, round the house and take in big gulps of air before going to bed. She would get hold of Poppet who was in her basket in the kitchen and give her a second's fun.

As she turned the corner of the house—the one leading into the herb garden—she stopped dead. Her heart gave an ugly twist, and she clapped both hands to her lips. All the joy of the evening's fun was wiped out in a lightning flash. Her dislike of Miss Lawson returned in full force. Still more so, her suspicion and fear of her young stepfather. For the second time, the fifteen-year-old schoolgirl was faced with the deplorable sight of Mike and Jix locked in a passionate embrace. The two figures were like one, clinging convulsively, etched blackly against the starlight. A wave of scarlet spread over Maybelle's cheeks and through her whole body. She felt frightened and ashamed. She stood rooted to the spot, unable to move. It was then that Michael saw her.

His arms fell away from Jix and his lips from that hot hungry mouth. He had only been indulging in what he called 'a moment of harmless petting' (nobody knew more than he did how harmful this particular petting was both to Jix and himself—and above all to Venetia). What an infernal bore that the kid should have seen them—*she* of all people! He knew that he must act quickly. He tried to pretend that nothing was wrong.

'Hello, old Maybelle, come and join us and look at the moon,' he said in a blustering voice.

But Maybelle turned and began to run away. She did not want to speak to Mike—or to that horrid girl. Michael, cursing under his breath, ran after her.

'Maybelle, come back, you little idiot!'

There started an ignominious race. The young girl won it, reached the portico, ran in, slammed the front door behind her. Michael, white with anger, returned to Jix, who was trying to powder her face by the light of the moon. She threw him a baleful look.

'Now we've torn it. I told you to be careful, Mike.'

'How the hell was I to know Maybelle would come out here and spot us?'

'Well, she did, and that's that. And back it will all go to mother.'

'I'll break her neck if she says a word.'

'Don't be a fool. You couldn't blame her if she *did* tell. It would only be natural.'

Michael set his teeth. He was ready, as usual, to bluster and argue but he was badly scared. The girl, who knew him perhaps better than

202

anybody in the world, twisted her lips as she looked at him.

'Good old Mike! Aren't you a greedy boy! You want to eat your cake and have it. Rich wife and poor little Jix all cooked up together in a nice pudding.'

He swore at her. She shrugged her thin shoulder-blades over which she had thrown her shabby fur cape. She searched in her bag for a cigarette.

'Hadn't we better go in? You can say good night to your wife for me. I'm off home. This has rather spoiled my evening.'

'What about mine?'

'Well, you'll have to get out of it as best you can. I don't quite know how you will, my sweet. You *can't* break the poor child's neck, and you can hardly bribe her to keep quiet—so what?'

'Leave it to me,' said Michael with a confidence he was far from feeling.

Jix was only too right, he thought savagely. He *did* want to eat his cake and have it; to keep Venetia's love and trust and all that she gave him with it. And to keep this queer girl who had a spark in her which roused a similar flame within him. He agreed that Jix had better go straight home.

'See you at the Meet tomorrow,' she said.

She spoke in rather a tired flat voice. Being the illicit love of Michael Pethick had its points, but didn't make for peace of mind, nor

203

did it promise anything in the future but ashes. She wished she had the strength of mind to break away from him. She wished they had never started things up again. She wished she had never met Venetia nor realized what a sweet woman she was—really a damned sight too good for Mike.

Suddenly Jix reached up and kissed Mike on the mouth—a fierce, possessive kiss.

'You're a monster but I adore you,' she said in a muffled voice and was nearer to bursting into tears than she had ever been in her life. She was not the sort of girl to cry. Michael had never seen her shed a tear—even on the day when he told her he was going to marry Venetia Sellingham.

Michael did not return her kiss. He was too worried for anything of that sort. He bade Jix a brusque good night and walked into the house. His brain was a bit addled from excess of alcohol. He could not think clearly. He only knew that somehow or other he must get hold of Maybelle and try to prevent her from telling her mother what she had just seen.

CHAPTER SIX

The first person Michael met as he walked through the hall was Venetia, who came in from the reception-room on old Woolly's arm.

She was laughing merrily at something the Colonel was saying. The sight of her mature beauty angered rather than delighted Mike in his present mood of frustration and fear.

But it was obvious to Michael that Maybelle had not yet 'spilt the beans', for Venetia approached him with her lovely wise smile.

'Hello, darling—I think everybody's going. Come and do the perfect host and help me say good-bye. The orchestra's packed up.'

Michael glanced nervously at his wrist-watch. He hadn't realized that it was past midnight.

'O.K.,' he muttered. 'By the way, where's Maybelle?'

Venetia's eyes widened slightly.

'I sent her to bed. Why?'

'Oh, I was just going to ask her for a dance,' he mumbled.

Venetia was touched.

'That was sweet of you. But she had stayed up far too late already, and she was beginning to look blob-eyed.'

Michael cast a rapid glance in the direction of the drawing-room. Couples were beginning to drift into the hall. One or two women came down the stairs carrying their wraps. Yes, the party was breaking up. And he must get hold of Maybelle before it ended and she could speak to her mother alone.

'I'll be with you in a second, darling,' he muttered to Venetia, then tore up the stairs, two at a time.

It never entered her head to wonder why he was doing so and she turned her attention to the departing guests.

Michael, outside Maybelle's door, face puckered with worry, called out:

'Maybelle, are you there? I want you a moment.'

No answer.

'Maybelle!' repeated Michael on a louder note.

Then came the sound of a muffled voice. Maybelle was obviously crying.

'Oh, go away. I don't want to speak to you.'

To *hell*! ... that meant the young idiot guessed that something was wrong. She was only fifteen but he must presume that she had some knowledge of the world. It would not be much good telling her that that long, passionate embrace she had seen was just a kiss 'under the mistletoe'. He was in a quandary. His first thought was for himself; he wished to avoid being found out because he knew that Venetia would be aghast, not only because of his infidelity but because Maybelle had seen it. That precious daughter of hers ... he ground his teeth at the thought of the young girl. He had always known that one day she would get in the way and make mischief. Such was the fashion in which his mind worked that he felt no particular shame or remorse, nor did he bother about the fact that it might leave an indelible mark on the mind of the young girl. He thought only of what he, personally, might lose if the episode were brought to light. Venetia might suspect the worst between him and Jix. In her damned pride she might even take it into her heart to walk out on him and take her ewe-lamb with her. He had to ask himself a great number of questions during the short space of time that he stood outside Maybelle's door. And the chief one was whether he really loved the wife to whom he had only been married for six months, and wished to keep her. The answer was a decided 'yes'. He did love her—as far as his shallow nature would permit. They had nothing in common but he still found her desirable. Despite the way that so many of her attributes irritated him. He did not want to lose her regard and certainly not the many financial benefits that he gained through being her husband.

So he made a desperate effort to placate Maybelle.

He tried wheedling her.

'Look, ducks, don't be a little fool—open the door and let me talk to you for a minute. They're waiting for me downstairs. I'm in a hurry—open the door, will you?'

Silence again. Then from Maybelle:

'No I won't. Go away, I think you're absolutely *horrible*!'

Michael's face darkened with colour. He put

a hand inside his stiff white collar and tore at it as though it choked him. With his quick temper rising, he felt he would like to smash the door down and tell Maybelle in a few short words what he thought of her.

That other, and better, side of the man knew well the ugly thing he was doing, but there was no time for such feelings so far as she was concerned. He tried to be clever.

'Look, Maybelle, you don't want to hurt your mother, do you?'

That brought a swift and very schoolgirlish reply from Maybelle.

'No, I don't, but I bet *you* do!'

'Don't be idiotic. It's the last thing ... I want to explain and stop *you* from saying anything that is wrong and might upset her.'

This at last brought Maybelle to the door, which she unlocked and flung open. She was still in her party dress but had undone her plaits. A wet, unhappy young face streaked with tears was framed in the flowing blonde hair which made her look very much of a child. Through her tears, she glowered at her stepfather. Any affection or regard she had ever had for him had been destroyed. She was not a coward but she was still not old enough to be able to cope with Michael. What she had seen tonight had flung her back into the same state of confusion and mental distress that had been hers after that first occasion when she had surprised Michael and Jix in the woods.

Now she blurted out:

'I saw you—in the forest—before I went back to school. I think you're *beastly*, and jolly deceitful. I told my grandmother about it.'

Michael stared, flabbergasted. He had to rack his brains for a moment in order to remember the incident to which she had referred. There had been so many of them. Last summer, Burnt Ash forest had been a favourite meeting-place for Jix and himself. *When* had this little devil seen them? What a b—y bore! To him, what he had done with Jix was no heinous offence—although, of course, having a 'party' now and again with Jix meant, if one looked at it from all sides, that he had been unfaithful to Venetia. It just wouldn't do for her to find out. He tried to laugh things off.

'I don't know what all the fuss is about, or why you're bursting into tears, my dear. Anybody would think you'd seen something ghastly.'

'Well, it was,' said Maybelle sullenly.

Michael's brain was clearing.

'Did you say you told your *grandmother*?'

'Yes.'

He could willingly have hit her. Without Venetia's daughter, there would have been none of this trouble. He hadn't done any real harm and nobody would have known about Jix and himself. Why the devil did she want to go and split about it to the old ex-mother-in-law?

209

He was somewhat relieved when Maybelle suddenly volunteered some information on the subject.

'Ganny said not to interfere, and that I shouldn't tell Mummy.'

Michael's eyes brightened. Wily old woman, he thought. Rather decent of her too.

'That's right—your grandmother's absolutely right,' he said heartily. 'That's all it is. Poor old Jix has been in a bit of a fix and I've been trying to comfort her, that's all.'

Maybelle's eyelids dropped. She began to plait her hair nervously. From downstairs came the sound of laughter and voices. Cars were starting up outside in the drive. Then Venetia's voice sounded on the staircase:

'*Mike, Mike darling.*'

Michael put a hand on the child's shoulder. She flinched away from it which annoyed him. Sanctimonious little brute! It wouldn't be long before somebody ought to teach *her* a thing or two. Honestly he would have thought twice about marrying Venetia, for all her money and attraction, had he realized that he would be forced to lead such a pious existence just because there was this schoolgirl around the place. Rapidly he said:

'I've got to go. But I want you first to promise me that you won't mention this to your mother. She—she mightn't understand, like your grandmother did.'

Maybelle looked up at him. The big grave

210

eyes, pink-rimmed with weeping, roused in him no feeling of sympathy or kindliness. His only thought was how to save himself. He was no psychologist, anyhow, and the last one on earth to start worrying about Maybelle's mental state. He tried to smile at her and pat her shoulder again.

'Mum's the word, Maybelle. One day I'll tell you all about it—but let this be a secret between us for now, will you?'

'I don't know,' she said in the same sullen voice. She had a frank and affectionate disposition but Michael had a bad effect on her. She felt insecure and troubled, and it was against every instinct in her body to keep a secret from Mummy—in particular a nasty secret shared with Michael. The girl was fast growing up and the time spent in this house with her mother and stepfather had opened her eyes to many facts of life and love which had hitherto been concealed from her. She could not altogether believe Michael's explanation. It was obvious to her that Michael had been doing more than just 'comfort' Miss Lawson. Tonight, for a full minute unseen by them, she had stood watching their exchange of hot, sensual caresses. She could not get the picture out of her mind.

'Mike!' repeated Venetia's voice and now they heard it coming nearer. Venetia was on her way to look for the truant host.

He caught one of Maybelle's clammy little

hands and pressed it.

'Be a sport and say nothing. I'll talk to you when we go hunting tomorrow. You know, anyhow, don't you, that it will cause awful trouble if you mention a word to your mother? For God's sake use some common sense and shut up about it.'

He then turned and hurried down the corridor to meet Venetia, whom he at once embraced warmly, apologizing for his absence.

'Terribly sorry, darling. I suddenly developed a terrific headache. Been hunting for the aspirin bottle.'

At once she was all concern and with lovely anxious eyes looked up at his handsome face.

'Oh, my poor sweet! You *are* looking a bit pale. I'm so sorry. Cheer up—they're all going now. Then you can get to bed. Bennett's manoeuvring the cars. Everybody seems to have enjoyed themselves. But I wish you hadn't got a bad head.'

He gave a short laugh and went down the stairs with one arm around her waist, as though he were her fond lover.

Now, assuring Venetia that his head was better, he accompanied her downstairs to bid good-bye to their guests.

By the time he was back in the bedroom with Venetia, and the house was quiet and deserted, Mike's head began to ache in earnest. He was glad of the excuse to swallow a couple of aspirin and instead of being his usual talkative self, turned his face to the wall and asked that the light should be put out at once.

Venetia believed entirely in the 'headache story'. She had no cause to suspect otherwise. She, herself, slept deeply and dreamlessly that night for she was tired after the efforts of hostess-ship. But Michael, contrary to all habits, kept on waking and worrying. He was frankly scared. And long before Venetia had opened her eyes he got out of bed, put on a dressing-gown and strolled through the house in a gloomy state of mind. He entertained the fervent hope that his young step-daughter would also rise early so that he could talk to her again. Having a guilty conscience was no fun, he ruminated with some bitterness. He cursed his indiscretion in the garden.

Maybelle, too, had had a restless broken slumber. The young girl had pretended to be asleep last night when her mother had asked, softly, outside her door if she was still awake. She could not bear to face Mummy. She would have no excuse for those red-rimmed eyes. During the watches of the night she considered telephoning to her grandmother and asking for advice, then decided against this plan. Although she was only fifteen years old Maybelle had an unusual sensitivity. From both mother and father she had inherited that instinctive wish to avoid hurting others.

She fell asleep just before dawn, and was still sleeping soundly when a tap on her door woke

HPL

her up. Mike, after tramping aimlessly around the house looking with some loathing at the litter of choked ashtrays, dirty glasses, dying flowers and all the paraphernalia of 'after the party', had at last dared to go to Maybelle's room. He must see and speak to her before the day began—he *must*. What a Boxing Day! His cracking headache was not only the result of too much drink but of acute anxiety. And this should have been the best Meet of the year, he thought sourly. Now, at half past seven, the winter's morning was still dim and grey, but there was no sign of snow and last night's weather forecast had been good.

Softly he went on tapping against Maybelle's door, until at length he heard her voice.

'Who is it?'

'I just want a word with you—' he began.

Back came Maybelle's reply.

'Oh, it's *you*!'

'Yes—will you just have a word with me, ducks?'

He attempted a jocularity which he was far from feeling. The result was a dismal failure.

Then the argument of last night was repeated. Maybelle did not want to speak to him. He persisted. Finally she put on a dressing-gown and opened the door. Her childish face looked a trifle pale and blotchy. Plaiting the long fair hair, she gave her stepfather a sulky look.

214

'What do you want?'

He could willingly have hit her. It was damnable that a kid like this should have such control—of him. The thing was growing out of proportion. But, it was not only a few kisses that she had witnessed. It was that unrestrained embrace in the forest. He had been caught in *flagrante delicto*. He realized that Maybelle's knowledge now stood between him and Venetia and threatened his life's happiness.

He began wheedling Maybelle all over again.

'You don't have to be an old meanie and talk about me to your Mum, now do you?' he asked, grinning.

The jocular appeal fell flat on Maybelle's ears. She thought that Mummy's husband looked rather horrid with unshaven stubble on his chin and those puffs under his eyes. The memory of last night was still vivid for Maybelle. The way he was kissing Jix. And that other time—never really forgotten. Like an animal, she thought in childish disgust.

Her sullen silence reduced Michael to a state in which he lost control. No longer lowering his voice or remembering to be diplomatic, he seized Maybelle by the shoulders and shook her.

'You little beast—you *want* to get me into trouble, do you?' He almost snarled the words.

Maybelle backed into her bedroom, her fair

215

face crimson and her eyes widening into sudden fear.

'No, I don't! Leave me alone!'

'Then will you promise to say nothing?'

She hesitated. She was not the type to betray anyone easily, even someone she disliked. On the other hand, without any deep knowledge of life and the petty lusts and cruelties of man, she had also begun to wonder if she ought not to ask Mummy about it. She and Mummy had never had never held secrets from each other, and this one weighed so heavily on her that it was becoming almost more than she could bear.

She had reached no definite decision. Only now, when Mike began to shout at her, she grew frightened. Never before in her sheltered life, during which she had always given and received kindliness and affection, had she suffered bullying or unpleasantness. She burst into tears.

'*Please go away*. Leave me alone!'

'You little sneak. If you don't promise to shut up, I swear I'll see that you don't come next holidays. I know you don't like me. You've done your best to come between me and your mother and I suppose you think this is your best chance.'

'It isn't!' Maybelle choked out the words and scrabbled for a handkerchief in the pocket of her dressing-gown. '*It isn't!*'

The dispute went no further. Unfortunately

for Michael, it ended in the last way he desired. By his own loss of control he brought about the one disaster that he had been trying to prevent. For Venetia, having wakened and found him gone, had come to look for him, fearing that he might be ill. And as she walked with her light step along the corridor, she heard those raised voices coming from Maybelle's bedroom. She stopped. She heard Michael's last, ugly words. Appalled she stood there. Then she walked forward and confronted her husband and her daughter.

CHAPTER SEVEN

The scene between the three was brief and—for each of them—terrible.

Maybelle gave one startled look at her mother's face which bore a horrified expression and began to cry again.

'Oh, Mummy, *Mummy*!'

Then she turned and flung herself across her bed in a paroxysm of grief. Venetia ran to her, put an arm around the quivering figure and tried to comfort her. But she, herself, was in such a state of shock that she hardly knew what she was saying or doing. Michael began to talk in a loud, blustering voice:

'I don't know what this is all about. Damn it all, do stop howling, Maybelle! What is all this

217

fuss about? Look here! I am going to my room. I've had enough.'

Venetia took not the slightest notice of Michael. For the present her whole being was concentrated upon cherishing her young daughter. Never before had she heard Maybelle cry in such a fashion. She had been a placid, happy little baby. To hear those sobs torn from her was almost as dreadful to Venetia as the implication in what Michael had said. She kissed and comforted the girl. Maybelle flung her arms around her mother's neck and began to garble explanations. Michael kept interrupting. Finally Venetia, who could hardly make head or tail of what she was being told, recovered her possession and took command of the situation. She turned a white stony face to Mike. A face that looked like a mask at that moment; only the eyes were alight, and they shone at him with something near to hatred.

'Get out of here and leave us alone.'

'If I do, I get out of the house and stay out—' he began on a high note.

Venetia interrupted:

'I couldn't care less. Just get out.'

'You and your precious daughter...' began Mike in a crescendo of rage and frustration, checked himself and, turning, marched down the corridor. A door slammed—presumably his dressing-room door—with a force that reverberated through the house.

Maybelle clung to her mother, trying to check her hysterical sobbing.

'Oh, Mummy! I suppose you heard us! Oh, isn't it awful? I didn't mean to tell—I was trying to make up my mind what I ought to do, Mummy—it was so difficult—I knew you'd be upset and Ganny had said, when I told her about the other time in the summer hols, that you mustn't be hurt. But now you know.'

Venetia, confused and feeling a trifle sick, could only hold on to the girl's trembling hands and listen. Half of her shrank from hearing the things that Maybelle was stammering. Poor child, she thought. How ghastly that she should have been dragged into this sordid affair. Little wonder she was distraught. How could a schoolgirl of fifteen know best what to do under such circumstances?

'What did you hear him say, Mum?' Maybelle was asking, with a hiccup.

'I heard him call you a little sneak and that he would see that you didn't come home next holidays if you didn't promise to shut up about something,' said Venetia, quite unemotionally and with that same dead look on her face.

'Then need I tell—?' began the girl piteously.

'No,' said Venetia suddenly, 'not unless you want to.'

'I want to in a way,' came the even more pathetic reply, 'because it keeps worrying me and I hate having secrets from you, Mummy.

219

We never have.'

'No, never.'

Then Venetia added. 'What did you mean about Ganny saying that *I* mustn't be hurt, darling?'

'When I told her about the first time.'

'*The first time*,' repeated Venetia and her soft brown eyes held an expression of anguish. 'I don't quite follow, darling. And what happened last night, anyhow? I think you'll have to tell me now.'

So the whole story came tumbling out—disjointed—as a very young girl would tell it. The mother realized what an indelible mark it had made on that young unsullied mind. The first time—the sight of those two—her stepfather and Jix Lawson together in Burnt Ash Forest. The lies and the deception. The unhappiness she had felt because Jix came to the Christmas dance. ('Dear life,' thought Venetia, 'if I had known what I know now, that girl would never have come into this house and spoken to my child, let alone me.') Finally the episode of last night. Venetia could almost see those two standing there in the moonlight as Maybelle had seen them, pawing each other in that filthy way, indulging in their guilty passion. Her 'precious daughter', as Mike had just called Maybelle so savagely, had witnessed it. Venetia's head sank. Her pride—where was it? She had none left. Michael had dragged it through the mud; her young daughter's too.

For the latter sin she would never forgive him even if she could excuse his conduct towards herself. Of course he had been sleeping with Jix again. That to Venetia was now obvious. He had been unfaithful. So quickly—even last summer—soon after his marriage, he had gone back to his previous mistress. It must be so, otherwise he would not have been so frightened of being found out; he would not have threatened Maybelle unless he knew he was guilty.

It was not pleasant for Venetia to know that her young husband had been dividing his time between wife and girl-friend. It was so despicable of him; so humiliating for her. But the pain of her betrayal was not so hard to bear as the knowledge that Maybelle had been drawn into it.

At last Venetia quietened Maybelle. The girl calmed down.

'I want you to go back to bed and try to sleep, darling,' Venetia said in her dead voice. 'Don't think about this any more. It's all over now. But I do apologize to you'—her voice cracked a bit—'on Mike's behalf. He must have had too much to drink. I'm sure he didn't *mean* to be as awful as he was. Anyhow, you don't have to see him again if you don't want to, and whatever happens, I promise you you won't be forced to spend your holidays away from *me*—ever.'

'Oh, Mummy darling I'm glad.' Maybelle

221

cheered up considerably and flung her arms around her mother's neck.

Venetia said:

'I'll bring your breakfast up to you for a treat. I don't think I should go to the Meet if I were you.'

'I don't want to now,' said Maybelle and turned her flushed wet face to her pillow.

She was feeling vastly relieved. Devoted although she was, she was not experienced or old enough to recognize the full impetus of what was happening, and what it was likely to mean to her mother.

Venetia kissed her, added a few more soothing words and walked out of the room.

She made no attempt to find Michael. She went into her bedroom and began, like a dazed woman, to dress. In describing the whole affair at a later date to Barbara she said:

'I think I was slightly deranged. I didn't even remember to have my bath. I couldn't see anything and I can't imagine what my face must have looked like after I made it up. But I got dressed, and just as I was putting on my ear-rings the bathroom door opened and Michael walked in.'

That was the terrible moment—when Michael walked in. But he was self-possessed once more and all ready for the Meet. Debonair as ever, no one could gainsay the fact that he was extraordinarily good to look at in that hunting-coat, perfectly-tailored breeches,

222

well-polished boots. He was the type to look well wearing a cravat that was white against tanned skin. The blue of his eyes this morning was a trifle jaundiced, but he looked, Venetia thought dully, as though nothing was amiss and as if he were just about to enjoy a good day's sport. He even grinned at her; apparently he had had time to think things over and had decided to brazen them out; to take up the 'innocent boy' attitude.

'I say, darling—we all seem to have passed through a sort of cyclone. I feel quite uprooted. I don't know about you.'

Venetia was too staggered to reply. She was quite aware that Michael had a shallow nature and that he was possessed of such an ego that he might well imagine he could get away with murder. But his lack of sensibility this morning reduced her to a state of speechlessness.

'I really don't know what it was all about,' he went on, 'but I suppose you do. The kid's got some crazy idea in her head that I—'

He got no further. For then Venetia, usually the calm, the dignified and the restrained, interrupted. She blazed at him like a tigress defending her young. Her face was colourless. She shook with the anger that had boiled up in her. She called him every name she could think of. She ended:

'You're absolutely vile. I don't care nearly so much what you did with Jix as how you behaved with Maybelle.'

Now it was Michael's turn to be speechless. This was a Venetia he had never seen before. They had had rows but their differences were soon over, and he had always felt that he could 'handle' Venetia; that she would melt at a touch or suitable word from him. But this was an outraged woman, not nearly so easy to deal with. Obviously she suspected the worst. Nothing he could say or do would convince her that it was not so. He had had time to lie in his bath and think things over and he had decided that he had better go a bit more carefully. Attractive although Jix might be, he could not afford to throw in his lot with hers. He never had been able to afford to, otherwise he would have married her before he met Venetia.

There was also that side to Michael—the human and soft side—that belonged to Venetia and to no other woman. He had been sincerely in love with her in his fashion. He had never loved any other woman in quite the same way. Aggravated though he was by the existence of Maybelle he still had no serious desire to break with Venetia. Such an idea had never entered his head. He had gone into the affair with Jix in a casual, thoughtless way, gambling on the fact that he would never be found out.

He eyed his wife furtively through the thick curly lashes that she had always found so endearing. In rather a gruff voice he said:

'You're being a bit vicious about this, aren't you?'

Venetia caught at her gilt necklace and pulled it so violently that the clasp came undone. The chain dangled foolishly in her fingers. She flung it on the dressing-table. Her underlip was trembling. There was still no sorrow in her, only rage.

'How *dared* you talk to Maybelle like that?' she exclaimed. 'How *dared* you threaten her? Trying to intimidate her because of what you were afraid she might tell me. Could anything be more *despicable?*'

Michael reddened. However determined he was not to admit his guilt he began to see that he would have a hard task to explain the situation away. He began to mutter all kinds of excuses. He had drunk too much last night. This morning he had a hang-over. He met Maybelle outside her room on his way downstairs to get a cigarette. She had taunted him and said that she was going to tell her mother what she had seen in the garden. He couldn't stand sneaks and he had lost his temper and yelled at her. Naturally he hadn't meant a word he said. Didn't Venetia know him by now? His bark was worst than his bite. He never meant any harm to anybody. He was quite fond of the kid, but she did manage to rub him up the wrong way, etc. etc.

Stonily and without making comment Venetia listened to his spate of words. They had a hollow sound. She felt that there could be no truth in anything he said—not even half a truth—and she did know without doubt that Maybelle would not have been the one to start trouble. Also she had been more distressed about the idea of 'sneaking' than about the thing she had actually seen.

Venetia simmered down. She began to feel sick and wretched. The room was growing lighter. Oh, her lovely bedroom, she thought, which she had decorated and arranged with such loving care, and wherein she had started her married life. In here she had known what she had falsely believed the perfection of love, and of love's delight. She had given herself so willingly, so rapturously, to this young man who had done her the greatest wrong. Now, at last, the citadel of her anger was stormed by love's memory. It crumbled and the core of her grief was reached. Her legs trembled and refused to carry her. She sank suddenly on to the bed and covered her face with her hands.

'Mike, Mike, how could you have done it!' she whispered.

That desolate question seemed to unnerve him, for all his egotism and arrogance. He was made aware that he was an unmitigated cad. He had wounded to death this sweet, generous woman who had trusted him.

'Oh, God!' he groaned, 'Venetia darling, it's all a mistake, I promise you. I wouldn't have had this happen for the world.'

She made no reply. She was not crying. She just sat silent with her face hidden in her hands.

He seated himself beside her and tried to put an arm around her but she shuddered away from him.

'Don't, *please.*'

'I know you're upset by what you heard me say to Maybelle, but you can't judge me just on that. Give me a hearing, please.'

Her hands fell away from her face. He was shocked to see how old she looked. Older than her years this morning in the grey winter's light, and for all his faults he was conscious that he was responsible. It touched what conscience he possessed and made him feel uneasy and ashamed.

'Honestly, Michael,' she said, 'I don't see how you think you can talk your way out of *this.*'

'Not if you refuse to believe a word I say and insist upon believing the worst before you've even heard my side of the story.'

'Michael,' said Venetia in a quiet flat voice, 'I can't stand another scene and I don't want lies. If you lie to me, I shall know it, because I'm not quite such a fool as you may think, and using the brains God has given me it isn't really difficult for me to put two and two together.'

'What do you mean?' he asked.

'I heard you threaten to keep Maybelle away if she didn't shut up—those were the words you used, *"shut up"*. What had she to shut up about?'

'Hasn't she already enlightened you?' He

gave a short laugh.

'Yes. She said she saw you with Jix, not only last night in the garden, but in the forest during her summer holidays. On that occasion you appear to have been in a far more compromising position.'

'So *she* says!' began Michael. But more uneasily and guiltily now.

Venetia's eyes glinted. She broke in:

'*You're not to lie* to me, Mike. If you do, nothing can ever be right between us again, *nothing*. You may have pulled the wool over my eyes up till now but you can't do it any more. You know that I knew about you and Jix, anyhow.'

'That was before you and I were married. Even the most jealous wife shouldn't hold her husband's previous affairs against him.'

'I am not a jealous wife and I've never held the Jix affair against you—I once said I didn't want Jix in this house. I think that was natural. You continually accused me of being prudish and Victorian. So I gave in and asked her to our dance. I know the fact irritates you, but I have an adolescent daughter to think of. I don't think any decent-minded woman would particularly like her young daughter to meet her husband's former mistress. There is something sordid about it. But I trusted you and gave in. And yet you started to meet Jix again behind my back almost as soon as we moved in here. All the many days you were supposed to be hacking alone, I suppose you spent with *her*. My God, Michael!'

He got up and began to walk up and down the room, thumbs stuck in his pockets, jaw jutting out defiantly. His remorse was sunk again in a morass of his own feelings—his imagined wrongs. He made a poor effort to extricate himself from the tangle.

'What if I have been meeting her? Kissing a girl in a wood or in a garden doesn't constitute an act of adultery, my dear, no matter what your young daughter might imagine.'

Venetia looked at him, her cheeks flaming.

'Maybelle doesn't know the meaning of the word *adultery*. But I *made* her tell me what she saw that day in the forest and it was quite enough—you were lying there—shamelessly— with Jix.'

'Supposing I was? I tell you I had had too much to drink. Can't you forgive and forget something a man does when he's drunk?'

'Yes, but you were hardly drunk when you went hacking in the woods last summer.'

'Even lying on the ground doesn't constitute infidelity, and you're behaving as though I had been unfaithful to you.'

'Haven't you?'

He looked her in the eyes, trying to brazen it out.

'No.'

Dead silence. Her heart knocked. She knew that that 'no' was a lie. By every instinct in her,

229

she knew it and so was bereft of all faith in the love, the trust that she and Michael had once shared.

'It was all just fun and games, I assure you,' said Michael.

She twisted her lips scornfully.

'You have a strange idea of "fun and games".'

'Well, anyhow, you've no right to think the worst.'

'I have every right,' she said calmly. 'I don't think if it had been a question of a few innocent kisses you'd have been nearly so scared, or tried so hard to bully poor Maybelle into silence.'

'Poor Maybelle,' he echoed with a sneer.

'You really are eaten up with jealousy of my daughter, aren't you?' Venetia asked almost on a note of surprise. 'It staggers me. I don't know what Maybelle has ever said or done to make you feel that way. She hasn't tried to take up all my time even in her school holidays—and never wanted to come between us.'

'I didn't say she had but I suppose I'm justified in wanting my wife to myself,' he said in a loud voice which had a defensive sound. She thought it very revealing. She knew him now all too well. He was, of course, guilty, and seeking a way to defend himself.

'You amaze me, Mike,' she said, 'and I suppose your desire to be with your wife is the reason why you went on these jaunts with your ex-mistress.'

He sprang up and, crimson, furious, was about to become abusive when Venetia put a sharp end to it.

'It's useless going on like this. You've done something unforgivable and I can't believe you just *kissed* Jix Lawson.'

'I see. Well I repeat that was all I did.'

'What difference does it make really? Even if you could prove you hadn't actually gone the whole way with her after our marriage, I would still feel the same about you. But, what my unfortunate daughter saw is quite enough to convince me you have been sleeping with Jix Lawson again.'

Michael tried to control himself, but a look of fear widened his eyes. Venetia hated to see it and turned quickly away. She had loathed every moment of this scene. With every word that had passed between them she could see the end of her happiness. The citadel was crumbling in front of her eyes. Anguish to find that all that she had built up in her mind about Mike was sheer illusion. The person whom she had heard threatening Maybelle earlier this morning bore no resemblance to the charming young man with whom she had fallen so deeply in love. She had loved that Mike very much. She had been ready to gamble on being happy with a man so much younger than herself. But *this* Michael—what was he? She dared not think. She felt too ashamed of him and of her own madness in ever having linked her life with his. One of the most bitter facets of the whole case was the feeling that she had not only harmed herself by it but her child too. It had been horrible for Maybelle. Now the memory of Geoffrey returned to add to the torture. She hardly dared imagine what he would have thought about this—and in particular about Maybelle—his beloved little daughter.

'I've made a ghastly mistake,' she said aloud, suddenly.

'You mean by marrying me?' Mike jerked out the words.

Venetia stood up.

'Yes.'

Silence.

Her heart beat quickly and painfully. What a horrible thing to have said! Horrible that Michael should ever have made it possible for her to say it. She had known six brief months of blind happiness. But today as she looked back she knew that even those months had been punctuated by doubts and the constant fear that she had done the wrong thing. There were so many small ways in which Michael had disappointed her; by his selfishness, his greed, and most of all by his uncalled-for jealousy of her child. She had tried so hard never to allow Maybelle's existence to interfere with anything that Mike had wanted to do.

'I think we had better stop this and go down. You must have some breakfast,' she said

232

wearily, 'otherwise you won't feel much like hunting.'

'Do you think I intend to go hunting and leave you in this frame of mind?' he began grandly.

Then Venetia, who had been walking to the bedroom door, turned and gave him a look which penetrated even the husk of Michael's inflated opinion of himself. He never forgot it, and the slow red flush burned under his skin.

'Oh *hell*!' he muttered and for once was at a loss for words.

'I'm sorry, Mike,' she said, 'but you can't expect me to believe that you really feel like giving up a day's hunting just because *I'm* unhappy. If you'd ever seriously considered my happiness, you would never have done what you did.'

'Are you going to persist in thinking the worst?'

'You're going to persist in denying it, aren't you?'

'Anybody would imagine you hate me and *want* an excuse to crack up our marriage.'

'That,' said Venetia, with a short laugh, 'is quite funny.'

'Glad you see the joke.'

'Oh, don't let's go on in this stupid manner—it's so unadult,' she flared up, her whole being suddenly in revolt against him. 'That's the trouble with you, Mike. You've never really grown up. You will behave like a spoiled boy all the time.'

'And you—' he began, and stopped.

'And I am much older and more like your mother,' she said very coldly. 'Don't bother to say it. I know.'

He gave her a sullen look.

'That, of course,' added Venetia, 'has been the trouble all the way along. I was warned that it would be an ill-assorted marriage but I thought we'd make a success of it. We might have if you had known how to behave—but you—oh, what's the good of going on—it's all over now.'

He was frightened again. The naked truth was not attractive and Venetia had said some revealing things. He had thought he held her in the hollow of his hand because of her passion for him. He was not prepared for this cold contempt—coming from a Venetia who obviously despised him. He was a little shocked. He forgot the wrong he had done her or Maybelle. He was much more concerned with his own 'loss of face'. It was such a new experience for Michael Pethick to be made to feel small.

'Look here, Venetia,' he said, and now he came up to her and took her hand. She tried to draw it away but he retained it. 'Venetia— don't be so bitter—so hard on me. I know you're frightfully upset and angry and I know I've behaved like a b—y fool. I'm willing to admit it. But whatever you think about Jix and

234

me—it hasn't *meant* anything. It's *you* I love and you I've always loved. The whole thing was caused by my jealousy of Maybelle. I swear it. It may sound silly but I just couldn't stand the way *you* love and mollycoddle that girl. Believe it or not as you like, it's God's truth.'

'I don't believe it. I know the facts about Maybelle, and, if anything, I've neglected *her* for *you*. As for Jix Lawson—I really feel quite sorry for her. If she's at all fond of you it must be rather miserable to be treated by you as though one is a cheap tart.'

He stirred uncomfortably. The word 'tart' didn't seem to fit in with Venetia's habitual dignity.

'Will nothing that I can say convince you that I don't care a damn about Jix? I promise on my oath to give her up tomorrow if it will satisfy you.'

Venetia dragged her fingers from his as though she could not bear the contact with his flesh.

'You swore to me when we got married that you had finished with Jix.'

'Can't you forgive one little lapse? Won't your love stand up to it? Good God! It can't be worth much. You seem awfully ready to condemn me.'

'I am not, and I find the whole thing unspeakably sad. But you must realize, Mike, that it isn't really your one "lapse", as you call it, with Jix that has hit me so hard as your behaviour towards my child. I cannot go on living in the same house with a man who can menace a fifteen-year-old schoolgirl—in the way you did this morning. Neither can I risk you giving her another chance to see her stepfather gavotting around with women, and deceiving her mother. It's a pretty poor upbringing for her. You have made it quite plain that your love for me is as shallow as a brook. You want me—yes—and all that I can give you. But you want Jix and your old life as well, and I'm afraid that sort of marriage isn't good enough. I loved you better than anyone in the world. If I've stopped loving you, it's your fault, not mine—or poor Maybelle's—or anybody else's. Just *yours*!'

Her voice broke suddenly. *She* was near to breaking, and he saw the tears glittering in her eyes—saw her put up a hand to check them—and was stirred to a real and consuming remorse.

CHAPTER EIGHT

In Mrs Keen's private office of her Bond Street *salon* Venetia sat in an armchair opposite Barbara. The two women were drinking coffee and smoking. Venetia leaned against her cushions in an attitude of excessive fatigue. She

236

had taken off her mink coat. She wore a mushroom-coloured suit. A tiny velvet hat of the same colour was pulled low over her forehead. Her appearance had shocked Barbara when she first came into the *salon*— she had never seen Venetia look so ill or so sad; except after Geoffrey's death. But then she had been younger and was, perhaps, better able to stand up to catastrophic events.

Venetia had been here for half an hour. Barbara knew everything now. It was all she had expected. And if there was any mortal man whom Barbara loathed at the moment, it was Michael Pethick. Being a true friend and unwilling to hurt Venetia, she had not indulged in the luxury of saying, '*I told you so*'. But her strange bitter face contracted into a cynical grimace as she listened.

'I had to tell someone,' Venetia had begun painfully. 'It isn't that I want to be disloyal to Mike but I just *had* to talk this thing over. I couldn't possible do it with Geoffrey's mother. In fact, I haven't told her anything beyond the fact that Mike and I have had a misunderstanding. She's putting Maybelle up for a few days. I have just left the poor darling there. She was going to Ganny anyway next week.'

But Venetia added a description of the way Maybelle had cried while they packed up for a visit to Lady Sellingham.

'It isn't that I don't *want* to go to Ganny, you
237

know I do—but it's just that I feel so awful about *you*, Mummy, and I wish everything had been different about Mike.'

That was the pathetic part of it. Maybelle blamed herself for the quarrel with Mike; as though she could have been expected to maintain a complete poise and silence and behave at her age like a woman of the world, Venetia said to Barbara. But Maybelle had been very distressed when her mother had left her at Richmond earlier this morning. Lady Sellingham, with her usual tact, behaved as if everything was normal and gave her granddaughter a cheerful loving welcome. Only her gentle blue eyes had regarded Venetia with sadness and apprehension. She, too, had been shocked by Venetia's appearance. But as she had kissed her good-bye, Venetia had whispered:

'I expect it will all work out, Mother—don't worry and try not to talk to Maybelle about it. I want her to forget the whole thing as far as possible.'

'So you have left Mike,' Barbara said now to Venetia, and narrowed her eyes and nodded her smartly-groomed head, looking like a wise Chinese idol.

'Not permanently perhaps, but—I just had to get out of the house for the moment,' explained Venetia.

'And how did he take your exit?'

'Not very well,' said Venetia, with a short laugh.

She was feeling ill and exhausted from lack of sleep. She had been living at high nervous tension ever since Boxing Day. It was repugnant to her to recall the sequence of events since the Christmas dance which had proved so fatal to her marriage. Even now she could not believe that after six short months things could have reached this pitch. It seemed terrible that all the wonderful plans she had built up for living happily with Mike for the rest of her life should have disintegrated in such a brief period.

In the end he had stopped trying to deny his infidelity and to defend himself. He had started to plead for her forgiveness. Hour after hour on that Boxing morning, he endeavoured to regain Venetia's affections. She could see him now, sweating, greyish under the tan, genuinely upset. Genuinely afraid of losing *her*. She did not doubt it. And when he kept repeating that he really loved her and that Jix meant nothing—she believed him.

'But I can't trust you any more,' she had said. 'That is what is getting me down.'

He had, after all, missed the day's precious hunting and refused to leave her. That, Venetia said to Barbara this morning, with a bitter smile, showed how upset he must have been.

'But I know now that he isn't really a *man*. Oh, yes, he's an adult, but he's actually got the mental make-up of an immature schoolboy.

239

He was upset with me in the way a teenage boy might have been if the headmaster had sent for him and warned him that he was about to be expelled. At the same time, you know, keeping an eye on the clock, wondering if he might manage to get to the cricket match after all. Not worried deep down about his *wrongdoing.*'

Venetia was quite sure that Michael had secretly wondered how soon he could get out of his difficulties and join the Meet. He made a big show of ringing up the M.F.H. and apologizing for not turning up, 'because he had 'flu and a temperature and could not leave his bed'.

He did everything to show his remorse. He even wanted to see Maybelle and apologize to her. But that, Venetia prevented. She wanted Maybelle left severely alone.

Eventually Venetia found that she could not get away from Burnt Ash as soon as she wanted because Maybelle was ill and had to stay in bed for forty-eight hours. Maybelle was like that. When she was a very small child, after any upset she used to develop a temperature. In a way, Venetia was glad to keep her in her room with her new books, and some of her young friends came to see her. She knew that wild horses would not draw any gossip from the child. She need have no fear that the unhappy business with Mike would be discussed.

But Michael's jubilation because his wife

could not rush out of the house and take her daughter with her was short-lived. Equally so were any expectations that he would be quickly forgiven.

'Leave me alone. I must think things over,' Venetia kept repeating. 'Please don't try and force it. I've had a considerable shock and I've *got* to try and get over it, and think things over calmly.'

She abided by that, and, she told Barbara, now had no doubt surprised him by her stubborn refusal to capitulate.

'You were damned well right,' said Barbara in a terse voice. 'If I'd been you, I'd have given that young man a crack or two that he would never forget. I think that you were decent to speak to him at *all* civilly.'

'One must try and see things from both sides,' said Venetia. 'I suppose I was so much in love with Mike that I didn't realize right from the start that poor Maybelle would become a thorn in his flesh.'

'Well, where do we go from there?' asked Barbara.

'I don't know,' said Venetia, and hung her graceful head.

Barbara pushed in a drawer of her desk, scowled fiercely, jabbed a cigarette-end into an ashtray and walked to one of the radiators. She laid her hand on it.

'I must speak about this central heating—it's not up to standard,' she muttered.

241

But her mind was on Venetia and Venetia knew it. She knew, too, that the smart, bitter-tongued Barbara was a good, dependable friend.

'Dear Bar—don't worry about me,' she said, with a short laugh.

'I worry about you like hell,' said Barbara, 'you're too soft. You want a hard old witch like myself to deal with a fellow like Michael Pethick.'

'Well, I couldn't do more than leave the house, could I?'

'With every intention of returning and forgiving him, and letting him know how fascinating he is?' said Barbara, and her own laugh was sarcastic.

Venetia sighed.

'I didn't say so.'

'But you'll never cite your own child as a witness, and she is the only one you've got.'

Venetia put her face in her hands.

'Oh, my God, I hardly like to remember what that poor child blurted out. I *had* to drag it out of her. I shall never forget the horror of it but it will never be mentioned between us again, and I hope she will forget it in time.'

'It stinks,' said Barbara in her frank way. 'And my advice to you is to send Mr Pethick about his business and go back to your old life—even if it means you have to admit failure. You'll be happier than hanging on with *that* sort of man. If he can do a thing like this to you so soon after your marriage—he'll repeat it—and quickly!'

Venetia remained silent. She had been saying these sort of things to herself ever since the nightmare of revelation. Yet with her whole soul she dreaded the thought of putting an end to their marriage. Despite her disgust, her disillusionment, there was still some love for Mike left in her heart. It was like that! You believe in somebody and love them with great passion. Then you find that you don't believe in them any more, but somehow it doesn't altogether wipe out your passion. It's rather humiliating, thought Venetia, but one had to face facts. Why not *be* magnanimous, even though Barbara, who was so much harder and more ruthless, would like her to leave Burnt Ash and return to her former existence? One should never go back. One must go forward. Michael, himself, had said to her:

'If you love me, surely you won't seize the first opportunity to chuck me out. You'll give me another chance.'

She couldn't answer him then. She wanted to get away. She wanted to remain away, until she had had time to think things out. She did not even wish to stay in Richmond with Geoffrey's mother and her own daughter, as she would have done under normal circumstances. And she refused a bed in Barbara's flat. She took a room in a quiet hotel facing the Park—a place where she and Geoffrey used sometimes to stay. It was strange, she thought, how much she thought of her first husband who had died, and of all his tenderness and loyalty. What a terrible mistake she had made in thinking that Mike could ever take *his* place!

Barbara lectured her for a while and then a business representative from Paris was announced. The brilliant proprietress of the Bara Beauty Salon was forced to banish her friend.

'But I'm here when you want me, darling, and *don't* go back to Burnt Ash in a hurry,' she counselled. 'Whatever you do, let that young man stew in his own juice for a bit. Believe me, I am ready to accept the fact that he's sorry. He knows what he's lost; but even if you decide to give him a second chance—let him wait for it. It will do him a power of good.'

Venetia returned to her hotel. She had not told Michael where she was to be found. That had frightened him badly. She knew it. There could be no doubt whatsoever that Michael was ashamed and sorry and anxious for a reconciliation. And it all would have been so much easier, she thought desolately, had Maybelle not been so deeply concerned. Perhaps there was some justification in what Michael had said; Maybelle *had* come between them. The poor little thing—and she had done it so unwittingly.

Venetia lay on her bed trying to rest during the afternoon and to work out problems to which there seemed no solution. She could see plainly, however, that this was to be a battle between her love for Mike and her deeper and quite different love for her child. Oh, cruel of Michael to have put her in such a position, she thought, and dissolved into bitter tears.

By tea-time she was feeling horribly lonely and hating the impersonal hotel bedroom, despite its warmth and elegance. She wished she had not been so dramatic as to walk out of Burnt Ash or to refuse even to stay with Mother and Maybelle. She longed for the little white house at Richmond, yet she did not really want to face either Geoffrey's mother or Maybelle just yet. She was not sufficiently mistress of herself.

She wished Herman was in London instead of America. She could have talked to *him*. He would have been wise and sensible. Yet in the eyes of all her friends she could only suffer a deep humiliation which offended her proud, fastidious nature.

She thought a lot about Burnt Ash Manor— the lovely home that she had made more lovely for herself and Mike, *and* for Maybelle. She wondered what Michael was doing at this moment and if he had gone to the office today and if he meant to confide in Tony, his partner, although she did not think he would. The story was not to his credit.

'You can say that my ex-mother-in-law is ill and that I'm with her for a few days. That will

explain my sudden exit from Burnt Ash,'
Venetia had told him.

She had a vivid picture of the worried and
too-handsome face and the new rather shifty
look in the bright blue eyes ... She had not
liked it. It was horrible to know now that
Michael had it in him to lie and to betray. He
had said:

'Very well. I'll tell people that you're at
Richmond.' And added gloomily, 'I suppose
you're doing this to punish me.'

Dear life! She was punishing herself, too, she
thought, as she lay there on the bed in the hotel.
She felt the loneliest woman alive. It was a
nightmare. She wanted to wake up and find
that it wasn't true and that Mike was here
beside her and they were lovers again,
delighting in each other as they had done in
France on their honeymoon and during the
early days in their own home.

Should she lift the receiver, call his office and
say:

'Come and see me. We'll spend tonight
together and talk it all over and try to put
things right.'

She knew that that could bring him here
within the next half hour; that she had only to
say the words of forgiveness and accept his
promises to put Jix Lawson out of his life and
make a better show of things with Maybelle.
Why did she hesitate? She *wanted* him. The
answer was, of course, that she had been too

deeply hurt and shocked by the whole thing to be capable of taking him back to her arms quickly.

Margaret, the faithful Scots maid, was the only one who knew where Venetia was tonight. She had given Margaret her address and said painfully:

'This is if you want me for anything urgent. But please don't give it to anybody else, even Mr Pethick.'

She had made no further explanation. Margaret had asked for none but Venetia had seen from the grim expression on her face that the wise old servant knew that all was not well. And Margaret had never really liked or accepted Michael. Venetia knew that, too.

Pippa was of no account. But now Venetia had lost faith in Michael. Pippa was a young, pretty girl, and as he was to be alone in the house except for old Margaret, Venetia took the precaution of sending the Spanish girl to Richmond with Maybelle.

Then there was Bennett—the little groom was, perhaps, the one person in the world who had a deep motiveless affection for Michael. Michael himself had told her that Bennett had refused many better offers because he was such a loyal and devoted servant. Just before she left Burnt Ash, Venetia had gone down to the stables, where Bennett was swilling out Red Prince's stall, and said to him:

'I shall be away for a week, Bennett. Look

after Mr Pethick, will you?'

He touched his cap respectfully.

'Very good, milady.'

She wondered if it was fancy or fact that made her think *he* knew what Michael was really like, too; had always known. Jix Lawson knew him. Everybody knew him well except his wife, Venetia told herself painfully. She was beginning to see that he was and always had been a stranger to her.

Wretched and lonely though she was, she stuck to her resolution to remain in this self-imposed solitary confinement for a night or two, at least.

It was much later that evening while she was eating a lonely meal that a page-boy brought her two letters.

She glanced at them in amazement, for one was addressed to her in Michael's handwriting. How on earth had he known where to find her? She could have sworn that Margaret would not give her away.

Then she opened the other note, and all was made clear. It was from Margaret herself:

Dear Madam,

I am taking the liberty of sending these letters up to London by my nephew whom you know is on leave from Korea and came down ˢee me today. It was lucky because Mr k asked if I knew where you was, and if

*you don't mind me saying so, Madam, made
things a bit awkward for me because I would
not give your address. He said it was vital so I
said I would deliver his note by my nephew.
He's packed up, Madam, and isn't staying
here, but Bennett said he'd be down again on
Saturday for the hunting* (that made Venetia
smile faintly and sadly), *but I thought you
might want to get this letter so my nephew is
taking it to you and I hope everything will be
all right for you, Madam.*

> *Yours respectfully.*
> *Margaret.*

Venetia swallowed hard as she folded this
letter. The seemingly unsentimental
Scotswoman was her faithful ally. No amount
of 'awkwardness' from Michael would have
dragged that address from her, bless her.

Venetia could not open Michael's letter here
in a public restaurant. She ordered coffee to be
sent to the writing-room which was empty, sat
down at one of the desks, switched on the table
light and began to read what he had written.

There were four closely-written pages.
Michael had rather a small but untidy writing,
hard to decipher. It was, she thought, with a
deep sigh, a badly-phrased letter, as immature
as himself. He never had been a letter writer.
But she did feel that it was sincere, which was
something.

Venetia my darling,

I think it was a bit rotten of you to leave me like that and not let me know where you were going. I rang up Richmond but Lady S. gave me a complete raspberry and just said you weren't there. Honestly, darling, I know I've been frightful, but surely you don't want to make a terrific thing out of this damned Jix affair and ruin our lives.

You're quite wrong if you think I can muck about at Burnt Ash by myself just remembering what I've done to you. I can't and I'm clearing out, and if you want me I'm at Tony's flat. I'm not saying a word to anybody but I would like to know how long my punishment is going to last or if you mean to quit for good. Venetia, I've said I'm sorry and by God I mean it. I wouldn't have hurt you like this for worlds. It was a sort of madness but I've 'phoned Jix and broken with her for good and all. Naturally she's just as upset as I am and she's sorry you have been hurt. And I really think she is. But she isn't as sorry as I am. I must say I blush when I think about Maybelle. Do try and see that the whole thing was my damnable jealousy. But give me another chance. I do love you. I swear it. Do come back to me, Venetia, and let's start again. If you think it's better to stay with Maybelle and the old Lady S. until the end of the holidays I shall understand. Perhaps you don't want M. to be with me until she's had a chance to get over it. I feel a complete bastard

250

and I suppose I've made everybody miserable as well as myself. But whatever you think please don't imagine it's because of the difference in our ages or because I got tired of you. It was just a sort of thing I had about Jix but now it's out of my system for good and all. I swear it. You're the one I love. Oh, God, do believe me, and ring me up at Tony's.

Michael.

Venetia read and re-read this effusion until she almost knew it by heart. Each time she mentally digested the words she sensed the underlying note of sincerity.

She put her hand over her eyes, and as she drank the black coffee the waiter had set in front of her, tried not to give way to tears again. Barbara was right when she had said this was a time for strength and thought, and that it would be fatal to show weakness.

But there was something curiously touching about Michael's letter with its schoolboy flavour. The naughty boy again, anxious for pardon. Venetia had to face the fact now that she was married to a man on whom she could not lean, and who would always lean on her.

He had *some* understanding ... that suggestion, for instance, that she should stay with her daughter and Geoffrey's mother until the end of the school holidays. As for that naïve reference to her age ... Venetia's lips quivered. She started to read the letter once

251

more. He was so unhappy, poor Mike! Could she trust him when he said that he never intended to see Jix again? He was bound to see her as long as they were both members of the same Hunt. That 'thing' that he had about Jix—would it remain and be revived in time? There was a lot in propinquity. If she, Venetia, and Mike, had any differences of opinion in the future, would he not go straight back to Jix? It was obvious that the girl had an ineradicable passion for *him*, so she must, inevitably, remain a menace to their happiness.

Was the only solution to ask Mike to sell the Manor, and for them to start again in another place and make a new circle of friends? But wouldn't that be a lot to ask of him when it was his old home? And all the people around Burnt Ash were his old friends. They liked and admired him and accepted him as one of themselves.

'I wouldn't have any right to ask him to make such a sacrifice,' Venetia mused. 'I'm the one who ought to make a few sacrifices. If our marriage hasn't worked it's my fault, too, because I'm the elder of the two and I should have had more sense. Besides, why should I demand that he should lead *my* old life? He isn't a Geoffrey or a Herman. He's just Mike. I loved and married that Mike, and if I didn't realize what he was like, I've only myself to blame. Why should I try to change him?'

Perhaps the trouble was that she had been

too apt to compare Mike with Geoffrey, and too intent on living as she had lived in the past. That was unfair to Mike, and could never have worked. A woman must throw her lot in with the man she marries. It should, of course, be fifty-fifty. Perhaps Michael had tried to do what she wanted, and found it too much for him. Perhaps he *was* genuinely jealous of Maybelle, and she, the mother, too much of the mother to make any young man of Mike's age a good wife.

If she was ready to admit her own failure, one stinging and embittering fact stayed to help her hesitate to lift that telephone and recall Michael instantly to her side. The indisputable knowledge that he had been unfaithful to her. *The wrong he had done to their love.*

After a time Venetia reached a state of mind where she could no longer be alone or she feared she might put that call through to Michael.

In desperation she telephoned Jack Fuller, the architect who had helped restore Burnt Ash Manor and who had been Geoffrey's friend.

It was her intention to suggest that were he and his wife alone at home she would go round to see them. She knew them well enough for that. But the moment she heard Jack's voice she panicked. He spoke cheerfully. Of course, he knew nothing and took it for granted that all was well with her.

'How are you, Venetia? It's delightful to hear your voice. How is that attractive young husband of yours? Liz has got a "thing" about him and says it's high time we asked you both to stay with us. How about it?'

Silence from Venetia. She was gripping the telephone very tightly. 'Liz'—Jack's wife, Elizabeth—even older than Venetia; plump and comfortable and quite happily married to her architect and with a son at Cambridge. Even *she* had felt that tremendous sex attraction that emanated from Michael towards all women.

Venetia regretted having telephoned Jack. She knew she could not see him and act a part this evening. She talked to him for a moment with forced brightness.

'Yes, Mike and I will come down and stay with you both very soon ... sweet of you to ask us ... yes, we're both awfully well and so is Maybelle. Thanks awfully, Jack. Give my love to Liz.'

Jack, always charming and jolly, gave his friendly laugh and ended:

'And a spot of love from the handsome husband to keep Liz quiet, eh?'

Venetia echoed the laugh, 'But of course.'

Then she put down the receiver, and lying full length on the bed, turned her face to the pillow and lay very still.

But she did not give way to the temptation to ring up Michael.

CHAPTER NINE

'And might I ask how long you're to be kept in disgrace?'

Jix Lawson asked the question in a flat voice. She was feeling flat. She stood beside Michael in the bar parlour of the Horse and Hounds, which was a small pub—once an old attractive Tudor house—about half a mile from Burnt Ash Manor. The January night was raw. Michael had come straight here from the station. He had been staying up in London at his partner's flat all the week. This was Friday. He had come down in the hope of some hunting tomorrow. Although, as he had just told Jix, he hated going home. The Manor House was like a 'morgue'.

'Anybody would think somebody had died there,' he grumbled. 'Only that old spy Margaret mumbling around the place. Even Pippa's been banished.'

'I'm afraid your wife doesn't trust you,' said Jix, with a curt laugh, and drank her gin-and-French at a gulp.

Said Michael darkly:

'Maybe she doesn't, but I don't happen to be *that* bad, and I'm not interested in wenches like Pippa.'

'I don't think you're particularly interested in me either, at the moment. You're only concerned with getting back into your wife's good books,' said Jix with bitterness.

Michael did not speak for a moment but set his empty glass down on the table, lit a cigarette and spread his fingers to the fire. As a rule he rather liked the Horse and Hounds. It was quite a cheerful spot, in the saloon at this time of the evening. But he and Jix had wanted to have a talk, so they had shut themselves in this small room where the landlord had lit the fire for them. There wasn't much glamour about it. It was full of black oak. A low-powered bulb in the hanging lamp had a dirty yellow fly-brown shade, and the dim light was depressing. The pictures were all crudely-coloured advertisements of people enjoying some proprietary brand or other and smiling glassily. Michael did not feel that he had enjoyed life since Christmas night. That was a fortnight ago. It was nearly a fortnight since he had seen Venetia. He was surprised to find how much he had missed her. He had gone out on a party or two but it just hadn't worked.

'In my way I'm a faithful chap,' Michael gloomily informed himself.

Yes, in his way he still loved Venetia. But he also desired Jix. That was a passion of which, for some strange reason, he could not cure himself. Yet he knew that she did not hold a candle to his lovely and dignified wife.

He stared at Jix. She had just taken a cigarette from her own packet and lit it. He noticed as she threw away the match that her nails were dirty. She never used varnish. And there were times when she smelled of the stable … like old Bennett, he thought. Yet she fascinated him. Her legs were poems. He liked her thin flexible waist and boy's hips. He always had an insane wish, whenever he saw her, to grab a fistful of that short untidy hair and kiss her until she lost her customary look of sullen resentment and her mouth opened languorously to receive his.

With Venetia, even during their moments of shared passion, he experienced a faint sense of inferiority; the need to ennoble himself in order to meet her on her own exalted ground. He could not accuse her of being anything but generous in her response. They had had some wonderful moments together. But with Jix it was quite different; more vicious somehow— and he was always the one who called the tune. He knew that she was mad about him. She did not demand that he should reach the heights with her, but rather that they should sink together to the depths. She had a certain streak of coarseness that matched his own and she amused him. A chap ought to be able to have two wives, he thought moodily. He wanted both Venetia and Jix.

How well he knew that old tweed skirt that Jix wore tonight, rather tightly stretched around her flanks as though it had shrunk in the cleaning; she wore with it a yellow polo-necked sweater, and a duffle coat. She had come hatless and with a large Boxer at her heels—her latest acquisition. He lay in the corner, muzzle on big paws, blinking at them, wagging his stump of a tail now and again if he thought he was being noticed.

Michael knew that Jix was feeling sore because he hadn't seen her since that night that Maybelle had found them in the garden. He had spoken to her on the telephone and she had been as shocked as himself to hear that the young girl Maybelle had also surprised them in the forest last summer, and that Venetia now knew. What a damned awful thing to have happened, she had said to Michael, and seemed genuinely upset.

They had both agreed that it was 'a bad show'; but there was nothing they could do about it.

'I hate that little prig of a step-daughter of mine with a deadly hatred,' Michael had finished in a burst of temper. But Jix had scoffed:

'Don't be a fool, Michael, why hate the poor kid? It wasn't very pretty for her, and if you hate anybody it ought to be *me*.'

'So I do!' he had almost snarled the words. But she knew her Michael.

'Ring me up when you're in a better mood,' she had said and put down the receiver.

Then he had had that abominable ten days with Tony, always hoping that Venetia might get in touch with him—that the love which he knew she bore him would induce her to relent. But she had only sent one short note asking him to stay away from her for the moment.

Alternately he went out on drinking-bouts with Tony or tried to find Venetia by ringing up everybody she knew, including Barbara Keen, who refused to speak to him. So he knew that *she knew* and rang off, calling her 'an old witch' under his breath.

The one person he had not had the nerve to ring was Lady Sellingham.

He tried cajoling and bribing Margaret in order to get Venetia's address, but failed. Yesterday he had driven down to the Manor to make a personal attempt. Margaret, fixing a cold eye on him, had with the utmost politeness maintained that her duty was to 'Madame' and that Madame had asked that nobody should know where she was.

After that Michael had taken a look at his horses and unburdened himself to old Bennett.

'Women are the devil. What do you think I ought to do, Bennett?' he had asked.

'Nothing, sir,' was Bennett's sage advice while the two men watched Red Prince in the warm hay-scented stable, munching his corn. 'Milady will come back. She's a very nice lady if you don't mind my saying so, sir, and better for you than Miss Lawson.'

Michael left him, laughing. No doubt Bennett spoke the truth, but Michael went straight back into the house to telephone Jix and fix tonight's date with her.

He was beginning to feel more relaxed now.

'I don't know when the hell Venetia's going to forgive me,' he said, and added, 'If ever, but *if* she doesn't, I'll damn-well get a divorce and marry you.'

Jix flushed dully but laughed, without humour.

'Don't be a B.F., darling. We can't afford to get married and you know it.'

'Are you suggesting I should stay with Venetia only because she's got money?'

Jix shrugged her shoulders.

'Oh, no, I'm sure *she* attracts you madly. She's a very beautiful, kind woman.'

'All the same I can't live with her, that's obvious,' muttered Michael.

'Well, you might think of me for a change. I'm sick of the whole set-up,' said Jix. 'It's no fun being just "the little woman round the corner" waiting for the odd crumb. And it's quite obvious that Venetia *won't* divorce you because she won't want to drag her daughter into it. And rightly. But if she *does* forgive you and offers to start again—what sort of a lookout will I have? You won't be allowed to see me again so that'll be that.'

'I suppose she'll want me to sell up, and take her away from this district,' said Michael.

'That's what I've been thinking, and if she does—will you?'

Michael looked into the girl's narrow hungry eyes, then stubbed the floor with the toe of his shoe.

'Oh, God, I don't know. It's all such *hell*! But I suppose I'll have to do whatever she wants. I'm not anxious to muck this marriage right up.'

Jix gave her derisive laugh.

'Are you not, dear? Well, you seem to have made a very good shot at it.'

'You know why, you little devil.'

'Because I sit on a horse so prettily?' she jeered and flung her cigarette-end in the fire.

'You know it's not that.'

'Well, I'm through,' she said and suddenly choked on the words and her eyes glittered with tears. He never remembered seeing Jix cry before. 'I broke with you before you married her and then you would start it all up again. But now it's over. I'm not going on, I'm *not*. I can't stand it, Mike. I like Venetia, which makes it all the worse. She was so nice to me at that dance. Oh, go away and leave me alone!'

She turned and put her arm on the mantelpiece and hid her face against it. But the old passion was stirring in Michael. He was unhappy. He was not a type who could bear to be unhappy, or feel himself unwanted. He had arrived at the Horse and Hounds half an hour before Jix and had that much start on the drinking. He swung easily from remorse to resentment against Venetia, whom he had

261

wronged, rather than Jix, who was the cause of the trouble. He caught hold of her and tried to kiss her.

'Let's cheer each other up, for heaven's sake,' he muttered.

She tried to break loose.

'What's the good, Mike?'

'I'm still damned fond of you and you know it.'

'I'm in love with you, too, and always have been,' she said huskily, 'but it's too much of a good thing. If you want Venetia back, well, you'd better go all out to get her, and leave me alone.'

'Venetia doesn't seem to want me. You do.'

'I don't know that I do any more—' she began. But he felt her slight body trembling, and suddenly he put his hot face between the small breasts over which the thick woolly sweater was tightly stretched. His passion was mounting. He thrust the vision of Venetia's beautiful, reproaching face right out of his memory. He was miserable and unsure of himself. He felt there was nothing he wanted more than Jix tonight, her unstinted passion, her strange misplaced fidelity. He had treated her badly and yet she was still his, body and soul, and he knew it. She loved him, *knowing* him. He was not an heroic figure. He was well aware of that, too, and he need not pretend with Jix. But he could never possibly be of the stature that Venetia admired.

'You and I are going to spend tonight together, Jix,' he said thickly, 'even if it's the last.'

'No . . .' she whispered.

But the struggle was of short duration. She had never been able to withstand Michael in this mood. After a moment she stopped fighting him and lay against him, thin arms twined about his neck, and a big hungry mouth moving hungrily under his hot kisses.

At last he raised his head.

'That's better,' he said thickly.

'You're a monster, Mike,' she whispered the old epithet.

'But you love me.'

'Yes, God help me.'

'Where shall we go?' he muttered.

'I'll have to let them know at home that I'll be away for the night.'

'Can you cook up something?'

'It's going to be a bit difficult as it's such a last-moment affair.'

'I wish I'd thought of it before,' he said.

'I *did*—I've been thinking of it every night since you told me that Venetia had gone away. But I didn't dare suggest it—I didn't think it was my place.'

He pulled her back to him again.

'I don't think I can ever really let you go, Jix. You're in my blood.'

'Well, this time you'll have to and I'm going to see to it,' she said, struggling with her tears.

263

'The future must take care of itself.'

'It never does,' said Jix with a sob in her throat and ran her small, hard fingers through his thick curls; 'it's a thing that wants taking care of—believe me.'

'Venetia's asked for this,' said Michael between his teeth, trying to justify himself. 'She can't expect to keep me in purdah for the rest of my days whilst she makes up her mind what she intends to do about me.'

Jix drew away from him.

'Let's not talk about her any more tonight, please, Mike.'

'That suits me.'

She looked in the mirror over the fireplace, smoothed back her hair, then glancing at him, pulled a handkerchief out of his pocket and attended to a smear of lipstick on his chin.

'Give me some pennies for the 'phone.'

'What are you going to do?'

'Ring up a girl friend of mine. She's a good friend—I don't think you've met her; Ann Collings. She's secretary to a doctor in London. We were at school together. I'll ask her to stand alibi for me. She has a tiny flat in Chelsea. You've got the car, so if you don't mind going all the way back, we'll drive there. If it's okay with Ann, I'll tell Mummy that I'm staying the night with her because she's not well or something.'

'Can't we find a place down here—?' began Michael.

But Jix was a woman and with feminine perspicacity intended to be more cautious than that.

'Not on your life, my boy. We're far too well known in this district. You can lose yourself in London better than anywhere else.'

He shrugged his shoulders. He could see himself missing the hunting again tomorrow. Something always seemed to stand between him and his hunting. What a curse women were! But he wanted Jix tonight and he was going to have her; if only to spite Venetia in his mind.

When Jix returned from her telephone call, she was looking a trifle pale but she wore the old derisive smile.

'Okay by Ann. What's more, she is going to be very obliging and leave the flat to us and take herself off to some aunt or other. She's a wonderful friend.'

'So it would seem,' said Michael and glanced at his watch. 'Seven. I must 'phone through and tell Margaret I don't want her b—y dinner. She can bleat about it for all I care or tell Bennett to eat it. We'll eat *en route*, then at our leisure drive on to your accommodating friend's flat. What about the dog?'

'He can go with us,' said Jix and whistled to the Boxer. He sprang up and bounded to her.

They walked into the bar together. Michael paid for the drinks. One or two of the 'locals', drinking beer, looked curiously after the couple.

'That's Mr Pethick from the Manor House,' said a farmer, as the door closed on the two.

'Oh, and was that his wife?' asked the other, who did not know the district so well.

The landlord of the Horse and Hounds, wiping a glass vigorously, winked an eye.

'I'll say it wasn't.' He laughed.

The three men all laughed together, with lewd humour.

Out in the darkness Michael paused to light another cigarette. He flung away the match, turned up the collar of his coat and glanced sideways at the girl beside him.

'Ruddy awful night—raining again.'

'You can take me back home if you like,' said Jix coolly.

For an instant he hesitated. She felt her heart miss a beat with fear. But he opened the door of the car for her.

'Get in and shut up,' he said.

CHAPTER TEN

Venetia was playing the piano in Lady Sellingham's drawing-room. It was warm and beautiful in this room which she knew so well, and loved. The piano was one that she had often played in the past. Geoffrey's mother sat on the Chesterfield, finishing a tapestry cover

266

for a footstool. Opposite her sat Maybelle, with Poppet stretched on the rug at her feet in front of a big log-fire. They had just finished dinner. It was Minnie's night out. Maybelle, as a great treat, had been allowed to make an omelet. It was a dish upon which she prided herself, and this evening it had come off rather well and been warmly received by her mother and grandmother. Maybelle had also insisted upon doing the washing-up.

Venetia, whilst she played one of her favourite Chopin nocturnes, glanced towards her young daughter and was thankful to see that the child looked happy. With the resilience of youth and that wonderful ability to throw off depression, Maybelle was herself again. It had done her a lot of good staying with her beloved 'Ganny', and Venetia was glad that she, too, had, in the end, decided to spend a week or so at Richmond. She had known from the start that it was useless trying to find any peace of mind alone in a London hotel. But the last ten days in this lovely little tranquil place where she had always known contentment had done much to restore her sense of well-being. Michael's name was not mentioned—by any of them. They were together, just the three of them, as they used to be in the old days before Venetia's ill-starred second marriage. Once or twice some of Lady Sellingham's friends had dropped in for drinks. And Venetia and Maybelle had been to the local cinema and to an ice show which Maybelle particularly wanted to see.

Things were, Venetia thought as she played the piano tonight, as they used to be again, yet so terribly different. Maybelle, thank God, had all her life ahead of her and would soon forget what she had had to suffer through Michael. Lady Sellingham was concerned only indirectly, but she, Venetia, was dreadfully and painfully concerned. For although she did not speak of Michael he was always in her mind. He was in her heart, too. Faithless and shallow, all that she had discovered him to be, he still remained the handsome, charming young man she had so passionately loved. She could not sever herself from him.

After a moment she stopped playing and sent Maybelle off to bed.

'Oh, Mummy!' said Maybelle with a sigh. 'I wonder if I shall *ever* want to go to bed.'

'When you're my age, you certainly will,' said her grandmother.

'All right, you go now, Ganny, and I'll stay up with Mummy,' laughed Maybelle.

'Off you go, you young rascal,' said Lady Sellingham.

'Will you come and tuck me up, Mum?' Maybelle turned to her mother.

'Yes, darling.'

Maybelle hesitated then looked back at Venetia again.

'Mummy, will we be going back to Burnt

Ash before the end of the holidays?'

Venetia looked, not at her daughter, but into the fire, conscious of her mounting colour.

'I hadn't thought of it.'

'It's jolly rotten not being able to see Jock any more,' said Maybelle wistfully.

'He's quite all right, you know, I had a note from Margaret this morning and she said Bennett told her he was in fine form.'

'But it's not much fun having a pony you can't ride,' sighed Maybelle.

Venetia bent and put another log on the fire. Somehow the very mention of returning to Burnt Ash caused a feeling of panic in her heart. Now Maybelle, with a child's lack of tact, added:

'I do wish we could go back there by *ourselves.*'

Lady Sellingham coughed and stuck the needle sharply into her tapestry.

Then Venetia with a fast-beating heart turned and faced her daughter.

'Darling, I know how you feel, but it isn't very easy for us to live by ourselves in a house that belongs to someone else.'

It was Maybelle's turn to feel uneasy and to colour.

'I thought it was your house, too, Mummy.'

'I—you—' Venetia stuttered, shrugged her shoulders hopelessly and looked as though for support at Maybelle's grandmother. Lady Sellingham in her quiet soothing way said:

269

'I think you ought to run along to bed, darling child, Mummy and I will talk about what can be done. We might even have your pony brought here and put in a local stable.'

After Maybelle had gone, whistling Poppet to follow her, the two women looked at each other in silence. Lady Sellingham laid down her tapestry. She had a shrewd idea what was going on in the mind of the younger woman who was, to her, still so young. A loved and much-to-be-pitied girl.

The tragedy of Venetia's marriage to Michael Pethick was a personal tragedy, also, for Lady Sellingham. She had been deeply shocked by what had taken place and particularly in relation to Maybelle.

'Of course,' she said suddenly, 'you couldn't let Maybelle come in contact with Michael again.'

Venetia flushed vividly.

'But Mother darling, I can't go on like this. I know I can't. It won't be fair to Michael.'

'But my dear child,' exclaimed Lady Sellingham, 'you would be perfectly entitled to divorce him!'

'I just—can't,' said Venetia in a muffled voice.

Lady Sellingham sighed.

'You're still in love with him.'

'Not as I was,' said Venetia. She rose now and folding her arms on the mantelpiece leaned her head on them and stared blindly into the fire. 'Oh, no, not as I was—one can't be in love with a man one doesn't respect, but you know there are a thousand reasons why I won't consent to a divorce. I wouldn't drag Maybelle into it and she is my witness. I'm hoping daily that she will have forgotten about it or at least put it into the back of her mind.'

'She never mentions it, certainly.'

'Barbara told me the other night that she had spoken to a psychiatrist who said that if we made no fuss, never alluded to it ourselves, and let things go on normally, she *would* get over it and it would leave no scars. Occasionally she might remember it as something...' Venetia swallowed hard ... 'something *filthy*. But memories grow dim and please God that one will fade.'

'Please God,' echoed the older woman with a sigh and took up her tapestry again. 'It would have been so awful if it had had a lasting impression and spoiled her romantic outlook for the future.'

'There wasn't much romance in what she saw.'

'Oh, my dear!' said Lady Sellingham painfully.

Venetia drew a long sigh.

'And yet, Mother, I can't hate Michael—I can't.'

'Unlike the young man, you have a faithful nature.'

'Yes. I have a faithful nature and I am still

271

fond of Mike in my way. I feel it must have been my fault as well as his. They say you always get what you deserve in this world, so I must have deserved what he did to me.'

'Absolute nonsense,' said Lady Sellingham. 'I am not usually cynical but I do feel doubtful about the laws of compensation. Far too many of the wicked prosper and far too few of the good and patient reap a reward.'

Venetia turned and looked at Lady Sellingham with a faint smile.

'Oh, darling, it's not like you to speak *that* way.'

'No, it isn't, but it's the way I feel at times, I'm very sorry to say, my dear. And why should you feel it is in any way your fault? Michael may act like a stupid undergraduate but he is a man of thirty-four and ought to know better.'

Venetia narrowed her eyes and returned to her unseeing stare into the wood-fire.

'It's a funny thing but since I've been away from him for so long and had time to think it all over, I've come to the conclusion that my feelings for Michael are more maternal than anything else. As though he were my son and not my lover. He has so much good in him but he's just utterly irresponsible and spoiled and I was the wrong woman for him. He was quite happy until I married him; that's one of the things that makes me feel I must be tolerant. I feel almost as though I did him a wrong in marrying him. A different sort of wrong from the one he did me—nevertheless, I'm not altogether guiltless in this affair.'

Lady Sellingham shrugged her shoulders.

'Sometimes, my dear,' she said in a humorous voice, 'I think I've lived too long. I'm so old-fashioned that I cannot understand you young people with your modern psychology. If I had ever been mad enough to marry Mr Michael Pethick I'd have wrung his young neck for him by this time.'

Venetia relaxed and laughed with her, but the laugh had a hollow sound. She felt hollow, she thought, depleted; and yet with anger against Michael receding into the background, other emotions were surfacing. Other memories ... not of his infidelity and vicious dislike of Maybelle ... but of the young and handsome man who had shared so much love and delight with her in those honeymoon days that had ended at Deauville.

'If one could put back the clock,' she thought hopelessly, 'if I could only begin again with him. I must have gone wrong somewhere. Perhaps I was too smug and self-confident and tried too hard to make him the man I wanted. I didn't realize I was doing it—but I did, and that is what a woman should never do ... choose her man, then try to turn him into someone else.'

Suddenly Venetia pulled a letter out of her bag which she had left on the Chesterfield. It bore an American stamp.

'Mother,' she said, 'I don't often show Herman Weissman's letters to other people but I want you to read it. Begin on page two. The first won't interest you—it's about his plans. He's coming back to London next month. You know how he loved Geoffrey. I wanted his counsel. He's old and so wise and good. Geoffrey valued his opinion. I didn't tell him all that happened—I couldn't. I wrote him a guarded letter—just to let him know that I'd found out that Mike had been unfaithful to me and that I didn't know what to do about it, and that his jealousy of Maybelle had reached such an extreme I could no longer cope with it.'

Lady Sellingham took the letter and began to read the page indicated, written in Herman's fine sloping Continental hand. The calligraphy was remarkable for a man of his age, and exquisite.

Your news about your husband grieves me because I know that you, my beloved Venetia, have been pitchforked from your paradise into the outer darkness where you must inevitably suffer for a time. Because you are a woman of great affections and loyalties and sincere passions—the pain will be intense. Alas, it is a pain that I, who long to help you, cannot alleviate by mere words. It is something you must bear alone. But if my love, my sympathy, and my understanding count—they are yours in abundance.

Who should know better than I the bitterness of human sorrow and the anguish of loss? These were my portion when my beloved Naomi and little son were taken from me. And when dear Geoffrey died, and you and I were united by our common sorrow, I helped you then but it is more difficult for me to help you now. This new sorrow is of a kind less ennobling and regenerating. To lose the one you love by death is one thing—to lose him in the manner in which you have lost your Michael is another. But most of all it is your pride that will suffer. You have been robbed of faith which is in itself a tragedy. My poor Venetia! Your happiness was short-lived and all too quickly your rose-coloured spectacles were smashed. When originally you asked me if I thought this marriage would be wise I found it hard to give you encouragement. I doubted, but because you were so much in love and, indeed, because I thought that he would grow of greater stature through his love and his association with you, I hoped for the best. Alas, my hopes were not fulfilled.

I pity you most deeply, but when you cry from the depths of your heart 'What shall I do?' nothing of my learning and experience of life helps me to answer—except with exceeding caution and some apprehension.

But this I do say. If I pity you, my heart turns with compassion also to him. Does this surprise you? Why should I, who hold you so dear and in such deep regard, feel sorrow for him? Yet I do. Let me explain. Michael Pethick was never the young god you imagined him. He never even had the greatness of the lesser gods. He is and always was of the earth, earthy. Without spirituality, lacking in ideals. He is as millions of other men who are born and who live and die in this world, generation after generation, neither a creature of the higher world, nor of the lower, of the Light or the Darkness. But as those described so ably by Rupert Brooke, 'wanderers in the middle mists'.

All his life Michael Pethick must have wandered and been unable to help himself, for he has not the eyes to see nor the ears to hear, and it will never be given to him to have the tongue to speak. He is a pagan and an egotist. Not even a supreme egotist, but a little selfish man whose littleness was at first hidden from you behind the mask of boyish charm and what is undoubtedly his sincere desire to please. He likes, pathetically, to be popular. He likes to enjoy himself. He saw an immense opportunity to enjoy himself with you who could provide not only beauty and experience and a deep devotion, but the good things of this life that money can buy. Forgive me if I hurt you but I must always be honest. He did not love the essential you whom Geoffrey loved, and whom I with deep respect will always love, old man though I am. He loved what you could

276

give him, then once married to you he found that it was not enough. Like the child that he is, he tired of his new toy and returned to an old favourite. Spoiled and possessive—he did not even wish to stand aside and make room for your child. He did not love you well enough to want to share with you the great happiness of your motherhood.

But should he, and he alone, stand accused? You are older and you took on this great responsibility—this new 'child'—when you married Michael. Now that he has grieved you, deceived you and proved less easy and sympathetic than your Maybelle—have you a right to desert him? Is this not the supreme test of your love—that love that led you into uniting your life with his? Great woman that you are—will you fail this poor young man who must need all the moral support you can give him and whom you say has asked you to allow him a second chance? Do not let your pride and anger or even your love for Maybelle make you intolerant. Do not lose sight of what you owe to him. Would it be trite for me to remind you that 'to err is human and to forgive divine'? You have the divine spark somewhere, Venetia. It must not remain hidden. If you part from Michael now he will go downhill and you will be as responsible for his eventual downfall as a mother would be for an erring child upon whom she turns her back.

I do not like Michael. You know that. I do

not think him fit to touch your shoes. Yet somewhere there is something likeable in him or you would never have given yourself to him. I think if you go back to him now and take on this great responsibility you will lose your feeling of disappointment and dismay and of mistaken superiority. You will grow more humble perhaps, and be more proud. You will stoop to forgive him and live with him again and that should elevate him in his own sight as well as yours. Can you understand what I am trying to say? I hope so, my very dear. And I feel that what I am saying is right even though I send you this letter in fear and trembling lest it should be wrong. And how wrong all we poor misguided human beings can be!

He wishes you to go back, then go, and try to be happy. You have it within your power; of that I am certain.

Strangely enough I am not even angry with Michael for he has done only what I expected—true to type. A purely physical type. It may take him a lifetime—or many reincarnations before he becomes capable of looking at you with the eyes of truth and an understanding that is of the spirit only. Who knows? But because you have loved him do not abandon him and retard his spiritual progress.

God bless you. You can count on me at all times.

Herman.

Lady Sellingham returned the letter to Venetia. Then she took off her glasses and wiped her eyes.

'That is a very beautiful letter, Venetia. A very deep and touching one.'

Venetia's lips were trembling but she did not weep. She tapped a thumbnail against one sentence and read it aloud:

'*If you part from Michael now he will go downhill and you will be as responsible for his eventual downfall as a mother would be for an erring child upon whom she turns her back...*'

Then Venetia looked at Geoffrey's mother.

'You see—that is what Herman thinks and what I also feel. It is why I must not stay away from Michael any longer.'

'I will try to understand,' said Lady Sellingham with an effort.

'Herman is a wonderful person. He always knows what one should do. And I know that he is right in this. People like Barbara tell me blithely to go and get a divorce and be rid of Mike and start again. But Barbara, dear friend of mine though she is, sees life in a narrow way. Herman has broad, tremendous vision. He is right, *right*...' Venetia beat one fist against the other ... 'I married Mike. I took on the responsibility. If he is not what I thought him that is *my* fault and not his. He was happy before I met him. I must go back and try to make him happy again.'

'This is all a little beyond me, my dear,' said

Lady Sellingham, 'but I am trying to understand.'

Venetia sat on the stool now at the feet of the older woman, and taking one of the fine cool hands laid it against her flushed cheek.

'Mother, Herman is right,' she repeated.

'But Herman did not know—about Maybelle—'

'He does not know that Maybelle was unfortunate enough to be a witness—'

'Maybe if he knew that, he would have written in another vein.'

'I don't think so. I think Herman would consider it a dreadful and abominable thing, but at least it was not Michael's intention that Maybelle should have been a witness, and I know from what he has said to me that he was genuinely shocked and distressed about that.'

Lady Sellingham leaned forward and touched Venetia's cheek with her hand.

'My darling, do as you think best—go back to him if you feel it right.'

'I will telephone his office tomorrow,' said Venetia as though she had reached this decision suddenly. She spoke in a firm clear voice: 'I shall tell him that I wish our marriage to have another chance. But, in return, he must do something for me which I know he will find painful. He must leave Burnt Ash. There, I cannot expect him to put Jix Lawson out of his life. She lives in that district and they hunt together. He must sell the Manor. We will start again somewhere else.'

She walked across the drawing-room, turning back at the doorway to smile at Lady Sellingham.

'I'm going to tuck Maybelle up. I shall tell her she must sacrifice having Jock these holidays. I do not wish to take her to Burnt Ash just yet. By the time the Easter holidays come, we will perhaps have moved, and she can start afresh with Michael. I shall try to prepare her mind to accept him as a friend in the way she used to.'

'If you think it wise,' said Lady Sellingham.

'I loved Michael very much when I married him; I cannot desert him now,' said Venetia, 'I *cannot.*'

The little household was shrouded in darkness and a gusty wind tore through Lady Sellingham's garden, driving an icy rain against the window panes, when the telephone bell suddenly shrilled through the night.

Venetia, a light sleeper, was the first to hear it, switched on her light, threw on a dressing-gown and hurried downstairs, dazed by the suddenness of the awakening. She had glanced first at her bedside clock and seen that it was nearly two o'clock in the morning. She wondered who on earth could be ringing. At the back of her mind was the thought that it might be Michael. He might in one of his crazy moods have been thinking about her and decided to telephone her even at this nocturnal hour.

But when she lifted the receiver—the telephone was in the hall—it was a woman's voice she heard, not Michael's. However, the call concerned him. Venetia was totally unprepared for the shock she was to receive.

'Am I speaking to Mrs Michael Pethick?'

'Yes.'

'This is one of the Sisters from St Mary's Hospital just outside Forest Row.'

'Just outside Forest Row?' repeated Venetia rather stupidly.

'Yes—not very far from East Grinstead, if you know that.'

'Yes, I know it well, but why—?'

'You must prepare yourself for a shock, my child,' broke in the gentle voice. 'I am the Assistant Mother Superior of this Convent. We are a Nursing Order. Your husband was brought to us here by ambulance an hour or two ago.'

Now Venetia's heart seemed to turn over.

'My *husband*!'

'Yes, Mr Michael Pethick of Burnt Ash Manor. That is the correct name—and address—is it not?'

'Yes.'

'He was involved in a serious motor accident on the crossroads half a mile from us. It is believed that his car skidded and hit a lorry and the smaller vehicle, of course, got the worst of it.'

The colour left Venetia's face. Shivering she clutched her dressing-gown around a body that was ice-cold.

'How badly is he hurt, Sister?'

'Very badly, my dear.'

'Is he—dead?'

'No—but he is in a critical condition.'

'You mean he is—dying?'

'We do not know. It is in God's hands. We are praying for him and you must do the same.'

'What do the doctors say—what are his injuries?'

'The main injury is to the spine. But he is cut and bruised all over. He has several fractured ribs. Mercifully his face is untouched. He has lost a great deal of blood and has just had a transfusion.'

'Then there is a hope?'

'Yes. The doctor says he obviously has a strong constitution.'

'Is he conscious—was he able to tell you who he was?'

'No,' came the answer in a low voice, 'he has not regained consciousness. But he had a passenger.'

Venetia licked her lips with the point of her tongue. Her heart hammered.

'Who—was it—do you know?'

'A Miss Lawson.'

Now Venetia shut her eyes and clenched a hand so tightly that the points of her nails hurt the flesh of her palms. '*Oh God,*' she thought,

283

'*oh dear God. What was he doing with her, at such an hour?—driving up to town I suppose.*'

Then came the second shock.

'Miss Lawson was more badly hurt than your husband, Mrs Pethick. She recovered consciousness a few moments ago, but died immediately after she had given us the information we needed.'

'*Died!*' repeated Venetia.

'Yes, poor child. She was terribly injured. It is a mercy that she has been taken to Almighty God.'

The soft calm voice of the religious woman, to whom death meant only an awakening to a better life, restored some calm to Venetia. Her teeth were chattering. Her numbed senses quivered to the shocking thought that Jix Lawson was dead. It was not easy to believe; that young strong girl about whom she had been talking to Lady Sellingham only a few hours ago—Jix, whom she had regarded as a potential menace, whom Michael must have loved in his curious way.

Venetia shut her eyes. The nun spoke again.

'I dare say you would like to come to the hospital immediately, Mrs Pethick?'

'Yes,' said Venetia, 'of course.' She added, 'Who gave you my telephone number?'

'Your housekeeper at your home in Burnt Ash. We telephoned there after receiving that poor girl's statement.'

'What a shock for Margaret,' thought

Venetia dully.

A moment later she was rousing Geoffrey's mother. Lady Sellingham by this time was awake. She heard the voice downstairs and was wondering what had happened. Only Maybelle, the child, went on sleeping.

When Lady Sellingham heard what Venetia had to tell her, she clasped her delicate fingers together and bowed her head.

'The ways of God are strange and sometimes terrible,' she whispered. 'Poor girl—poor girl—to die so suddenly and violently.'

Venetia had lit a cigarette with trembling fingers. She smoked feverishly. Every nerve in her body jangled. She said:

'Michael may be going to die, too. This was something we never thought of. Mother, what a terrible disaster! The nun said that he is still unconscious and that his spine has been injured.'

'My poor child,' said Lady Sellingham in a shaken voice, 'I'm afraid you have much to go through. I wish I were not so old and helpless and could be of use to you.'

'I shall be all right,' said Venetia. 'You know me. I can manage alone.'

Lady Sellingham sat up in bed and put a woolly wrap around her shoulders. Her face was ivory pale in the light of the lamp that burned beside her. Terrible, oh, terrible the things that can happen in this world of mad speed, of mistaken values, she thought. This, indeed, was retribution. Michael had been with that girl—for all his promises, his assurances to Venetia, that he meant to turn over a new leaf—he had been taking Jix Lawson out—driving with her to London. No doubt he had had more than enough to drink and been careless on the wet roads. God be merciful to them both, thought Lady Sellingham, and to that young girl's mother who would know now that her only daughter had been hurled suddenly into Eternity. She said to Venetia:

'Go, my dear, and I'll look after Maybelle. You need not worry about her—don't wake her. I will explain in the morning. You may want to stay at the hospital.'

'I rely on you, as always,' said Venetia.

While she drove her car through the rain—out of Richmond and made her way towards Sussex on roads that were deserted at this hour—she thought, as Lady Sellingham had done, of the terrible thing that had taken place.

It did not seem to matter any more that Michael had broken his word about Jix. Jix would never betray her with Mike again. She was dead. With her vivid imagination Venetia saw the crash between the beautiful sports car Mike was driving and that lorry. He always drove too fast. She used to tell him so. And she, too, guessed that he had been drinking heavily. Perhaps he had been going up to London with Jix with every intention of staying the night with her. Venetia could almost hear the crash;

it made her feel sick. The black sleek Lagonda was now a shapeless wreck; the two occupants who had been laughing and talking together flung into a mist of pain and blood. Now, for one, had come total oblivion.

There was no room in Venetia's heart for resentment or bitterness. She felt only a profound and hopeless pity for both Jix and Michael. Wrapped in a fur coat, her hair tied up in a scarf, she drove steadily and carefully through the unceasing rain.

CHAPTER ELEVEN

One brisk morning, at the end of April, Herman Weissman opened the carriage door of the train at Lewes station, waving and smiling as he did so, at the figure of Venetia, whom he could see walking towards his carriage. The train slowed down. He stepped out.

Venetia did not look too badly, he thought, after all she had been through. She was as elegant and beautiful as ever, although when he was within closer range of sight he could see a change in her. She looked much older and far too thin. But she had a warm colour and a bright smile as she approached him with outstretched hand.

'Herman, *my dear!*'

'My dear,' he echoed the words and kissed her on both cheeks, then dropped another kiss on the gloved hand.

'It was good of you to come all this way,' she added.

'Of course not. I had to see both of you and *him*. How is he?'

'Just the same. He'll never be any different,' said Venetia.

For a moment Herman did not speak except to comment on the beauty of the spring morning down here where a stiff breeze blew freshly through the budding trees, and where the gardens of the houses which they drove past were filled with daffodils. The fields looked exquisitely green; the sky was a pale clear blue. There was nothing like London and the Sussex Downs in the spring, Herman reflected. It was an especially welcome sight after America. His tour of the United States had been successful but he did not like America and he had taken a secret vow never to return there. The life was too fast and furious for him. People could complain about England, and the Government, and the frustrations of existence over here, but it was always England that he loved best. Old, tired man though he was, he felt that his heart must ever rejoice when he returned here. Especially when he could look upon Venetia again.

She was telling him about Michael.

He was in a spinal chair and could be

wheeled around the house and into the garden. He could use his hands, but from the waist downwards he was totally paralysed. He had not responded to any treatment. Venetia had spent a small fortune on specialists but one after the other they had given the case up as incurable. Michael would never walk again.

Herman, his broad-brimmed hat pulled over his head, listened and felt that deep compassion which he never failed to experience in the face of human suffering.

The poor young man! Whatever he had done—he was paying for it most tragically. What could be worse than for a man of his particular type—a sportsman—wedded to horses and hunting—to be struck down and condemned to total disablement for the rest of his life? A life that might last a very long time, since he was not yet forty.

'He is well in a sort of way,' said Venetia, 'but perpetually depressed. It is very hard to keep his spirits up, and find fresh things to interest him. He doesn't like books or good music, which makes it so much harder.'

'Ah, yes,' murmured Herman.

'He doesn't even like people any more,' went on Venetia. 'and you know how keen he used to be on parties and entertaining. Well, I started by filling the place with his old friends. They all came, of course, to try and cheer him up. Every member of the Hunt put him- or herself out to do what could be done.

Everybody was sorry for him—so kind. But nothing really amuses him any more.'

'I can understand that,' said Herman.

'If it had happened to me,' said Venetia, 'I could still have been happy listening to music and with my books. I try to make Mike read but he does not really care about literature, and sometimes I feel he is really unable to concentrate. His head seems full of thoughts he can't express and he is very excitable at times, and difficult, too, which I understand is all part and parcel of the complaint.'

Herman thought: 'That is putting it mildly, I am sure. From what I can gather after my conversation last night with Lady Sellingham, Venetia has now become a martyr to a more than ordinarily difficult invalid.'

Poor lovely Venetia! She seemed doomed to unhappiness. First the death of her beloved Geoffrey, and now this tragedy—with her second husband. Herman felt there could be nothing worse than for Venetia to be forced to spend the rest of her life nursing the unhappy paralysed young man who, when robbed of all that his once vigorous body used to afford him, had nothing much left. They could not even be lovers any longer. They had no link—either physical or spiritual.

Death in life for them both, thought Herman. In a detached way he pitied Michael but with all his heart and soul he deplored Venetia's personal tragedy. Yet he could see that she was enduring it with courage, and as he listened and talked with her, he even began to believe that she was extracting something from the wreckage. She no longer had a husband she said, but a sick child to nurse and care for.

'You will remember, Herman,' she was saying, 'that letter you wrote telling me to give Mike another chance because I was much older than he, and morally responsible for him. On that very night of the accident, I had made up my mind to take him back and start again.'

'So now you are the mother—of two children,' said Herman, with a faint smile.

Venetia, turning the car into the gates of Burnt Ash Manor, gave him a quick smile.

'Exactly,' she said.

'And Maybelle?'

'Maybelle has been perfectly wonderful. In a strange way this disaster has forged a new bond between her and Mike. That is one of my compensations. It might have been very difficult—you will know how difficult—for us three to have lived together as a trio, as we did before the accident. Mike never liked Maybelle then and she no longer trusted him.'

'And now—?'

'Now, Maybelle, too, regards Mike as her child. It is quite touching to see her maternal regard for him. When she was home for the Easter holidays, she spent an incredible amount of time sitting beside his spinal

carriage. He seemed to like her to be near—
even better than having me beside him,' added
Venetia with a faint grimace—'but that is
understandable. Maybelle's youth and natural
gaiety provide an entertainment in themselves.
She laughs and she makes Michael laugh. They
play foolish games of cards, or dominoes, and
so on. They watch the television together. She
plays for him—the sort of light records he likes
to hear. She is, in fact, a better companion for
Mike than I am. He can hardly bear Maybelle
out of his sight. Is that not strange?'

'Strange and touching,' nodded Herman.

'Pippa has gone. We have a local daily now
and there is always Margaret, my old Scots
servant, whom Mike used to hate. She used to
loathe him—but now they are the firmest
friends. His incapacity has brought them
together, too. We wanted to have a male nurse
in the house—but our faithful Bennett, the
groom, has turned himself into Mike's
attendant and does all the lifting and carrying
for Mike. Margaret does the rest. To hear them
together is quite comic. He curses her—and
calls her an old Scots devil, and worse than
that. She soothes him down and says, "Now,
Mr Pethick, you don't mean it," and then
sometimes she gives him back as good as she
gets and they have a first-class row. But it does
Mike good. He always sends for her and
apologizes.'

'The whole house revolves, of course,

around him.'

'Yes,' said Venetia quietly.

'He is lucky to have you and such a staff *and* the wherewithal to make the days easy for him, under the circumstances.'

Venetia drew the car up before the front door. The garden of Burnt Ash Manor was a blaze of spring flowers. Herman had never seen anything more beautiful than the cascade of purple and pink aubrietia tumbling over the old stone walls. Venetia, drawing off her driving gauntlets, opened the car door for her passenger and said:

'Money helps, of course, and we all do what we can. But dear life! Think what it means to *him*. The hunters have been sold. There are terrible moments—moments when Mike realizes that he will never ride again. I dread the hunting season beginning again because of the effect it may have on him. My poor, poor Mike.'

'And what of my poor Venetia?'

She turned away.

'At first I wondered how I was going to get through,' she said in a low tone, 'it was so hard. He is not the easiest of patients. There seemed nothing left. But I've been lucky. I have been able to find a queer sort of contentment and peace in looking after him, and knowing that he needs me. He's very grateful. He tries to show it to me in his own way.'

'And rightly,' said Herman in a dry voice.

'He is singularly fortunate to have you and Maybelle.'

Herman stood a moment with his tired face lifted to the warm sunshine. He heard, suddenly, a voice breaking the peace of the spring morning.

'Oh get out you b—y old fool and leave me alone!'

Venetia smiled and grimaced at Herman.

'There we are!'

'Michael,' said Herman half to himself.

While they waited the front door opened and Bennett wheeled a long spinal carriage out into the drive. Herman saw with pity the outline of Michael Pethick's wasted frame lying under a rug. That fine body that once had been so full of life and energy. Then he saw Michael's face—hardly recognizable—it was thin and haggard—and *bearded*. Herman caught Venetia's eye again and she whispered quickly:

'Yes, I forgot to tell you about the beard. It all started because he didn't want the bother of shaving.'

'It suits him,' murmured Herman.

It did in fact give Michael the appearance of an Elizabethan giant struck down; all the old vitality had gone to that thick beard which was bright and curling, with a reddish tint to it. His face bore a look of fierce discontent which made Herman's heart ache for Venetia as well as for the invalid himself.

'You've been the devil of a time at the

station, Venetia,' were Michael's welcoming words. Bennett touched his cap to Herman and moved away. Michael then added, 'I suppose your train was late and—' He turned grudgingly to Herman, 'How-d'you-do?'

'I am well, thank you,' said Herman, and moved to the side of the spinal carriage and extended a hand. Michael shook it limply. It was no longer the brown and muscular hand of the old Michael. The fingers were thin and white with that translucent look of the invalid who performs no menial tasks. Now Herman with intense compassion felt moved to speak very gently to the man who had caused so much havoc in Venetia's life and his own.

'Believe me, dear boy, I am deeply concerned that this tragedy should have befallen you,' he said in the old-fashioned and courtly way he had of speaking.

Michael shut one eye and looked out of the other, quizzically, at the pianist who had been Geoffrey Sellingham's friend.

'Thanks. Not so sound in wind and limb as I was when we last met, eh?'

Herman found nothing to say. Venetia came forward and laid a light hand on her husband's hair, ruffling it as she would a child's.

'Shall we push you on to the lawn or just leave you here like this outside the french windows? This is the sheltered side. You won't feel the wind, and you'll find the sun quite hot.'

'I don't care where we go,' he said irritably.

'Then let us all sit out here and have coffee,' said Venetia.

Now Herman saw Michael reach up and take those fingers which caressed his hair and pull them down against his cheek.

'Okay, darling,' he said briefly, and turning back to Herman, added: 'She's been an angel, you know. I must be hell to live with these days but she never bats an eyelid.'

'Nonsense,' said Venetia and looked quite pink and embarrassed.

But Herman thought:

'He *is* hell to live with, but he loves her now very much. She is his rock of refuge and he could not do without her. Good has sprung from evil.'

Herman was convinced that they had found something, these two. When Michael was well and strong and able to move those now wasted limbs, he and she might so easily have parted for ever.

As he sat talking with them—he and Venetia on either side of the spinal carriage—he became increasingly convinced that Venetia's lot was not as tragic as might first have been supposed. The flashes of irritability—the childish display of cursing and swearing in which Michael indulged—were to relieve his feelings, and of no importance, and did not seem to affect Venetia. But he clung to her hand, he showed by every sign and gesture that he could not bear her to leave him, and that

296

made her happy. There was a warmth, a glow in her eyes which Herman attributed to the absoluteness of her mother-love. To passion, to feverish emotion she had said a long good-bye but she had found this in its place. She was secure. For as long as she lived this big, bearded, helpless man was completely hers. It could not be gauged how long he might live. Sometimes the paralysed go on to old age, Herman reflected. But at least for Venetia there could be no more jealousy, no fear that any younger woman could ever take him from her.

The midday post brought a letter from Maybelle, who had just returned to school. And this was the time when Herman Weissman saw proof of the new affection that had sprung between the young girl and her stepfather. Michael's gloomy bearded face lit up and he held out a hand for the letter after Venetia had read it. He even chuckled as he reached the end.

'Good girl! That essay she wrote on hunting has shaken her teachers. I knew it would. You know'—he glanced up at Herman—'young Maybelle rides like Diana herself—all under my instructions. I may be a log but I know the things to tell her, and she's quick to pick them up.'

'Michael sold his hunter and bought a most charming little mare for Maybelle,' added Venetia.

'I can see that my godchild will become a spoiled young woman,' said Herman.

'She's a damned nice child,' said Michael quickly.

Venetia said:

'Michael's taken to landscape gardening. He's going to design a rock garden and fishpond down there through those poplars. He's got it all worked out and Maybelle's very keen on it, too.'

'I shan't do much digging,' said Michael with a grunt for a laugh.

'But he'll direct operations,' observed Venetia.

'One must do something,' said Michael, and lay back on his cushions and scowled up at the blue cloud-flecked sky. Then suddenly he looked towards Herman. 'You wouldn't like to go and bang the old ivories for me, would you? I rather like to hear music.'

Venetia felt her colour rise and looked anxiously at the world's greatest pianist. Herman was smiling; he who a few months ago would have winced and writhed at being asked to play in such a language as this. With immense good humour he rose and said:

'If you would like to hear it, I shall "bang the old ivories" especially for you, my dear fellow. I have always enjoyed playing Venetia's piano.'

Venetia hurried into the drawing-room after Herman and lifted the lid of the Bluthner.

'Are you sure you don't mind?'

He laid a hand on hers.

'I shall play for you as well as for him and it will be a pleasure. You know one cannot help liking your Michael—your bearded Elizabethan—who has been struck down. He has courage. Of that I am sure.'

'Yes, he has courage. It must be very hard for him,' she said in a low voice.

Herman seated himself on the tapestried stool and ran his beautiful strong fingers over the keys. Venetia watched him only for a second, for she heard Michael's voice calling her. Always he seemed to be calling her. She hastened to his side.

'I'm here, darling, I was just settling Herman down.'

'I want my dark glasses,' he said.

'I'll get them.'

'No, tell that old basket Margaret they're on my chest of drawers. Don't you waste your energies. You look tired this morning.'

She laughed but was pleased. It always pleased her when Michael showed consideration for her. But in the end it was she who fetched the glasses. He put them on.

Now the sunlit morning was filled with the sound of music. The man whom other men all over the world paid to hear, and paid dearly, was giving of his best to his friends. Even Michael, who knew nothing much about classical music, was fascinated.

'What's that he's playing? I like it.'

'Ravel's *Ondine*.'

299

'That doesn't mean a row of pins to me,' said Michael, 'but I do like it.'

Venetia, sitting beside the spinal chair, lifted one of her husband's hands and toyed with it.

'I am glad. So do I.'

'He isn't a bad little chap,' added Michael.

It was grudging praise, but coming from him she thought it meant a lot. She thought of the last time the three of them had met. Not such a propitious meeting in many ways, perhaps, as this one. For then she, blindly and passionately in love, had taken Michael for the first time to meet her old friend and Herman had been disappointed, apprehensive for her future. How right he had been! But the situation had resolved itself. Time had done much to hurt— and to heal.

Maybelle's opened letter still lay on Michael's rug. It was a happy letter. Thank God, Maybelle was very happy again, and thank God, thought Venetia, for the blotting out of the past nightmare, for the establishment of understanding and friendship between her husband and her daughter.

Herman's music filled her with delight. She closed her eyes, and felt something approaching real contentment. She wondered what Michael was thinking and feeling. Haunted, maybe, by the ghost of poor little Jix, who had once ridden with him so madly and gaily through this green countryside; Jix, whom he had wronged; Jix, who in turn had wronged her, his wife. Poor broken Jix, now lying in her quiet grave. Surely he must remember her sometimes! But he never spoke her name. He seemed to mind nothing except the moment when she, Venetia, left his side.

'I have eaten the fruit and found it sweet,' Venetia thought as she closed her eyes and the haunting *motif* of the *Ondine* drifted out to her through the open windows. 'Dear life! the core was bitter. Perhaps it has all been worth while.'

Suddenly Michael touched the side of her head and said in almost a shocked voice:

'Good lord, do you know you've got a whole lot of grey hairs? I've never noticed them before.'

'I have,' said Venetia, opening her eyes and smiling. 'Do you mind?'

Michael yawned and shook his head.

'No, I like it. It suits you.'

Herman stopped playing. Michael added:

'That was terrific. Ask him to play something more, then get old Maggie to bring out the sherry.'

She went obediently to do as he asked. Now she, herself, touched the grey threads in her hair, glancing in the hall mirror as she passed into the cool, gracious house. But she could not see very well, for her eyes were full of tears.